South San Francisco Public Library

3 9048 07636018 3

P9-COP-119

S.S.F. Public Library
West Orange
940 West Orange Ave.
South San Francisco, CA 94080

JUN   2010

every little thing in the world

nina de gramont

atheneum books for young readers
new york london toronto sydney

• • • •

to my mother and father

"For Each in the loved Home—
Tell me any service and my Heart is ready."
—Emily Dickinson

• • • •

acknowledgments

First, thanks will always go to my great friend and amazing agent,
Peter Steinberg. He, of course, led me to my warm,
brilliant, and insightful editor, Caitlyn Dlouhy.

Thanks to friends and readers Mel Boyajian, Alicia Erian,
Rebecca Lee, and Hannah Abrams. Thanks to Carmen Rodrigues,
for all kinds of advice, and Danae Woodward,
for all manner of support. Thanks to Planned Parenthood,
Canada, for graciously answering all my questions.

Last (and biggest) thanks will always go to
David Gessner, my favorite storyteller.

chapter one
not telling

Natalia and I stole her mother's new blue Cadillac and drove out to Overpeck to find Tommy. Natalia steered inexpertly, lurching her way from the luxurious oak-lined streets of Linden Hill, New Jersey—lush lawns and stately manors—to the spindly birch trees and ranch houses of Overpeck, aluminum siding and green awnings everywhere.

"Are you sure Tommy will be at this party?" I asked her.

"Pretty sure," Natalia said. She drummed her French-manicured nails nervously on the wheel. I couldn't tell if her uneasiness stemmed from our mission or from driving itself. This was our first night together after being grounded for two weeks, and we had promised Natalia's parents we wouldn't set foot outside the house. Natalia had a newly minted learner's permit, but no license. As I wasn't due to begin driver's ed until school started again in the fall, I didn't exactly qualify as the licensed driver who was supposed to be sitting beside her.

It was late in the day, hours after dinner, but the sun still hung stubbornly in the sky. I loved this time of year, early summer, with months of leisure and possibility still ahead. My part-time job—lifeguarding at the local country club where most of my school friends belonged—didn't start for another ten days, and it would mostly involve dozing behind sunglasses and working on my tan. Even the prospect of confronting Tommy couldn't entirely interfere with the happiness this kind of bright summer night infused in me. Sparrows perched on swinging telephone wires, and the dull slant of sunlight promised that although darkness was taking its time, night would arrive before too long.

The car rattled over potholes and a crooked set of railroad tracks. Natalia parked between an ancient Toyota truck and a battered Chevy Impala. We stepped out of the car and slammed the doors, gravel crunching underneath our feet. Next to the collection of hand-me-down vehicles, the Cadillac looked elegant and out of place. Not unlike Natalia herself— lean, sleek, and raven-haired—picking her way over the splintery post fence and gliding through the tall, wet grass on the strappy designer sandals that had originally belonged to her older sister. Natalia had a funny, endearing face. Her dark eyes were a little too far apart. She had a pronounced bump on the bridge of her nose, and a gap between her two front teeth. Despite her slim body and beautiful clothes, other girls never noticed Natalia until they registered every guy in the world swooning as she walked by.

"Come on, Sydney," she said, waving her arm toward the woods ahead.

I lagged behind her, my sneakers instantly damp and

squishy. We crossed a rickety old playground and followed the voices. I could smell a festive blend of wood and cigarette smoke, possibly cigars and pot.

The scent reminded me of Tommy, and I felt suddenly ill. "Natalia," I called. "Wait up a second."

Natalia stopped, looked at my face, and backtracked to my side. She put her hand on my shoulder as I wrapped my arms around my own middle.

"I'm not sure I can do this," I said.

"What's wrong?" Natalia said. "Are you nauseous? Is it morning sickness?"

I looked at her as if she'd gone completely insane. "No," I said. "Definitely not." I uncrossed my arms and started walking again. Natalia's hand slid off my shoulder, and she strode back to her place in front of me.

No matter what she might think, no matter what the pregnancy test had told me, I knew that the prickly nausea in my middle was most definitely not morning sickness. Apart from my missed period, I had zero symptoms. There had been no barfing, no craving pickles and peanut butter, no swollen breasts. No nothing. I felt so exactly normal that I still didn't really believe it, even though I'd used all three of the sticks that came in the EPT box, and every one had produced two pink lines. It didn't seem possible that something so huge—so catastrophic and monumental—could be going on inside my body, while I looked and felt exactly like my usual sixteen-year-old self.

I had taken the tests at Natalia's house on the very day I was supposed to get my period and fully expected the results to relieve the vague anxiety I'd felt these last two weeks. Afterward, Natalia and I lined them up on the bathroom floor. Then we called the 800 number listed on the box. We sat next to each other, our backs pressed up against the pink porcelain bathtub with lion's feet. Natalia's parents were very old, and from Hungary. They spoke in thick accents and decorated with lots of gilt and animal figurines, the kind of details my mother considered tacky.

Before we called, Natalia had promised me that she would do the talking. But as soon as the customer service rep answered, she thrust the phone into my hands.

"Hello?" the customer service rep said, to my silence.

"Um, hello," I said. "I just took a pregnancy test? And there are two lines, but the second line is faint. It's very, very faint. So I was wondering, is this a positive result?"

"If there are two lines," she said, "it's a positive result, no matter how faint the second line is." I could hear all sorts of sympathy in her voice. No matter how low I tried to pitch my voice, whenever I answered the phone at home, whoever was calling always said, "Is your mother there?" Obviously the customer service woman could tell I was not some twinkling bride, all giddy to give my husband the joyful news. "You do need to see a doctor to confirm," she said, which sounded vaguely hopeful.

After I thanked her and hung up, Natalia dug her mother's extra car keys from her bedroom bureau. We left our cell phones—which our suspicious parents had equipped with GPS tracking devices—on Natalia's frilly canopy bed. (Natalia always apologized for that bed. "I know," she would say. "It's completely childish." But her mother considered it the height of girlish luxury, and Natalia couldn't bring herself to tell her it was a total embarrassment.)

Now we walked through a muddy state park, toward the keg party that Overpeck High School seniors threw at the end of every June. It was here that Natalia had met her boyfriend, Steve, last year, the two of them becoming the Romeo and Juliet of the twenty-first century.

I held the white pharmacy bag that contained the EPT box and used tests in my right hand. I hadn't brought them along as any kind of proof for Tommy, I just didn't want the evidence within a ten-mile radius of Natalia's house or mine. The first garbage bin I saw, I opened up the lid and pushed the bag deep inside, burying it under McDonald's wrappers and dented soda cans. The odor of garbage didn't help the swirling, nauseated ball in my gut, which was not about being pregnant, I still felt sure, but the anticipation of seeing Tommy again. Not that he was a bad guy. It was just that I hardly knew him. It felt wrong and bizarre, telling him something so personal.

"This seems really pointless," I said, positioning myself directly behind Natalia. "I don't see what he's going to do. I don't see why I should even tell him."

"Of course you have to tell him," Natalia said, striding forward with great purpose. "He's the father."

The nausea widened. If Tommy was the father, what did that make me?

Almost as soon as we stepped through the trees, the blue sky gave way to dusk. I could see Steve, standing by the keg. He wore a white T-shirt cut off at the sleeves, and a knit wool skullcap, even though it was about eighty-six degrees. I don't think I ever saw him without that cap. He waved at us, or at Natalia anyway.

"Don't tell him," I hissed at Natalia.

"I won't," she said, not looking back at me, but walking straight into Steve's arms. He held her tight, the muscles on his forearms taut and sinewy, the set of his jaws and his closed eyes looking totally sincere in his happiness at her presence, and in his love for her. My own chest tightened as Steve's eyes fluttered open—shimmery, gray-blue eyes. He nodded hello at me, his True Love's best friend.

Steve poured a beer for Natalia and one for me. "Is Tommy around?" Natalia said casually. She dipped her fingers into the cup of beer and flicked the foam to the ground. "Sydney needs to talk to him."

"Sure," said Steve. "He's around here somewhere. I think I saw him head down to the railroad tracks with a couple guys."

"It's not important," I said, sipping my beer without getting rid of the foam. I could feel the mustache forming on my lips. "If he's busy."

Steve shrugged. "They're probably just getting high."

He put his arm around Natalia's shoulders, and I wiped my

mouth and followed them down the hill. Now that it was dark, people were arriving by the carload. I jostled my way through laughing bodies, not recognizing anybody. Even in Linden Hill, Natalia and I would have been strangers in a gathering like this. We went to the private day school, where parties mostly involved stolen bottles from our parents' liquor cabinets. Last year Natalia and I had come here with my then boyfriend Greg, who'd heard about the event from one of his older brothers. Natalia and Steve had locked eyes immediately, and over the summer she had—in quick succession—lost her virginity and ruined her relationship with her parents. They didn't want her to have anything to do with a borderline juvenile delinquent who was not Jewish and whose father worked at a gas station.

Usually when a friend got a serious boyfriend, it meant seeing a lot less of her. But Natalia and Steve's relationship required so much plotting, it had brought Natalia and me closer together than ever. Natalia's romance with Steve somehow made all our lives much more exciting, our evenings fueled with the arrangement of secret meetings and plans. Twice she and Steve had run away together—both times discovered before daybreak (the Overpeck police knew Steve well, and they were always glad to help Natalia's parents keep her away from him).

I didn't know if trains still ran over the Overpeck railroad tracks. Part of me thought I had heard them in the distance on some of these foggy, partying nights. But maybe that was just my imagination. They certainly didn't look fit to hold any kind of weight—crooked and cracked, with ancient wood slats crawling with ants and termites. I let Natalia and Steve cross the tracks, then I stood on that rotting wood a minute, almost like I hoped one of those phantom trains would come hurtling down the tracks and mow me down, saving me from all this: the supposed life inside me and all the miserable errands it would require. I could see three teenage boys by the brook that trickled over flat rocks and moss. They all looked completely alien. I couldn't imagine that I was here to tell one of them this terrible secret about myself, one that I still didn't totally believe.

"Sydney," Natalia called. "Come on."

I walked forward. At the sound of Natalia's voice, all three boys looked our way. I heard them say hello to Steve, and then Natalia. They weren't passing a joint back and forth like I'd expected, but a bottle in a brown paper bag. I recognized Tommy, leaning against a tree as if he needed it to hold himself up.

He had shoulder-length hair, not thick and curly like Steve's but fine and shiny. He was short and slight, not much bigger than myself. I'd first met him a month or so before, at a pizza parlor in Overpeck when Natalia and I skipped third period so Steve could pick us up and take us to lunch. That day I'd thought he was very cute in a boy band sort of way, with puppy-dog eyes, smooth skin, and perfect teeth. Afterward, through Natalia, Tommy had relayed messages of how hot he thought I was, how nice and pretty. A week or so later Natalia slept over at my house, and we snuck out after my mom went to bed. Steve and Tommy picked us up at the end of my street and we drove to Flat Rock Brook Park. While Steve and Natalia disappeared up the nature trail, Tommy and I sat on the swings and shared a pint bottle of peach schnapps. I ended up kissing him, and then having sex with him, not because I especially liked him, but because I was flattered by how much he liked me.

I know how that makes me sound. But I wasn't a slut. I had never been a slut. The only other guy I'd ever had sex with had been my boyfriend Greg. We'd gone out all last year, and we'd been in love—not a great romantic drama like Steve and Natalia, but still in love. It had taken me months to decide whether to sleep with Greg, and when I finally did, it was a big event, with roses and soft lights and good French wine stolen from his dad's cellar. Then we broke up, because of a blond cheerleader who now held hands with him in the halls at school.

So when I found myself making out with Tommy in the park, kind of drunk—adored again, for a minute anyway—I went ahead and had sex because that was what I did now. It was like after all those months with Greg, I'd forgotten how *not* to have sex. It was only afterward, picking the dry leaves out of my hair and saying an awkward good-bye—that I realized the whole thing had been, if nothing else, entirely unnecessary. I wasn't even sure if I wanted to see him again. But then the next weekend rolled around, and Natalia had the bright idea that the four of us should go to her house at the shore. It seemed like so much fun to be part of a foursome—with my own Overpeck boyfriend, instead of just being Natalia and Steve's third wheel.

Who knows? I thought. Maybe Tommy and I could be Romeo and Juliet too, except for the fact that my mother would probably like Tommy, who looked so generally harmless.

We took the bus down to Red Hook, where we met the boys and took a taxi to Natalia's. Thank God we didn't get caught until Sunday afternoon. While we were heading back on the bus, Kendra Hirsch's mom had called mine for a copy of the summer reading list. No, she said, Natalia and I were not with them in the Berkshires that weekend. Luckily, by that time Natalia and I could pretend we'd gone to the shore with just each other—earning us two weeks of being grounded instead of a firing squad.

Of course if we'd been caught on, say, Friday, with or without boys, I might not have been standing here, supposedly pregnant from those few attempts at my own wayward romance. I stared at Tommy, who in the hazy dusk looked not only very cute, but extremely drunk and about thirteen years old. I wondered what telling him could possibly accomplish. What was he supposed to do? Marry me? The idea brought a faint, scratchy laugh to my throat. Unlikely as that prospect was, Tommy was equally unlikely to have five hundred dollars, or however much it cost for an abortion.

"Tommy," said Natalia. She reached out and put her hand on his shoulder. He seemed like he needed to be woken up. "Look. Sydney's here."

He raised his eyes to mine. They looked filmy and unfocused, like they probably had the three or four times we'd been together. His skin looked flushed, a faint patch of pink on each cheek. Although he'd probably started shaving as a point of pride, he definitely didn't need to. His face looked very young, very open, and nothing whatsoever to do with me.

"Hey," Tommy said. He pushed himself off the tree and stepped forward with a lurch. "Hey, baby," he said, then tripped over a root and fell flat on his face, landing splayed out at my feet. The bag and bottle slipped out of his hand, not breaking on the soft ground, but seeping through the brown paper and soaking my already wet sneakers with a pungent smell that I'd never be able to hide from my mother.

I stepped back, defeated. "Forget it," I said to Natalia, handing her my half-drunk beer. "Let's just forget the whole thing."

I turned around and ran back over the railroad tracks, over the sprigs of poison ivy and jagged stones, back to the party. I could hear Tommy's friends behind me, laughing and helping him up. I could hear Natalia's light voice calling me, and I pictured Steve holding her arm, escorting her and her stupid shoes around every hole and bump. It wasn't fair. If Natalia were pregnant, Steve would take care of everything. They might even run away and get married, catapulting themselves out of the hell of high school limbo, these stupid parties, and the stupid rules that made them exciting in the first place.

As I ran up the hill, my blood began pumping in a pure and liberating way. Even though it was impossible to the point of ridiculous to think that I might actually be pregnant, this image appeared in my mind for one split second, of a little baby floating around on an umbilical cord, getting bounced and jostled because I was fleeing from half its DNA.

"Sydney," Natalia yelled, and I stopped, not so much because of her order but because I'd reached the threshold of the party, and bodies stood too thick to run through. I waited for her and Steve, my chest rising and falling with labored breaths.

Natalia's face when she reached me looked pink and exhilarated. I couldn't blame her. It was thrilling, all this drama. She still had a beer in one hand, but she placed her other hand on my shoulder and looked directly into my face, searching. "Are you all right?" she asked.

"I'm fine," I said. "But I think I need a plan B."

She nodded and said, "It's not like we really had a plan A," which was true. We hadn't worked out anything besides telling Tommy, as if he would take over the problem and make it right, like some kind of wonder parent. We both laughed now at our lack of logic and foresight.

"We should get back to your house anyway," I said. Natalia's parents were due home from their dinner no later than ten.

While Natalia and Steve began their lengthy and tongue-thrusting farewell, I sidled my way through the party. As I stepped out of the trees and onto the playground, I could see the silent, whooshing lights of a parked police cruiser. I stood there for a minute, watching the red and yellow shadows pulse across the dented metal slides, the merry-go-round's sad and chipping horses.

"Shit," Natalia said, coming up beside me. "Do you think they're here for us?"

"That would be my first guess," I said, "given my recent luck."

There was no point ducking back into the woods. We joined hands and walked toward our decidedly less luxurious—but much safer—ride home.

Natalia's parents were a strange combination of strict and good-natured. They laid down firm laws and drastic repercussions but always did it with sweet, giggly smiles on their faces. Whereas my mother would get angry—screaming and yelling and listing hurt feelings—they would just issue their edicts as if Natalia's adventures were as understandable and expected as they were punishable.

When they'd come home early from dinner, they found our cell phones on Natalia's bed and the new Cadillac missing from the garage. They called the Overpeck police, who discovered the car almost immediately in the playground parking lot. I rode back to Natalia's house in the back of the police car, while Natalia drove the Cadillac sitting next to the younger of our blue-capped escorts. I imagined him flirting and giving her driving tips, while my officer lectured me all the way home.

"You smell like a brewery," he told me. He had a thick New Jersey accent. He sounded a whole lot like Steve and Tommy.

"Someone spilled whiskey on my shoes," I said. I held up

my brown-stained sneaker so he could see it in the rearview mirror.

"You've got no business hanging around kids like that," he said. "A nice girl like you."

I put my foot back on the floor of the car. Where my sneaker had been reflected, I could now see my face, which certainly looked like it belonged to a nice girl. I had big brown Bambi eyes. I had round apple cheeks. I had lips that would not hold any color of lipstick, because my too-big front teeth rested naturally on my bottom lip and couldn't resist scraping it off. I had curly, shoulder-length brown hair. Everyone thought I looked sweet. Innocent. I had "girl next door" written all over me.

"I'm sorry, officer," I said. "I won't do it again. It wasn't much fun anyway."

He laughed, not sure whether I was conning him but charmed anyway. The kids he was used to dealing with were like Tommy and Steve, usually drunk, not politic enough to mind their manners.

When we got back to Natalia's house, her parents stood together between the elaborate columns of their front porch. They waited for us with their arms crossed but big smiles on their faces, as if our disobedience was the funniest thing in the world. Mr. Miksa was somewhere in his sixties, Mrs. Miksa not far behind. Natalia had an older sister, Margit, who was thirty-three and married to a bonds trader named Victor. They had a fancy apartment on West 59th, a block from Sutton Place. Margit had sleek blond hair, a floor-length mink coat, and an incredible collection of shoes—many of which she wore once before handing them down to Natalia.

The year before, we'd watched a show on the Biography channel about an old movie star who found out that his sister was actually his mother and his parents were actually his grandparents. Ever since then, we had decided this must be the case with Natalia and her family. Last summer she had planned to confront them, but her romance with Steve had caused so much trouble, she'd put the revelation on hold.

"Seed-ney, dahling," Mrs. Miksa said. "Your mother will be here in one minute."

Natalia shot me a look of deep, devastated apology. Until that moment, the chance had existed that only she was busted. Mr. Miksa spoke to her in Hungarian. The tone was full of fond hilarity, but the words must have been severe. Her shoulders sagged as she followed him inside.

I stood in the quiet dusk with Mrs. Miksa. Her plump, aged face was pleasantly made-up, her bleached hair swept into an elaborate bun. Even when she came to the pool with Natalia, she always wore heavy, swirling gold earrings. She would do a breaststroke in her thick, bosomy bathing suit, her head carefully perched just above the water.

Now she pinched my cheek and pressed my cell phone into my hand. "I don't tink you'll have this long," she said cheerily. I nodded and stared into the forsythia bushes. After the police car left, the motion-sensor lights had turned off. Only the faint porch light shone above us. I could hear the whistling chirp of cicadas. A stand of honeysuckle braced the west wall of the house, and in the blossoms I saw the summer's first firefly light up, dim, and light again.

"Don't look so stricken, dahling," Mrs. Miksa said. "It won't be a life sentence."

I raised my chin and smiled at her bravely, as if the worst of my problems lay outside and in the present moment—instead of far off in the future, and very deep inside.

chapter two
parents

My mother wasn't the worst in the world. I knew all about those, thanks to broadcast news. Every couple of years there would be a big story about a mother who'd snapped and done away with her kids. One time a mother pushed her car into a lake with two little toddlers locked inside. Another one shot three of her kids in the head, then claimed she'd been mugged by a black man wearing a ski mask. There was one mother who drowned six little kids in a bathtub, and all these women staged protests at her trial—as if being a mother was such a horrible and hair-raising job, who could blame someone for drowning her kids. Every so often this woman would get a new trial, and when she appeared on the TV screen—all beleaguered and bedraggled—my mother always said, "The poor thing," in this tone that made me surprised she ever paid for my swimming lessons.

That night in the car on the way home from Natalia's, and back in our living room, I listened to my mother lecture. I watched her fume and pace—the same old accusations about how I was spoiled, and selfish, and immature. She talked about the weekend Natalia and I went to the shore, and how scared she'd felt when she didn't know where I was. She talked about underage drinking, and she talked about lying as if truth was her religion. All I could think about was what she would say if she knew I was pregnant. Of course I knew what she would do: She would schedule me for an abortion as fast as humanly possible. The thought flooded me with relief, all this worry ended, the procedure paid for and taken care of.

But the hurdle I'd have to jump to get to that point might as well have been Everest. I sat on the comfortable lilac sofa that she longed to have reupholstered (just one in an endless list of sacrifices she made in order to send me to private school), and listened to her rail against me. She kept karate chopping one hand with the other, making her case for my general rottenness. I'd noticed in the last year that the line that appeared between her brows when she was angry had etched itself there permanently. If Mom was this mad over a party—a stupid party that I'd attended for exactly twenty minutes—what would she say if she found out I was pregnant? I thought about that movie star on the Biography channel, how his grandparents raised their daughter's illegitimate child as their own.

Every day my mother made it clear: She'd had it with sacrifices. In a thousand years, in a million years, she would never for a second consider doing something like that for me. Not that I'd want her to. But still. Wouldn't there be something, some deep and important meaning, in the willingness itself? Instead of these daily meltdowns, letting me know how my existence made her life a misery. Sometimes I wondered why she even cared if I snuck away for a weekend or went to a keg party. If I was so much trouble, why not just leave me alone?

I remembered another news story we'd watched together, a long time ago, about a teenage girl who'd hidden a pregnancy. The girl ended up giving birth at her prom. She went into the bathroom and had the baby, then shoved it into a trash can and went back to dancing.

I tried to remember what Mom had said at the time, if she'd been sorry for that girl the way she was for the mother who'd drowned her kids. But I couldn't recall her saying anything, just a sad and curt shake of her head. I guess I could have told her I was pregnant. But I couldn't help feeling that would be handing over the cherry to top off the ice cream sundae of my rottenness.

"Mom," I finally said. "You know I could sit here all night listening to what a terrible person I am. But it's getting late. Do you think we could cut to the chase? Is there going to be some sort of punishment?"

Mom lowered herself into the armchair and stared into my face. It was funny, sometimes, how I could see my own self in her—my own exact eyes looking back at me. My mother and I had been living alone together in this house, since I was eight. I could remember the first couple of years after my dad was gone, how she would let me sleep in her bed, and how at times it seemed like this fantastic boon that I got to keep her all to myself. I couldn't say when exactly she had gone from that familiar comfort to this raging witch. But right now I didn't have the energy to figure it out.

"Sydney," she said, in this pained little voice, "could you please just once cut me the slightest little break?" As if *I* had just been lecturing *her* for the past half hour.

"Me cut *you* a break?" I said. "That's funny, Mom. That is just completely hilarious."

For a second she almost looked like she might cry. "Do you think this is fun for me?" she said. "Do you think I'm enjoying this?"

"No." I slumped on the sofa and tried to look remorseful. It would serve me better, I always realized too late, to act more like I had with the Overpeck police, instead of fighting her every step of the way.

"I don't know why such a smart girl does such stupid things," Mom said. "Sometimes, Syd, I think that's your problem. Everything comes too easily. You don't have to try. You don't have to *do* anything."

"Just because I don't do exactly what you want," I said, immediately forgetting politeness, "doesn't mean I don't do *anything*. I do plenty."

Mom dropped her head onto her hand. In the broad wing-backed chair, she looked small and tired. I felt sad that I'd spoken, and sad that she didn't have nicer furniture. I felt sad that she worked so hard at her stupid and thankless corporate job, and that she hadn't found someone to remarry. Last fall one of the vocabulary words on my PSAT study cards had been "uxorious,"

which means "overly fond of one's wife." Reading that defini-
tion, I'd felt a drop in my stomach, like this word had nothing
to do with me or my mom, like it was from somebody else's
life and we weren't good enough for it. Mom had been single
forever, and frankly I had a hard time imagining my father ever
even liking her. And the whole time I'd considered myself the
perfect girlfriend—had worked so hard to be everything Greg
wanted—I hadn't been able to hold on to him, either.

Mr. Miksa was probably uxorious. Steve would be, if he married Natalia. But at this point, there probably wasn't anybody
who would ever be uxorious to my mom. Or to me. I felt sad
for both of us that on top of this I had somehow turned into
such a burden for her.

"Look," said Mom, not knowing anything that was going
on in my head. "We'll talk about punishment later. Tomorrow
morning you're going to Mr. Biggs."

I stared at her. "Mr. Biggs" was what she had called my dad
since their divorce, a sarcastic kind of snarling, like no one in
the world could be smaller or less significant. She had changed
her name back to Sincero and had tried to have mine changed
legally too. Since she failed, it always struck me as weird that
she used my own last name as a method of distancing herself,
and me, from the man she'd once loved enough to marry.

"You called Dad?" I said. Usually it was a point of pride with
her to leave him out of my situations.

"I did," Mom said. "Because honestly, Sydney, I am at my
wits' end. I don't know how to reach you. If I punish you for

lying, you just lie to avoid the punishment. There's no apology, no remorse. Just that blank, angry stare, like I'm some kind of jailer. I don't have any interest in being a jailer, so I'm going to let your father have a try. He thinks he knows how to save the world? Let him start with his own daughter."

For the past few years, all visitation with my father had been entirely up to Mom, and she usually only doled it out when I asked her. The thought of her relinquishing me to him wasn't terrible in practice, even though it would mean sleeping in a full-size bed sandwiched between his three-year-old twins. The chaos of Dad's household seemed like exactly the distraction I needed. But there was something unsettling about her willingness to hand me over, after all those years of fighting against exactly that. It felt like a kind of disownment. If I'd considered for the barest second telling her about being pregnant, I knew now that it was out of the question.

"How long will I stay there?" I asked. My dad didn't even own a computer. Without my cell phone, I'd be cut off from the entire world.

She raised her hands in an open question, looking pleased that I seemed worried.

"We'll see," she said.

"But I have to be back by the end of next week," I said. "To start at the pool."

"The pool," she echoed. "We'll have to wait and see."

"But Mom . . ."

"Good night, Sydney," she said, her voice flat and emotionless.

I stood up, recognizing this as my dismissal, and went to my room, strangely sad that the lecture was over and nothing had changed.

My mother took my cell phone, but she forgot about my laptop. I waited until I heard her go to bed, then IM'd Natalia.

They're going to do it, she wrote me right away. *They're sending me to Switzerland.*

All year, with Natalia sneaking around with Steve, this had been the threat: that they would ship her off to boarding school in Switzerland. "It vill be fun!" Mrs. Miksa would say. "It vill be glamorous! You can ski every day!"

To us it didn't sound fun or glamorous. It sounded like a strange, wintry exile. How could I ever be expected to live without Natalia? How could she be expected to exist an entire continent away from Steve? Away from our friends, our whole world? Switzerland might as well be the moon, without gravity or oxygen.

They're just pissed, I wrote back. *You can talk them out of it.*

No, she wrote. *It's for real this time. I know it is. But what are we going to do about you??????*

I can't talk about it here.

Time is of the essence, she wrote. *We have to get you to P.P.*

I shuddered at how decodable this message was and gave a little prayer of thanks for my Mom's IM cluelessness.

Can't tomorrow, I wrote. *Going to Dad's.*

What??!!! That's so wrong.

I know. I'll call you from there.

I signed off before she could write anything further. Then I stashed the computer back under my bed. My heart did a funny, runaway kind of pounding. I rested my head on my pillows and did my yoga deep breathing to calm myself down. Soul-cleansing breaths, my teacher called them.

Abortion was all about the first trimester. That had to be at least twelve weeks. The night in the park with Tommy had been just over three weeks ago. I had the entire summer, which meant I had all the time in the world.

Two days later I sat in my father's kitchen with Rebecca, my eight-month-old half sister, in my lap. My stepmother, Kerry, worked on dinner.

"So what's so bad about this guy Steve?" Kerry said. She stood over the long kitchen table, rolling out dough for an apple pie. Strands of blond hair fell into her face. Her arms were almost as white as the flour that covered them, and they jiggled as she pounded out the crust. At twenty-nine, Kerry still had a pretty, unlined face, and she loved listening to my high school gossip. But in the past four years, since the twins and then Rebecca, she had gained over a hundred pounds. Her flesh moved in a strangely graceful rhythm, and she made little puffing noises while she worked.

"For starters," I said, "he's not Jewish. And he goes to public school. Natalia's parents think he's a thug."

"Is he?" Kerry asked.

I considered this, bouncing the baby on one knee. I thought Steve was very nice. He had a slow, kind smile, and those pretty blue eyes. He didn't speak well—his accent was pure New Jersey, and his diction was terrible—but sometimes he would make surprising observations, about a fish swimming upstream in that sad Overpeck brook, or about a scene in a movie that he'd snuck into after our parents had dropped off Natalia and me. I knew he had a police record, but only for petty things, like underage drinking, maybe a shoplifting incident or two. Once he had been suspended for bringing a gun to school— they'd found it in his locker—but it hadn't been loaded. He said he only wanted to show it to a friend whose uncle collected antique weapons.

"Maybe a little," I said.

"Still." Kerry sat down and pushed the hair out of her eyes with her forearm. "It doesn't seem fair that you would be in so much trouble. It's not like you're the one with the inappropriate boyfriend. You were just helping out a friend."

Kerry loved making this kind of dig at my mother, like she was the cool friend and Mom the evil disciplinarian. In the past, I might have made the mistake of defending my mother, pointing out her valid reasons for being angry at me—the fact that I'd lied about where I'd be, and that I'd been drinking. But by now I knew that Kerry would report the conversation word for word to my father, so I just shrugged in agreement at the injustice of it all.

From the next room, we heard a gigantic crash, and then

one of the twins—Ezra or Aaron—started screaming. "Oh, no," Kerry said, and dashed out of her chair surprisingly fast for a two-hundred-pound woman. At the loud noise and her mother's departure, Rebecca started screaming too. I stuck my finger in her mouth, but it didn't help at all. Kerry was a big believer in breast-feeding, and the only thing that ever calmed her babies down was one of her giant boobs. I stood up and patted Rebecca on the back, walking her up and down the kitchen. I sang a little, but without much feeling, knowing nothing I did would make a difference until Kerry returned and peeled off her shirt.

"Did anything break?" I called to Kerry. My dad did all the deliveries for the Bulgar County Farmer's Market. He and Kerry lived in the refurbished barn that belonged to Bob Pearson, one of the bigger farmers. Almost none of the furniture belonged to them, and they lived in constant fear of destroying things.

"No," Kerry called back, thinking I meant one of the kids' bones. "Ezra just banged his toe when the loom fell over."

Rebecca kept on wailing, and I started to feel this very frantic sense of panic deep in my gut. Like if she didn't stop crying, my head would explode. "Come on," I whispered to the baby. "Come on, you can stop it now." I hardly ever thought of my dad's kids as my sister or brothers. To me they didn't seem much different from the little kids at the pool, or the neighbors whom I occasionally babysat. They were just children, cute when they were laughing or snuggling, unbearable when—like now—they were screaming.

"Okay, Kerry," I called. "I think she's ready for her mom."

Kerry whisked in and plucked Rebecca out of my arms. In one smooth motion, she sat down, popped out a boob, and dropped it into the baby's mouth. Rebecca transformed from squalling anguish to blissful relaxation, her eyes half-closed and glazed in a happy stupor. She reached her chubby baby hand toward her mother, and Kerry absentmindedly twined her long, fat fingers into the baby's short fat fingers. The gesture from Rebecca, holding hands like that, seemed impressively human. It always took me by surprise, those moments when I realized my dad's kids were actual little people and not glorified pets.

I wondered if Kerry would take my baby if I ended up having it. This morning I had read in one of her baby books that it was possible for a woman who already had biological kids to breast-feed an adopted child. The sucking triggered the hormones, or something like that. So theoretically, Kerry would be able to supply milk for a baby she hadn't actually borne.

In the same baby book, I read that you start counting weeks for a pregnancy on the first day of your last period, which essentially meant I had been robbed of two weeks. According to the long list of authors on the front of Kerry's book, I was now nearly five weeks pregnant. The logic of this—counting back to before the thing even existed—struck me as ridiculous and unfair. Across the country politicians and Christians fought over whether life began at conception. Apparently they didn't know the medical community had already decided: It began two weeks before.

From outside, we heard Dad's truck rumble over the long, dusty driveway.

"Shit," Kerry said.

My dad had this thing about whole, unprocessed food. Once when I was about eleven, he sat me down with this very serious look on his face. I thought he was going to give me a lecture on the birds and the bees. Instead he told me about the modern wasteland that is the chain supermarket, and gave me very specific instructions on navigating it by sticking only to the very perimeter of grocery stores. "Never go down the aisles," he told me. He sounded so serious that I always battled a pang of guilt if I turned from the main course into the pasta aisle, or even to buy a package of toilet paper.

The food thing was one of the reasons my parents had broken up. "Your father becomes very fixated," my mother always said. Though I took much of what she said about him with a grain of salt, I knew that she was right about this particular trait. Way back when we all lived together, and my father had worked keeping books for an architectural firm, he had read this article about the cattle industry, how the cows were overdosed on antibiotics and growth hormones. He started taking out books from the library and clipping newspaper articles about E. coli, and the next thing we knew he had quit his job and begun working for a guy who distributed grass-fed beef.

"Grass-fed beef," my mother said, "grass-fed beef. Those were the only words I ever heard come out of his mouth. We could start out talking about the Dalai Lama, or our honeymoon in Barbados. It always led back to grass-fed beef. It was enough to turn me into a vegetarian, all the ins and outs of those stupid cows."

The grass-fed beef obsession had long since given way to peak oil and self-sustaining communities, but Kerry still spent half the day doing what my mother had gotten divorced to avoid: making elaborate, organic meals from scratch. They were never ready when my father walked through the door, and he always heaved a sigh of disappointment at the world's inability to measure up to his high ideals.

Kerry stood up and placed Rebecca back into my lap. The baby sighed and flopped her head against my stomach, sleeping happily.

Kerry peered into the oven at the meat loaf she'd made from hormone-free (and of course grass-fed) beef, pureed onions, and broccoli florets. The vegetables were from my father's garden, but I happened to know the meat loaf also contained a secret cup of Heinz 57 sauce. I'd seen Kerry hide the bottle in the garbage underneath the plain brown meat wrappers.

"I promise," she said to my father, "dinner will be ready in thirty minutes."

"That's fine," Dad said. "I want to talk to Sydney for a while anyway. Syd? You up for a walk?"

We went outside together, into the broad, bright evening. My dad lived a forty-minute drive from my mother's modest but well-kept house in the neighborhood she couldn't really afford. But Dad's life seemed so many miles farther than that, away from the suburban lawns and microwave ovens. He never allowed me to bring my computer, or my cell phone, or my iPod, which meant—among so many other reasons—that I hardly ever visited. And when I did, I felt like I'd entered one of those reality TV shows, where for no good reason people pretend they're living in 1632.

Dad and I walked down the dirt path from his house onto the dusty road. I could smell some sort of roast from the main house, battling the rich waft from Kerry's meat loaf. I knew this was the sort of thing a pregnant woman should be bothered by, these dueling odors. But I felt fine, only mildly hungry. Beyond the two buildings, horses grazed in a meadow and rows of corn stretched out to the horizon. Nobody would guess that New York City was less than an hour away, never mind the industrial chimneys that lined the New Jersey Turnpike.

Dad kept his hands in his pockets. His eyes fixed on the road in a habitual squint, as if something perplexed him, or he needed sunglasses. I tried not to fidget or look away from him. The truth was, under the best of circumstances I dreaded time alone with my father. Even though I had no particular emotional attachment to Kerry, I found her company much more natural. With her love of gossip and the built-in conversation piece of her children, Kerry was easy to talk to, whereas with my father I always found myself worked into a mild panic, racking my brain for something to discuss. It almost made it easier knowing that he had a particular grievance.

We stopped at the top of a low hill just beside his vegetable garden. Rows of tomatoes and lettuce were lined up neatly and impressively. He let his eyes rove happily over the sprouting plants with their neatly lettered signs, a kind of satisfied pride I never noticed when he observed his children. Then he knelt down and pulled a head of Bibb lettuce from the ground, lovingly brushing dirt away from the roots. In half an hour, these greens would be a salad at the center of our dinner table.

"Grab some tomatoes," he said, and I bent down to inspect the stalk for ripe ones. Dad watched me, but I couldn't tell what, if anything, he was thinking. He didn't tend to speak much unless sparked on one of his pet topics. I could never tell exactly what would do this. Once when he took me fishing on Redtop Lake, I'd worn a "Life Is Good" baseball cap. He'd ranted on and on the whole afternoon, about how he hated my hat because life wasn't, in fact, good. It might be good, if only we could do away with corporate greed, and processed food, and the industrialized world's addiction to fossil fuel.

Dad had this whole apocalyptic theory about how oil would run out in the next few years. Suddenly the supply would just stop, and almost immediately our entire culture would crumble. Nobody would be able to get food or clean water, there would be riots in the streets, and everybody who didn't know how to can fruit and grow their own produce would perish. The year before last I'd started coming home from our scheduled visits with nightmares about being stuck in the city when the oil ran out. I'd dream I was fighting my way to the old railway tracks, where people were being loaded aboard a train like some old World War II movie. Three nights in a row I woke up screaming, so my mother called her lawyer. In the affidavit for his appeal, my father wrote a defense of my nightmares—how they were grounded in coming events. The family court judge stripped him of visitation rights, so instead of staying with him every other weekend and over holidays, I saw him only when my mother decided it was appropriate, meaning convenient for her.

Like now. "The thing is," my father said, "kids in the suburbs are separated from the natural world. When you don't know where your food comes from, when you're not connected with the practical strength of your own body, you have nothing to do but look for artificial ways to expend your energy. It's like keeping a border collie for a pet. The dog was meant for working, and if it doesn't have work, it ends up chasing a tetherball round and round till it wears itself out."

I plucked two pale orange tomatoes and held them up to my nose. They smelled sweet and grassy. I didn't remember much about when my father lived with Mom and me, but I knew there had been a family next door to us that owned a lunatic border collie. The dog was obsessed with the tetherball set in the backyard, and from morning till night it would chase the ball back and forth, like the polar bear that swam endless laps at the Central Park Zoo. Even at seven years old I had recognized this behavior as perverse, disturbing, and very sad. I felt insulted and confused that my father would compare me to that neurotic dog.

"The other night was really not such a big deal," I said. "We just went to a party. It wasn't even late. We were back before nine o'clock."

"You took a car without asking," my father said. "Your friend drove without a license—as if this nation doesn't waste enough gas with the licensed drivers on the road. The police brought you home. And you'd been drinking."

At this last he looked at me, particularly disappointed. Dad didn't believe in putting anything into the body that didn't have nutritional value. He himself wouldn't eat Kerry's apple pie— disapproving of sugar, even the raw brown sugar that she used to placate him. His own body was very lean from following this diet, not the barest ounce of fat. Clothes hung from his sharp edges in straight, neat lines, no extra flesh to interrupt gravity's pull. The rest of us couldn't help but feel soft and hedonistic in his presence, dependent on the world's pleasures instead of its healthful possibility.

"I'm sorry," I said. "It won't happen again."

"But it does happen again," he said. "It happens over and over again, and you end up in the same place. You end up with your parents disappointed in you."

I waited for him to say something else, to elaborate—with specific instances, or his own opinion—but he didn't. He turned and headed back to the house, as if our main objective had been gathering food and the conversation only a way of passing the time. I stood watching him for a second, then ran a few steps to catch up.

My father was quiet a minute. Then he said, "Bob Pearson has a friend who runs canoe trips up in Canada from a place called Camp Bell. Kids spend the summer paddling on a lake in Ontario, camping out on islands. No electronics. No motorized vehicles."

"Huh," I said. I didn't take the information as any sort of suggestion. Dad often held up other people's activities as examples of the wholesomeness I lacked.

He didn't say anything else on the way back to the house. It occurred to me that I had no idea how he felt about abortion. Whatever the recent divide between my mother and me, I knew her very well. I could write a term paper on almost any one of her opinions, political or otherwise. I knew exactly what she thought about reproductive freedom, and how deeply she believed in what she would call "a woman's right to choose."

But with my dad—apart from foreign oil, processed foods, and the "Life Is Good" logo—I knew very little about what he thought about anything. I wondered what he would say if I told him I was pregnant. I wondered if he would want me to have an abortion, or keep it, or have someone adopt it. In my head a funny sepia image appeared of an old-fashioned home for unwed mothers, and me standing at a sink, washing sheets for the nuns.

We walked inside, and Dad handed me the lettuce. I went to

the sink to wash it. I chopped up the tomatoes and tossed them with vinegar, oil, and fresh herbs in the wide, cracked wooden salad bowl. Kerry's meat loaf sat cooling on a rack, inches away from where I worked, and it was all I could do not to plunge my fist into the brown, gelatinous crust—shining with a pool of broccoli-flecked gravy.

That ten-minute walk might have been a twenty-mile hike through the desert. I couldn't wait to sit down to dinner. I was ravenous.

chapter three
my fate, their hands

While I was at my dad's, my mother sent me a letter that read like a rap sheet, listing everything I'd done wrong in the past year. I had been caught spending the night at Greg's when his parents were away and I was supposed to be at Natalia's. Three times I had been caught in lies, covering for Natalia when she was secretly meeting Steve. My grades had slipped, and I had waited two full weeks before telling her that I quit the swim team. "These instances only represent your getting caught," she wrote. "I suspect they represent a very small fraction of unsavory and habitual activity."

I wasn't sure about her word choice. Unsavory? But if she meant drinking and sex and occasional mild drug use, of course she was right. Her biggest grievance was the weekend I'd gone to the shore with Natalia.

It frightens me that for two entire days I thought you were one place, only to discover you were someplace else. It frightens me to realize the extent to which I cannot trust you. I feel that you have been slipping

away from me and that coddling and protecting you
is no longer the best course of action.

She went on like that, laying on some very heavy guilt about how hard it was to raise a child all by herself, let alone keep me in private school.

I'm becoming increasingly reluctant to do this. Your
father has always refused to contribute to your
tuition. It is an enormous expense for me, and it
doesn't seem to be doing you any particular good.

My heart sank. I had been at Linden Hill Country Day since pre-K. I had a regular spot at the best lunch tables, and this was not just a matter of status. It was a matter of all my friends, some of whom I loved nearly as much as Natalia. For the past few years these girls had been the heart of my emotional life, more than either of my parents or my tiny half siblings. It was bad enough Natalia's parents might send her away. I couldn't imagine being ripped from the school I'd attended since I was four years old, to be sent instead to a public school with bells and crowded hallways. And Natalia thought she had it bad, threatened with ritzy exile among wealthy Europeans!

My hands shook as I read my mother's letter. I was sure she couldn't wait to start spending the money that had been set aside for my tuition. I imagined her at that very moment, sending our furniture out to the upholsterer while she drove into the city for a shopping spree at Bloomingdale's or Talbots or wherever she bought her lame clothes. But of course she disguised her giddiness by trying to sound 100 percent stern:

> *I'm going to wait on making that decision. In the meantime, I'm going to leave it up to your father as to what to do with you this summer. If he wants to keep you there as a mother's helper, that's fine with me. If he wants to send you to some free-range veal cooperative to give back rubs to baby cows, I'll agree. But for now, you're not coming back here.*

I put down the letter and marched straight to the phone. Mom picked up at work and spoke in her fake professional voice, all silky and confident. "Alicia Sincero," she said.

As soon as she heard it was me, her voice turned from silk to sandpaper. "Sydney," she said, "my mind's made up. For the next two months you belong to your father. If you have any problems or complaints, I suggest you bring them to him."

"But what about the pool?" I said. "They're expecting me to start next week."

"I've already told them that won't be possible."

A surge of fury overwhelmed me. That was *my* job. I'd earned it by spending last summer measuring the pH balance of the pool, skimming leaves, and bussing outdoor tables of potato chip bags and soda bottles. Sometimes I'd been able to sub for one of the regular lifeguards, wearing a red suit and a shiny whistle. Everyone I knew was jealous of my job. I'd worked hard for it. She had no right to tell them I wouldn't be there, and I told her so.

"I think you have a very skewed idea about what I have the right to do," said Mom. "You are a minor child. I am your mother. I am fully within my rights making a decision about what you will do during the summer."

I started to say something about her being a hypocrite, preventing me from making money when she claimed it was so hard sending me to private school. But then I remembered that in the few jobs I'd ever had, babysitting or working for the country club, I'd never given a penny of what I earned to my mother. I'd never pitched in for my own necessities, but just spent the money on little luxuries. Most of my friends came from such wealthy families. It never seemed fair that I couldn't have the things they took for granted. Why shouldn't I spend the money I earned on myself? It was just the barest fraction of Natalia's weekly allowance, which her parents immediately supplemented whenever she asked.

"This is completely unfair," I told my mother. I knew the words were cliché teenager, but they were so accurate—so true—that I couldn't prevent them from coming out of my mouth. I was equally powerless over the petulant, tear-shaky tone of my voice.

"That's a very predictable reaction," Mom said, predictably, and below her icy tone I could hear a faint note of glee that she had gotten to me. "I'm sorry that you feel that way, but I can only hope this will make you think for a moment the next time you feel like stealing a Cadillac and attending a keg party."

Tears sprang to my eyes. It was so . . . unfair. That was the only word. I hadn't had any choice about that party and taking Mrs. Miksa's car. I was pregnant. Telling Tommy had seemed, at that moment, like the most important thing in the world. It had almost felt like my only responsibility had been getting to Tommy and telling him I was pregnant, and then the whole situation would somehow, magically, disappear.

But of course I remembered how that had gone. And I admitted to myself that if I hadn't been pregnant, Natalia and I would probably have gone to the party anyway, and we probably would have stayed a whole lot longer.

"Sydney?" said Mom. "Are you still there?"

I made a little noise in my throat.

"I have to go back to work now," she said.

"Fine," I said. "Thank you so much, Mom, for all your help. I feel like a better person already. I feel reformed. I'm going to run right upstairs and start working on the New Me. I think first I'll end world hunger, then start writing my application to Harvard. Because your new method of discipline, it's just taught me so much about myself and the kind of person I want to be. It's given me so much wisdom and maturity."

"Good-bye, Syd," Mom said. And then she hung up.

I slammed down the phone. Even though my mother didn't know I was pregnant, I still felt like she was abandoning me when I needed her most. It didn't matter that she didn't have all the information. The fact that I couldn't tell her—that she made it impossible to tell her—felt like its own kind of cold, uncaring desertion.

It seemed to me that everyone always focused on the wrong things. For example, Mr. and Mrs. Miksa thinking that Natalia shouldn't date a boy who wasn't Jewish. What did it matter? It wasn't like she was going to marry someone she met when she was sixteen, or have his children. They didn't care that I, her best friend, wasn't Jewish. So what did it matter about Steve?

My mother was all hung up on obedience and truth. My father was obsessed with values and ideals that no normal person could ever live up to; even his wife snuck products containing high fructose corn syrup into the meat loaf, and I knew she kept a stash of Snickers, Pop-Tarts, and Marshmallow Fluff hidden under the floorboards of the Pearsons' chicken coop. I had sat out there with her on rainy days, dribbling melted chocolate and marshmallow onto frosted raspberry while the twins tormented the roosting hens.

I didn't exactly know the alternative, what my parents should be focusing on instead of the incident with the car. But I knew there should have been something—something that would make it possible for me to explain my situation. Because talk about focusing on the wrong thing! Here I stood, steaming at my mother because I'd lost my summer job, when what I really needed was a Planned Parenthood, pronto, because the secret inside me would grow bigger and closer to reality with every day that passed.

I looked through the kitchen drawers and found an old, frayed phone book. To my surprise, "Abortion" was the very first heading in the Yellow Pages. I would have thought that word would be too obvious. But there it was, the first word on the first page. Abortion. The first organizations were actually under the heading "Abortion Alternatives," which had three listings. One was called A Woman's Concern. Then there was Birthright of Northern New Jersey, and New Jersey Citizens for Life. I knew that if I called any of them, I would get a lecture on the evils of abortion. They'd call it murder. Being against sex education themselves, they probably wouldn't have taken it, so they might not know it was illegal to inform my parents. Probably they would drop the name Jesus Christ into the conversation and tell me that fetuses screamed during D & C's. I'd learned in health class that this was false. It's not possible to scream if you don't have functioning lungs.

At any rate: The New Jersey Citizens for Life would pretend to care about me, but their real goal would be nine months down the road, a nice white baby for a nice white—and Christian—family.

So on to the next set of listings: "Abortion Providers." These had friendlier and more familiar names, like Women's Health Services and of course Planned Parenthood. All of them were located in West Falls, a town I'd never even heard of. I dialed each number, only to receive that annoying succession of tones and a recorded voice telling me I had to first dial a 1. If I did this, the numbers would show up on my father's long-distance bill. I had no idea what his habits were regarding that particular document, but I couldn't take the chance that he went over it the way my mother did—like an Al-Qaeda operative lived in the house. She always dialed any unfamiliar numbers.

Besides, what would calling Planned Parenthood do for me? I had no car and no driver's license. I still didn't know how much an abortion cost, but I guessed it was more than the eighteen dollars in my wallet—all the money I had to my name before my job at the pool started (or didn't start) next week.

It seemed ridiculous that I didn't know exactly what to do and exactly how to do it. After all, Linden Hill Country Day was a good, liberal academy. Starting in seventh grade, we'd had health class, otherwise known as sex education. The teachers had drummed certain facts into our heads, repeating them over and over again. We knew that we should always use condoms, *always*, because one time was all it took to get pregnant or catch an STD. We knew that coitus interruptus was no form of birth control, because that tiny drop of semen at the end of an erect penis contained about a zillion sperm. We knew we were legally entitled to private birth control counseling, and also private abortion counseling. I could walk into any clinic in the country and get birth control pills or an abortion without my parents ever finding out.

I'd thought I knew everything there was to know. Until those two pink lines came up on that stupid stick, I considered myself properly educated. My education had, after all, served me well with Greg—who had been in the very same Health class. Whenever we had sex, we always used a condom plus an extra dose of spermicide.

But with Tommy, I hadn't felt like I knew him well enough to remind him about the condom issue. It seemed so stupid now, but at the time it just felt so priggish to raise the topic, as priggish as saying no would have been. There were Natalia and Steve, all rapturous and adventurous and in love. I would have felt like such a killjoy bringing up a technical and unromantic word like "condom."

Tommy and I had had sex a grand total of four times. After the first time, I thought, *Next time I'm going to tell him.* But somehow time number two rolled around and I just didn't, maybe because nothing really bad had ever happened to me. In my head I knew the right words to say, and the right precautions to take, but I had a hard time believing they actually mattered. I could think a thing, I could worry about it, but I still wouldn't believe anything like a pregnancy would ever happen to *me.* It was sort of like thinking Margit might be Natalia's mom. An interesting idea, maybe even a probable one, but too huge and troubling to ever seem real.

At Natalia's beach house, I'd finally taken out a couple of condoms and put them on top of the bedside table. Tommy had looked at them and shrugged, like what was the point now, but then bit off the wrapper at the appropriate time. Talk about too little too late. And now, after all that careful education, it turned out that the only thing I knew about abortion was that I was allowed to have one. Thanks to that great sex ed program, none of my friends had ever gotten pregnant. I didn't know anything about the procedure, if I'd need to stay in the hospital, or if they'd just let me go home on my own afterward. Would I need painkillers? Would I bleed for a long time? Would it be like an operation, or would they just give me one of those pills I'd heard about when my mom listened to *All Things Considered*?

I closed the phone book and crammed it back into the drawer. Upstairs, I heard Rebecca waking up from her nap.

"I'll get her," I called outside to Kerry, who was playing with the twins on the front lawn.

I trudged upstairs toward the wailing baby. One thing was clear. In order to take care of my current state—in order to end my pregnancy—I had to get back home. At home I could work to get money. My friends could help with transportation. I could figure some way to get an abortion.

Rebecca slept in a plain wooden crib next to Dad and Kerry's bed. To my surprise, she stopped crying when I peered in at her. She looked up at me and grabbed her feet, a big smile on her drooly face. She had big dark eyes, which was funny because I always thought I'd inherited that feature from my mom.

"Hi, baby," I said to her.

She reached out her fat little arms in a way that so clearly said, *Pick me up,* I had to laugh. I hoisted her onto my hip, which seemed to have a little groove that was tailor-made for carrying babies. Rebecca grabbed a piece of my hair and put it into her mouth.

"Ouch," I said. "That's gross." I could feel her soggy diaper—cloth, of course—seeping into my clean jeans. Hauling her over to the changing table, I peeled off the diaper and threw it into the hamper. My dad didn't believe in diaper services because of the chemicals they used, so Kerry washed every single one by hand. She had done this even with the twins. When I told my mother, she laughed. "So much for virtue being its own reward," she said.

I cleaned Rebecca up and slathered her with Butt Balm—she always had a screaming red rash, which I knew came from wearing the cloth diapers instead of the disposable ones. As soon as I had her all diapered and fresh, she started screaming, like she'd just realized she was hungry and knew there was nothing I could do for her in that department.

"Okay, okay," I said, carrying her downstairs to her mother. If Rebecca were my baby, I thought, there would be no one to hand her off to. If I had a baby next year, she would barely be one year younger than my own sister. The idea would have made me wail right along with Rebecca if it still didn't feel so untrue. In my heart, I couldn't quite make the idea of a baby seem real. I felt totally normal, not at all like my body was busy spinning little fingers and toes and internal organs.

I carried the crying baby out into the bright sunlight, back into the arms of her rightful owner.

When my dad's truck pulled up that evening, I was waiting

for him in the driveway. Kerry worked in the kitchen, basting a free-range chicken while the twins played with wooden blocks underneath the table. I had Rebecca on my chest in a BabyBjörn. Kerry had filled her up with mother's milk before strapping her onto my body and shooing me out the door.

Dad climbed out of the truck and squinted at us, his two daughters, as if trying to remember exactly who we were. "I have to talk to you," I said to him. "I spoke to Mom today."

"She told me."

"She did?" The thought of my parents talking—maybe even agreeing—was as unbelievable as my pregnancy.

"She called after you spoke. I told her what I had in mind for you, and she thought it sounded like a good idea."

"Listen," I said, the panic rising again. "I think the best thing would be for me to go home and start my job. I can probably still get it back. What if I promised that I'd give everything I made to Mom to pay for school?" As soon as I spoke, I saw my money for the abortion flying out the window. But as long as I could get home, I knew I would find the resources to take care of myself. It was only being out here, stranded, that made me helpless.

"I don't know how much they're paying you at the country club, but I don't expect it would make a dent in your tuition."

"But you know," I said, "it would be good for me, to work and to make sacrifices."

"I don't see sitting on your ass watching rich people swim as much of a sacrifice," Dad said. I stared at him. He almost sounded angry, which was at least an emotion. I reached up and took hold of Rebecca's hands, which she had been waving in an effort to get his attention. So far, he hadn't seemed to notice.

"I could help Mom around the house," I said, my voice getting fainter, the fact of my losing battle more and more apparent. Dad just stood there squinting at me, like a cowboy in some black-and-white Western.

"Remember I told you yesterday about Bob Pearson's friend who runs canoe trips in Canada? It's called Camp Bell Wilderness Adventure."

I could hear a cow, lowing off in the distance. A quieter, mewling sound answered its call. A mother, probably, searching for a wayward calf.

"Well, Pearson's friend—his name is Campbell—has a farm not far from here, just a mile or two up the road."

"Campbell," I said. "I get it. Camp Bell." Dad put his hands in his pockets, and I could tell even he agreed this was unspeakably cheesy.

"Pearson takes care of his place in the summer, when Campbell's up in Canada," Dad said. "I've worked out a deal with them. You can leave next week to spend July in Canada, canoeing on a lake in Ontario. Then when you return you'll work at Campbell's farm in August to pay him back. You'll live here and spend the day working in his vegetable gardens, weeding and picking, and selling produce at his roadside stand."

I tilted my head. "I'm going to spend a month canoeing?"

A quick time line formed in my mind. Five weeks plus one week plus four weeks.

"You used to like it," he said. "Being on the water."

The first three summers after my parents divorced, Dad had taken me river rafting on the Green River in Colorado. We went with one of his friends, a divorced father who had two kids close to my age. We would spend a week winding our way down the river and camping every night in tents on the bank. Before I'd discovered boys, and beer, it had been the most fun I'd ever had in my life. It surprised me that my father knew this. It surprised me even more that he'd want to give it back to me now. From his perspective, it must have seemed more like a gift than a punishment. And even though I knew the idea should send me into a giant panic—weeks lost, farther and farther from any chance of abortion—for some reason it flooded me with calm.

"I think it will be good for you," Dad said, as if reading my mind, "to get back to something healthful, something physical. It will be good for you to go to sleep outside with aching arms. No cell phones. No Internet. No TV. Just campfires and constellations. I'll give you a map of the summer sky to take with you. It seems to me you've got so much noise in your head, you can't even remember who you are. Maybe this will remind you."

My eyes filled up with tears. I pictured myself as the person I wanted to be—not pregnant and escorted home by the Overpeck police, but strong and wholesome, my arms cut and brown from a month of rowing and living on the water.

I wondered what the other kids would be like, the ones on the trip, and imagined the cool new friends I'd make. It was so unexpected, this sudden adventure. I couldn't believe my dad would think of it, that he'd want to send me on a trip like that instead of making me work at his place—the Cinderella stepsister, tending babies and sweeping out the fireplace.

I thought about myself just floating down a river. Not worrying about where the water would take me, but just letting myself be carried away. It seemed so easy, so effortless.

"That sounds amazing, Dad," I said. "Thank you so much."

He smiled. Probably he'd expected me to be indignant instead of grateful. He patted me on the head, an awkward attempt at affection, and I stepped forward and hugged him. I put my arms around his waist and pressed my face into his chest. Rebecca squeaked in protest, squished between us.

Dad thumped my back in an uncharacteristically natural gesture. "Come on," he said. "I'm starving." He didn't know that dinner was more than an hour away.

Which didn't bother me, because I wasn't hungry in the slightest.

That night, after everyone had gone to bed, I snuck downstairs and risked my dad's phone bill review by calling Natalia. Unfortunately, her cell phone had been canceled. The next morning, after Dad went to work, I asked Kerry if I could call my friend. "Sure you can," she said. "I know how it is."

Of course, they didn't have so much as a cordless phone. My

only chance at privacy was their bedroom, while Kerry played downstairs with the kids. "Hello, Mrs. Miksa," I said, when Natalia's mother answered.

"Seed-ney, dahling! How is the farm?"

Several niceties later, Natalia came on the line and I told her about my father's plan.

"Oh my God," Natalia said. "We have to come up with something. I'm going to find a way to get my mom's car. I'll come out and get you, and take you to a clinic. Then we can spend a night in a hotel somewhere. They'll know we ran away, but they never need to know why."

I twisted the phone cord around my finger. If we ran away, there was no way I'd be allowed to go on the canoe trip. I told Natalia this.

"Fuck the canoe trip," Natalia said. "You need to get that baby out of your body."

"Shhh," I hissed, not knowing whether her parents could hear her. "And don't call it a baby."

"A baby is exactly what it's going to be if you don't do something very soon."

"That's not true," I said. The way I figured, I had plenty of time. Postponing my abortion four weeks—even, worst-case scenario, seven weeks—should not be a problem. "I've got till, like, twelve weeks," I told Natalia.

"You're crazy."

"Anyway," I said, "I don't have any money."

Natalia paused. Through her parents, she had regular access

to small amounts of cash, but nothing like what we'd need for the abortion. "Maybe I could take something from around here," she offered. "Steve could sell it for us. There are so many knickknacks, they'd never miss one or two."

"Well," I said, "maybe we can plan that for when I get home. The beginning of August, when I get back from Canada, you can come get me and I'll have the abortion."

"That would give me more time to collect money," Natalia said. "I can just keep putting cash aside, and maybe sneak some from their wallets here and there. I should be able to save a few hundred in a month."

"Okay," I said. "Then it's all set."

"Another idea," she said, "is that I could come on the trip with you."

I hated this immediately, which surprised me. Usually distance from Natalia made me feel lost and panicked. But if she came along on the trip, I would have to talk about being pregnant every day. I realized that one of the things I'd really been looking forward to was just not thinking about it for a while.

"If you come on the trip," I said, "how would you get the money?"

"I'll think of some way."

"Your parents would never let you come."

"Maybe not," Natalia said, instead of arguing. I could tell she felt a little hurt that I hadn't jumped at the thought of her coming along. "Do you feel all right?" she asked. "Do you feel sick?"

"Not a bit," I said, which was true. I felt light and airy, as if the pregnancy had already been terminated. "I'm just fine."

"Sometimes I worry," she said, "that you're going to turn into one of those girls who pretends she isn't pregnant and then throws the baby into a Dumpster."

A cool summer breeze drifted in the window, making the fish mobile over Rebecca's crib sway and circle. Her tiny patchwork quilt was tangled around the worn, eyeless bunny that Aaron used to chew on constantly. He'd called it the Love Bunny.

"I would never do something like that," I told Natalia.

We spoke for a few minutes more. I told her I'd try to call again before I left next week, but that I couldn't make any promises. It was only after we'd hung up that I realized I'd forgotten to ask about Switzerland, or if she'd had a chance to rendezvous with Steve.

I walked downstairs to see Kerry and the kids. She was sitting on the floor stacking wooden blocks with the twins. Rebecca sat in her lap, chewing on a splintery red triangle.

"How'd that go?" Kerry asked.

"Fine," I said, and she smiled.

"Do you ever think about using disposable diapers when Dad's not around?" I asked, thinking about how Kerry loved to be sneaky, and how she still loved being on the receiving end of girlish gossip.

She sighed. "I sure do," she said. "But I've never figured out a way to hide them. One goof would be all it took, and he'd hit the roof. I'd wind up canoeing with you in Canada."

I laughed. "That might not be so bad."

"That's true," she said, rolling her eyes. "Forget the mosquitoes and the rocky ground. It would be the first time I'd slept in three years."

She pushed lank blond hair out of her blue eyes. Her pretty, plump face suddenly looked to me like it belonged to a rebel. When she and my dad met, she'd been a marathon runner and a vegan, as passionate about organic food as he was. Like Aaron and Ezra, Kerry was an identical twin, and her sister—who didn't have children—still looked spare and athletic, a weird ghost-version of the woman Kerry used to be. Clearly Kerry's new, fleshy body was a way of thumbing her nose at Dad and his impossible principles.

I could tell her right now, I thought. I moved my tongue around, testing the words inside closed lips. *Kerry*, I could say, *I have something to tell you. I'm pregnant.*

Maybe she would stand up then and there, brushing off the dust and flour that always clung to her clothes. She would go to some cookie jar, or underneath her mattress, and come back with the money I needed. We would drive together to the town called West Falls, and Kerry would sit in the waiting room with the three kids while I underwent the procedure. From inside the doctor's office, I'd be able to hear their familiar whines and chatter. Kerry would check in on me in the recovery room and get all the directions from the nurse about taking care of me. Then she would help me to the car and drive me back to the farm. Maybe on the way we could pick up some soup that she could pretend she'd made herself. *Sydney's not feeling well,* she would tell my father when he came home. *I'm just going to heat up this soup for dinner and take her a bowl in her room.* I would recover for a couple of days while Kerry secretly tended me, and then I would go off on my canoe trip without a care in the world, all my problems—or at least the worst of them— solved.

"Kerry," I said. She looked up again, her eyes bright and expectant.

It was too big. I knew that if I told her, she would definitely get to her feet. But she would march directly to the phone and dial my father's cell phone number, the one we were only supposed to use in case of emergency. Or worse, she would call my mother. The whole world would come crashing down on my head.

"I'm really looking forward to this trip," I said, and she smiled.

chapter four
surprise, surprise

M r. Campbell, the guy who ran the camp up in Canada, sent a list of things I needed to bring: no more than could fit into a single, midsize pack. My dad loaned me camping equipment, and my mother mailed a box with my passport and some warm clothes (Mr. Campbell's letter warned that Canadian summer nights were chilly). Although I didn't want to hear anything Mom had to say, it was a reflex to sift through the package and look for some kind of card.

When I didn't find one, I automatically felt dejected and dissed. I thought that if I ever had a kid, I would punish her without being so emotional about it. The way my mother used anger to make points struck me as mean and even childish. It reminded me of the way Greg used to deal with me when I did something to hurt his feelings. He would freeze me out with these stony silences, attempting to make me feel worse and worse about what I'd done and who I was. My mother did exactly the same thing. If she thought that would make me have any kind of sympathy for her, it just had the opposite effect. I had hardly any sympathy and almost no respect.

I decided to concentrate on getting ready for my trip. I jammed a warm sleeping bag, two bathing suits, three T-shirts, four pairs of socks, two pairs of shorts, a sweat suit, a pair of sneakers, a raincoat, a fleece jacket, a hat, and mittens into my dad's external-frame pack. I would wear my jeans and hiking boots on the plane.

Kerry made a little packet of the toiletries I'd need. In the front pocket of the backpack, she zipped a bottle of Dr. Brauner's peppermint soap, a toothbrush and toothpaste, bug repellent (deet free at Dad's insistence, despite Campbell's recommendation), sunscreen, a Ziploc baggie full of Stri-Dex pads, and a box of o.b. tampons. That was the brand Mr. Campbell's list recommended, because they didn't have applicators. I watched Kerry tuck the box discreetly into its own separate compartment and thought how weirdly convenient it would be not to have to deal with my period on the trip.

The morning of my departure we woke at dawn. Dad drove me to the airport in Newark. We didn't talk much on the drive, which took more than an hour. He listened to *Morning Edition* on NPR, shaking or nodding his head vehemently at any mention of global warming or the Middle East. There was one segment about public schools replacing sex education with abstinence-only programs. I watched Dad's face for any sign of opinion, but he only hummed and looked out the window. Apparently this topic struck him as too frivolous to even listen to.

For the past few days, I had almost completely stopped

worrying about my pregnancy. Maybe it was because I still couldn't feel it in any kind of physical way. Every morning I stepped on the scale in Dad and Kerry's bathroom, and I hadn't gained an ounce. I'd even lost weight, despite Kerry's buttery cooking. I thought about what my father had said about me being distant from my own body. But I didn't feel distant from my body. I was a good athlete—not a great one, but competent enough to make the swim team and JV lacrosse. I tended to do best at individual sports, like diving or skiing. Although I had hated track the one term I'd joined the team, I liked to run. I felt aware of living inside my body, which had always done more or less what I wanted.

I had seen this kind of reasoning backfire in my friend Ashlyn, who was one of the best swimmers on our team. She always got chosen for national meets, and she was the one who always saved us when the rest of the team lagged behind. She also played field hockey and varsity lacrosse. Last year at an away meet for the swim team, Ashlyn and I shared a double bed at the New Haven Sheraton. We stayed up whispering long after the other girls had gone to sleep, and Ashlyn told me she'd been raped by this guy who lived in her old neighborhood. She told me that she should have seen it coming, because he used to follow her every day from the bus stop to her house.

"I never really worried about him," Ashlyn told me, "because I always felt like I could take him. He wasn't that much taller than me, and I knew I was so much stronger than the average girl. I worked out every day. I felt sure I could run faster than him if I ever needed to, and that I could fight him off. My body always did exactly what I told it. I thought I was invincible."

She never told her parents that the guy was stalking her because she knew they would freak out. She thought she could handle it herself. The freedom she had, walking around on her own, still felt new; she didn't want her dad to start escorting her like she was a little kid. But one night when Ashlyn got home late from lacrosse practice, the guy jumped out from behind a tree. He dragged her into the bushes of a house that had been for sale for months. Ashlyn was amazed by how much stronger he was. He pinned her fast underneath him, his body unmoving when she tried to push him off, his hand over her mouth stifling her screams.

Ashlyn's family moved not long after this, and the boy never got in any kind of trouble. "I just never wanted to see his face again," she told me.

I wondered if my confidence that this pregnancy would work itself out sprang from the same sort of delusion that had kept Ashlyn quiet. But even as I questioned that confidence, I couldn't veer away from it. I'd read in Kerry's pregnancy book that one in four women miscarried before the tenth week. Those odds did not seem so bad. Maybe I would be one of the lucky ones and lose the baby before I got back from Canada in August.

Because of my age, Dad was allowed to come with me to the gate. The first flight would take me to Toronto, where all the campers would meet, and we would fly on a chartered plane to a little town called North Bay. After that, a chartered bus would take us to Camp Bell on the shores of Lake Keewaytinook. If it had been my mother, she would have gone over the printed sheet of instructions—meeting place, passport, tickets—a thousand times. But my dad just handed it all to me, trusting that ten years of private education had left me capable of reading.

We got to the crowded gate and sat down to wait for the plane. As soon as I was settled, two soft, cold hands covered up my eyes.

"Guess who?" said the familiar, silky voice.

I circled my fingers around slim wrists and pulled the hands away. When I whirled around, there stood Natalia. She had the same gap-toothed smile, but she looked different somehow. She was pale, and I could tell she'd piled extra concealer under her eyes.

"Oh my God," I said. "What are you doing here?"

"I'm coming with you!" said Natalia. "Can you believe it?"

I really couldn't. For one thing, I'd never known Natalia to do anything remotely physical. After I'd quit the swim team I had to take gym class, and more days than not she would sit out with her period. Also, she had never been one to go without luxuries. I couldn't imagine her without her iPod, let alone minus a bed or running water.

I studied Natalia's face to make sure she was serious. She had on Lucky Brand jeans, a velvet T-shirt, and a cashmere shrug.

I wondered if she'd packed mascara and glitter blush in her own lightweight backpack—which I could see, sitting over by Mr. Miksa, who waved at me, was top-of-the-line Kelty.

"Dad," I said, "this is my friend Natalia."

Dad stood up and shook her hand. I could see he was seething. "Mr. Biggs," Natalia said, placing a second hand on top of his before he could pull away. "I'm so happy to finally meet you."

Dad pulled his hand away and nodded, mumbling something that sounded unconvincingly like "Great." Then he said, "How exactly did this happen?"

"I told my mom what Sydney was doing, and she called Ms. Sincero right up to ask about it. She thought it sounded like the perfect thing for me. I've been in a little trouble myself of late."

My father forgot civility altogether and frowned. If I were the sort of person to draw cartoons, my picture of this meeting would have used quite a bit of black ink for the huge cloud of smoke coming from his ears. No doubt my mother had poured herself a hefty glass of Chardonnay and had a good laugh imagining my father's reaction to this development: a primary character from my usual life landing smack in the middle of his plan to separate me from all things familiar. At the same time, I recognized Natalia's appearance as a nod from my mom toward me, maybe even a small bit of olive branch.

I introduced Dad to Mr. Miksa, who pinched my cheek and then pumped his hand enthusiastically. "Ve just love your little Seed-ney," he said. "The girls will have a grand time in the woods, yes?"

The gate attendant announced the first boarding call, which included minors traveling alone. Natalia threw her arms around her father's neck as Dad and I awkwardly kissed each other's cheeks. Next thing I knew we had displayed our passports and tickets and were walking arm in arm along the ramp to the airplane. It was completely surreal, and I couldn't decide whether I felt overjoyed or disappointed.

My seat was in the very first row of coach. Natalia had already worked out getting her seat assigned next to me, and we settled down together for the four-hour flight. She had gone to so much trouble in order to be with me that I felt guilty about my mixed feelings, which had nothing to do with her personally. I loved Natalia, and really there was no one in the world I'd rather see. It was just that I'd been so happy pretending not to be pregnant. It would have been so easy to keep doing exactly that with no one along on this trip who knew. But now Natalia would want to talk about it constantly. When really, what was there to talk about? Nothing could be done about anything till we got back from Canada.

I decided to level with her. "Look," I said, once we settled into our seats. Natalia had just turned to look at me with the most dazed and wide-eyed expression, and I knew she was about to ask how I was feeling. I would never last through a monthlong canoe trip if every time we had to portage Natalia started fretting about my so-called condition.

"I just want you to know," I said, "I feel perfectly fine. I don't feel weird or nauseous or anything. I just feel totally normal. And one thing I really want is for nobody else on this trip to know. I don't care how friendly we get with anyone, this has to be a total secret. Okay?"

"Of course," Natalia said. "But are you sure you feel all right?"

Truthfully, as the plane began to taxi down the runway and lift off into the sky, I felt a sinking, lurching sensation in my gut. But I had never been a good flier. I looked at the pocket in the seat in front of me and noted the exact location of the white tabs of my airsickness bag, sticking up from behind the airline magazines.

"I feel fine," I said.

She rubbed her hands nervously over her thighs. I looked at the fake-silver Irish wedding band Steve had given her, shining on her left ring finger.

"So this is going to be great, right?" she said. "Paddling from one island to the next. Camping out. It'll be like *Survivor*, except no one gets voted off."

She still didn't seem like herself. The words might have been enthusiastic, but her voice sounded strained. Maybe she was upset about the long separation from Steve, or else maybe she was scared of a month in the wilderness.

"Have you ever even been camping before?" I asked, though I knew perfectly well she hadn't.

"Don't you remember Kendra Hirsch's birthday?"

That had been in fourth grade. Five of us pitched a big tent for a slumber party in Kendra's backyard. Her mother had brought us hot chocolate and mint Milanos on a tray, and her father had sat awake all night in a lawn chair, standing guard with an industrial flashlight to keep kidnappers and pedophiles away.

"This will be a little more hard-core," I said.

"That's all right," said Natalia, in that same slightly husky voice. "I'm ready." She stretched out her arms and cracked her knuckles, something I'd never seen her do before. Her words spilled out in a weird staccato, like she couldn't stop herself. "This was a really ingenious plan of your father's," she said. "As soon as I told my parents, I could see all sorts of lightbulbs going off above their heads. There's no way Steve could track me down on a Canadian lake, so they'd finally know for certain that we were apart. I'm thinking, when I get back, I'll tell them I met some nice Jewish boy. They'll think I'm IMing him and talking to him on the phone, and they'll never know the difference."

"But what about this summer?" I said. "Isn't it your last chance to be with Steve before Switzerland?"

"Be with Steve? I haven't laid eyes on Steve since that night we tried to tell Tommy. They've got me under house arrest. No computer, no cell phone. I had to send him a letter to tell him about this trip, and then I got in trouble for sneaking out to the mailbox. But I'm thinking, maybe having me away this month will make them miss me. And if they think there's no more Steve, then why bother sending me all the way to Switzerland?"

"But there's still a Steve, right? You two haven't broken up."

"There's no way to contact him," Natalia said, "so I couldn't break up with him if I wanted to. Which I don't. We're still totally in love." She took a deep breath, and sitting so close, I could see that concealer masked tiny purple half moons beneath her eyes.

"But I haven't even told you the biggest thing," Natalia said. "I have news. Huge news. Monumental."

The seat belt sign went off with a little electric ding. Natalia unbuckled and said, "Just a second; I'm going to the bathroom. Get me a Coke if the drinks come by."

I watched her sashay unsteadily around the annoyed flight attendant. As she passed the little kitchen, she reached into the unattended drink cart and pulled out two of those miniature liquor bottles. I couldn't imagine where she would hide them— her jeans were painted on—but she disappeared so quickly into the lavatory, nobody but me could have noticed.

"We'll each have a Coke," I told the flight attendant when she came by with the cart. Natalia still hadn't returned. When she did climb in next to me, it took her a few minutes to dig the bottles out of her pocket.

"Unless," she said, her hand hovering over my Coke, "you don't think you should be drinking."

"Don't be stupid," I said, my tone unusually harsh. Her expression darkened for a second, from sadness to annoyance. I watched the emotional progression of her face, remembering my state and forgiving me. Then she poured the rum into my

Coke and disposed of the bottle—stashing it in the flap pocket of the seat in front of her in one fluid, secretive motion.

"I'm sorry," I said. "But you don't drink so as not to hurt the baby. And there's not going to be any baby."

"That's a little bit related to my news," she said.

"What do you mean?" I said. I wondered if she was pregnant too, and felt surprised by how the notion cheered me. Wouldn't it be wonderful not to have to go through all this alone?

Natalia picked up her drink but didn't take a sip. She just held it up in the air and furrowed her brow into a serious, faraway look. "Those days before I talked to you on the phone," she said, "all I could think about was how to work out your abortion. And it just got me thinking about teenage pregnancy, and the different possibilities, and our whole theory about Margit being my mother. So the day after you called me, I confronted my parents at dinner. I told them what we thought, that they were really my grandparents. And guess what? It's true."

"What's true?" I said.

"Margit is my mother."

"Oh my God," I said, feeling a strange combination of disbelief and envy. I imagined Margit at sixteen: a pale, blond version of Natalia. I imagined her on her parents' silk mauve sofa, a gilt-embroidered throw pillow in her lap, tears streaming down her face. I imagined the Miksas, all cheery and solicitous, offering to take care of everything.

Natalia took a sip of her Coke, then crinkled her nose,

something I didn't need to see to know the drink was strong. Just the smell of the rum wafting off the popping soda bubbles made me want to grab the air sickness bag and retch.

"I should have known," Natalia said, the shakiness returning to her voice. "I mean, I guess I did know. My mom is sixty-two years old. We had just sat down to eat, this horrible-looking chopped beef. And I told them about that show on the Biography channel, and that movie star, and I said that ever since I'd found myself wondering whether they were actually my grandparents. As soon as I said it, my mother burst out crying. The jig was totally up. I'm not supposed to tell Margit that I know until I get back. They're going to tell her while I'm gone so she has a chance to prepare herself."

"Wow." I couldn't think of anything else to say.

"I know," said Natalia. "So don't you think it would just be too weird for them to send me to Switzerland now? Maybe I can go live with Margit and Victor instead, in the city."

"Are you just completely freaked out?"

She took a sip of her drink, then lowered the cup to her knee. "Of course," she said. "But what's so weird is, nothing's changed. My mom still feels like my mom. I haven't spoken to Margit, but in my head she's still my sister. I can't think that will change. But then I look back at my life, and everything seems different from what I always thought it was. I feel so . . . tricked. You know?"

I just stared at her. Of course I didn't know. How could I? I didn't even know what to say.

"I'm going to write out a list of questions for her while I'm gone," she said. "I really want to know who the father was. My parents wouldn't tell me. And I want to know why she decided to go ahead with it. Having me, I mean. And then I think about your situation. It's not like abortion was illegal when Margit had me."

I felt another lurch in my stomach. Natalia put her finger into her Coke and stirred the ice and rum. "You know," she said, in her new, faraway voice, "I think I'd be a lot angrier at Margit if it weren't for your situation. I keep thinking about your plans, and then I feel sort of grateful. If Margit had had an abortion, I wouldn't even be here."

We had reached our cruising altitude by now, and as suddenly as it had started, my nausea vanished. I did feel intensely thirsty and wished I hadn't let Natalia spike my drink. The last thing I wanted at this moment was a cocktail.

"You wouldn't be here if Margit had stayed a virgin till she was twenty-two," I said. My voice sounded flat and strangely serious. I'd heard my mother make this kind of argument when the subject of abortion came up, and it felt weirdly natural to be parroting her. "You wouldn't be here if your parents, your grandparents, had never met, or if they'd stayed in Hungary. There are a million things that could have ended up in you not being here."

"I know," Natalia said. "But would it be different? Would I just not exist? Or would I be dead?"

I sat there beside my best friend, feeling cold and clammy

and longing for a glass of water. "You can't go all pro-life on me now," I said. "Please. Think about if it were you."

"If it were me, the father would be Steve," she said. "Maybe I'd get to marry him."

"Is that what you want?" I said. "To be sixteen years old and married to Steve? Living in some ratty house in Overpeck with aluminum siding and a screaming baby?"

Natalia put her hand on my arm. "Of course not," she said. And then, too loud, "I'm not saying you shouldn't have an abortion."

I was sure the people in the seats behind us could hear every word. "Shhh," I pleaded. Then I said, "You were certainly all gung ho about the idea when we spoke on the phone."

"I still am," she whispered, not sounding completely convinced. "It's just I've been thinking since then. Everything feels different. But you know I think you should have an abortion if you want. I totally do. It's just weird. It's just very weird and complicated. Don't you think?"

I reached up and pressed the flight attendant button so I could ask for a bottle of water. My throat felt dry as the Sahara desert. My head felt terribly light, like I couldn't keep my eyes open another second.

"I think I just need to sleep," I whispered. In my whole life, I had never been able to sleep on an airplane. But almost immediately a heavy fog settled around me, and I fell into a deep and dreamless sleep. I didn't wake up until the wheels hit the tarmac on Canadian soil.

chapter five
"o canada"

It took forever, the trip from Toronto to Camp Bell, and finally I was glad to have Natalia beside me. While I remained in a groggy stupor from my daytime sleep, she navigated our way to the chartered plane that would take us to North Bay. From there it was easy; we just had to follow the stream of teenagers wearing hiking boots and backpacks. My dad's ancient external-frame pack made me look sadly out of place in the middle of all the shiny new gear, and I was glad again to have Natalia so that I could absorb some of the glow from her brand-new, ultra-expensive equipment.

We reached Camp Bell's base camp on Lake Keewaytinook in the same dusky summer light I'd left behind at my dad's. The air felt crisper, more northern. Rustic as Dad's farmland might be, here the scent of pine was so much thicker. The daylong travels that rolled out behind us might have delivered us to another place in history, where houses existed in deeper thickets of forest, and nature had yet to be tamed.

Natalia and I stood in line, uncharacteristically docile, and gave our names to a counselor who checked them off on a clipboard—the only thing that marked him as an authority figure. Otherwise he looked as spindly and teenage as the campers surrounding him. There didn't seem to be any adults around, certainly not the fabled Mr. Bell, only teenagers like Clipboard Guy, whose red T-shirts bore the word STAFF in big white letters on the front and back. After Clipboard Guy had checked off the names of all the new arrivals, he told us that we would spend two nights here at base camp learning the rules of the water and how to pitch a tent—all the basics of living outdoors. We found out that we would be separated into groups of ten—four girls, four guys, and two counselors. Then we would shove off in our canoes to paddle for two weeks toward a supply drop point where we would stay two nights, then spend the next two weeks making our way back to the base camp. Clipboard Guy pointed us toward a bulletin board where the groups would be listed, then disappeared into the night as if all his responsibilities were complete.

"Crazy," Natalia said, trying to decipher the map that was posted next to the list of groups. When Natalia's parents signed her up, they made sure that she and I would be traveling together, so it was only out of a vague sense of curiosity that we had walked over to the bulletin board. We looked at the other names in our group, which of course meant nothing to us. On the charter plane from Toronto and the bus from North Bay, we had barely spoken to each other, let alone the other campers.

"I hope they're nice," said Natalia, running her finger down the list of names.

I shrugged. So far, the other two hundred or so campers seemed like the usual assortment of teenagers. Some looked barely out of diapers, some looked like they should already be trading bonds on Wall Street. Now that we'd arrived at base camp, though, I kept spotting guys who looked distinctly out of place. In the middle of the usual stream of Patagonia and Lucky Brand there would suddenly be a shaved head, or a pair of Carhartt's, or those weird gangsta turbans. About half of them were white, but they all looked like they would make my mother punch the automatic locks on her car. "They must have some sort of Youth at Risk thing going on," Natalia whispered, as other curious campers jostled us out of the way of the bulletin board.

We went to find beds in one of the girls' bunkhouses. It was first come, first serve, and ours was the last group to arrive. Finally we found two beds in the last bunkhouse, on opposite sides of the cabin.

"Totally unacceptable," Natalia said.

"It's only for two days," I said. "Let's go to dinner and deal with it later."

The dining hall—like everything else at Camp Bell except the great outdoors—was unimpressive, nothing but a wide wooden building. The small, dingy kitchen was empty of staff, and the dining area was filled with picnic tables. In the morning the cracks between the wall's slats would let in flies and daylight. Now, at night, mosquitoes and a chilly breeze slipped their way through the echoing room. Maybe tomorrow we would have actual hot meals, but for now we served ourselves cold-cut sandwiches from a long buffet table. Kerry's book had said pregnant women should not eat cold cuts, but I reminded myself I was only temporarily pregnant and helped myself to a pile of shaved turkey. The spread before us was my father's worst nightmare: a collection of processed meat, canned olives, and white bread. I bypassed all the iceberg lettuce and yellowed onions in favor of head-sized brownies.

Natalia and I sat at the end of an unoccupied picnic table. Before long, guys started drifting over, introducing themselves to her. Soon the table was full—me, Natalia, and about ten guys. Natalia never did anything intentional to attract this kind of attention; guys just gravitated toward her no matter what. She could wear baggy jeans and a T-shirt, her hair shoved under a baseball cap, and still they'd come flocking. Once at school, she and Ashlyn and I had been sitting in the bleachers watching a baseball game on an overcast autumn day. When a cloud blew over, opening up the sun's heat, Natalia had peeled off her sweater, revealing a Yankees T-shirt. Seconds later I could hear guys behind us whispering, and then a girl's voice, intentionally loud: "Who does she think she is?"

Natalia couldn't help it. She just oozed sex whether she wanted to or not. The rest of us could take off our sweaters when it got hot, but Natalia couldn't take off her sweater without *being* hot. So it surprised me when the guy to my right introduced himself to me first. "Hey," he said. "I'm Cody."

"Sydney," I told him, hiding my mouthful of turkey behind one hand.

"Sydney," he said, jutting his chin toward my tray. "You got the last brownie."

"There were more when I took it, I swear." When he didn't answer, I picked up the brownie, ripped it in half, and handed over the bigger piece. I expected him to protest—or at least offer to take the smaller half—but he didn't say a word, just balanced it on the edge of his plate beside his own heaps of food. I snuck one more look at him before going back to my meal. He was a medium-sized guy, with brown hair and nice hazel eyes. Despite, or maybe because of, his stealing my brownie, he seemed like the sort of person who'd be easy to spend time with. I tried to remember if the name "Cody" had been on the list for our group.

"So what's with all the thugs?" Natalia asked, when the guys told us this was their second summer at Camp Bell. She didn't have to worry about being overheard. The room had segregated itself into normal campers and boys from the hood. The latter took up a single table in the far corner of the room, while the rest of us spread out around the dining hall.

The guy sitting next to Natalia told her that Mr. Campbell gave scholarships to East Coast boys from the Youth at Risk program. "Campbell's from New Jersey," he said. I could tell he was about to put down our home state with the usual turnpike jokes, but Natalia quickly said, "We are too." So he just told us that every group would include one of these Youth at Risk guys.

"We each get our very own juvenile delinquent," he said.

Natalia laughed. "This information was definitely not relayed to my mother when she signed me up," she said.

"But it's not just juvies," Cody said. "Did you girls know there's a movie star at the camp?"

"No," said Natalia. "Who?"

"This guy Brendan Taylor. He had a recurring part on *The New Mill River*. And he's in that Alltel commercial for their family plan. The one with the lady in the sandwich suit?"

The New Mill River was a prime-time soap opera about teenagers that we all made fun of but watched religiously. "Oh my God," Natalia said. "Sydney, I think he's in our group. I'm positive that name was on our list!"

"Who was he on *The New Mill River*?" I asked.

"The English guy who got Carol Ann pregnant."

"No way. Is he really English?"

"I don't think so."

I turned around in my seat and scanned the milling teenagers. I remembered that character, a ridiculously handsome guest star with a very believable accent. I didn't see any sign of him in the dining hall. Apart from the Youth at Risk kids, who were immediately recognizable, nobody looked remarkable. I turned back to our table, where we exchanged the usual introductions—where we were from, where we went to school. It turned out that every one of us went to private school, and I imagined how I'd feel at moments like this if I ended up going to Bulgar County High, the school that pooled students from Linden Hill, Wallingston, and Halltown.

After dinner, our whole table walked back out to the bulletin board to check the group rosters. None of the guys were in Natalia's and my group, but sure enough, there was the name Brendan Taylor. "Oh my God," Natalia squealed, elbowing the cutest guy in the stomach. It irked me a little bit that she would already be flirting, as if the grand romance we'd sacrificed so much for didn't mean a thing.

By now dark had settled around the camp, making it about fifteen degrees colder than when we'd gone in for dinner. Natalia shivered in her little shrug, and I unwrapped the fleece jacket from my waist and pulled it over my head. The air smelled woodsy and fresh, full of pine and wildflowers. Above our heads, with no city lights to interfere, stars glowed by the thousands. From the lake, loons trilled to one another, filling the evening with a wonderful, ghostly vibe. I breathed it all in hungrily, like something I didn't know I'd been craving.

We walked down to the dock, where there were about a million bright blue canoes resting on their sides by the river bank. The guys started a rock-skipping contest. They went about it all wrong, hurling tiny round pebbles. I searched the ground for a broad, flat rock, and when I found the right one I sailed it over the top of the water. One, two, three, four, and then a last sailing skip before it plunged into the dark, silky depths. The guys whooped in appreciation. "That was awesome," one of them said. "What was your name again?"

"Sydney," Natalia told them.

"Hey, Sydney," said Cody, the guy who'd sat next to me at dinner. "Do you want to take one of these canoes out?"

"Are we allowed?"

He shrugged. "Probably not. But I haven't seen many counselors around. We'll just take it for a quick spin."

"Okay," I said. I could feel Natalia's eyes on my back, probably surprised that even one of the guys was singling me out instead of her. With Natalia around, guys never paid attention to me until it was clear she was taken.

Cody and I pulled one of the canoes from its resting place. I rolled my jeans up to my knees and we waded into the water. When it was deep enough for the canoe to float, we climbed in, me in the front and Cody in the back. Sound carries so well over water, I was sure they could hear the lap, lap of our oars all the way up at the dining hall.

Cody and I didn't speak at first, just drifted out on the water. Obviously he had learned a lot last summer on the lake. He didn't switch oars in that awkward way, but steered with expert J strokes. Up above the water, the night went even crazier with stars. Cody and I both stared up, transfixed.

"Look," he said. "There's the moon." I turned toward the bright crescent, nearly hidden in the spectacle of stars.

"It'll be amazing out here when it's full," I said. "Did you see the northern lights last summer?"

"Once," he said, "at the end of the trip. But last summer I came for August, so it was nearly September by the time we saw them. That's more the season."

"Oh," I said, disappointed. I stared up at the sky as if I could will the display to appear. Instead of lights there was an explosion of sound. We heard a chorus of bullfrogs in the reeds, and then a booming voice:

"Whoever's got a canoe on the water, you better bring it right back to shore."

The voice sounded weathered and distinctly adult. I wondered if it was Campbell himself and looked over my shoulder at Cody, who smiled at me. I smiled back. At camp barely three hours and here I was, in trouble again. But what did it matter? My feet felt chilly and wet from wading through the lake, and I could tell the faint breeze and mild exercise had turned my cheeks bright pink. Campbell's instruction letter had said the lake was fresh and bacteria free: The water wouldn't need to be boiled, and we could dunk our Nalgene bottles straight in whenever we wanted a drink. I stopped rowing for a second, cupped my hand, and dipped it into the lake. The water tasted fresh and cold, the purest stuff on Earth.

Whoever had called out didn't bother meeting us onshore for a lecture. Nobody greeted us on the dock, not even Natalia. I wondered where she had gone. Cody and I dragged our canoe to its original spot, then sat on the edge of the dock together, swinging our feet through the water and looking up at the stars. Every once in a while I would sneak a look at his profile. He looked much more grown-up than Tommy had, with a nice manly nose—a bump on the bridge, as if it had been broken playing sports. I resisted the urge to run my finger over it.

"How old are you?" I asked him.

"Sixteen," he said. "You?"

"Sixteen," I said.

"It's too bad we're not in the same group," Cody said. I flushed with the compliment. And then, with a fresh shock, I remembered the baby. As soon as the word formed in my mind, I shook my head. *The baby*. Since when was it a baby? I wondered if Natalia's pro-life moment on the airplane had somehow infected me. But it hit me with monster force, the memory of my pregnancy. It was weird and exciting enough, sitting here in another country, a cold Canadian lake under my dangling feet, and a cute, apparently interested guy beside me. But to remember that I was *pregnant*, that there was this possible other person along for the ride, brought the moment directly into the realm of surreal.

I thought again of Margit, pregnant with Natalia—who would grow into one of the most important people in my life. Where would I be now if Margit had gone the same route I'd mapped out for myself?

Something inside of me hardened, and I thought that if Natalia had never been born I'd have one less obstacle to ending this pregnancy. Not only that, but I never would have met Tommy, so I wouldn't be pregnant in the first place. Before I could get around to beating myself up for these thoughts, I reminded myself that my circumstances were completely different. Margit had been seventeen. Only a year older, but still—enough to make a difference. And her parents had been

79

willing to step up to the plate, something my mother would never do. Hadn't she made it clear every day that raising a child was misery? Kerry and my father might take the baby. But I wasn't sure how I felt about that. Kerry was so devoted to her own kids, mine might get lost in the shuffle. And I'd never especially enjoyed being my father's child; in fact, he had given me nightmares. Why would I leave a child in his care?

It felt bizarre to consider the future of this dust speck as if it were an actual person. If I didn't want it to be raised in a less-than-ideal environment, why did I feel fine about scraping it into medical waste?

"What are you thinking about?" Cody asked, a question I would have hated even if I weren't pregnant. I looked directly into his face. His eyes were so pretty, even in this starlit darkness, every possible color flecking and merging. Perversely, I thought that if we had sex this very minute, on the edge of this dock, I wouldn't have to worry about birth control.

"Hmm," I murmured, borrowing a page from Natalia's flirt book. "Isn't that kind of a personal question for someone you've known forty minutes?"

"Oh," said Cody, "I think it's been a lot longer than that. Dinner was like, an hour ago. And we shared a brownie. In some Middle Eastern cultures, that would be tantamount to an engagement."

"Tantamount. Did you bring along your SAT vocab cards?"

He tapped his head. "I've got it all up here, baby," he said, and I laughed.

From up on the hill—the same direction as the voice that had called us back—a bell sounded.

"You must know the significance of that," I said.

"Warning for lights-out," Cody told me. "But believe me, it's not strictly enforced."

"Still," I said. "Maybe we should head back." I stood up and rolled down the cuffs of my jeans, then pulled on my shoes. Cody did the same. I half expected him to try to kiss me before we went up to the dining hall, but he didn't—just thumped me on the back, between my shoulder blades, like I was his little sister.

"That was fun," he said. "Thanks."

"Any time." We walked through the dark in an unfamiliar direction, our hands swinging intimately beside each other, not touching, but still companionable.

Back at our cabin, Natalia had managed to trade beds with the dour, chubby girl who'd claimed the bunk below mine. We lay awake in the dark, crickets madly chirping outside our window. "They don't give us much direction around here," Natalia said. I hung over the edge of my bed and looked down at her, her long black hair spread across the camp pillow. She'd already complained about the pillow being too flimsy, and I didn't want to tell her that it would be the last one she'd see for four weeks.

"Did you kiss that guy?" she asked.

"No," I said. "He didn't even hold my hand."

"That's kind of romantic," she said, and I wondered if she'd heard me right. "He was cute."

"You think?" I said.

"I do. Very cute. I love his nose."

"Me too."

"Maybe you can hook up tomorrow," Natalia said. "At least you wouldn't have to worry about birth control."

Though I'd had exactly the same thought, coming from Natalia it sounded mean. I drew my head back without saying anything. At the same time, a girl from the next bunk shushed us. Natalia blew a light raspberry, and we both laughed before falling into obedient silence. Along with the racket of the crickets, bullfrogs gulped and loons trilled. A mosquito buzzed around my head and I batted at it for several minutes before smashing it, with a squelch of blood, on my forehead.

"Do you like it here?" I whispered to Natalia. But she answered only with a quiet snore, the traveling and the great outdoors working on her like a sleeping pill. In my top bunk I lay awake a long time, thinking about boys, and kisses, and all the appropriate teenage topics.

And then, for no particular reason, I wondered how high from the ground my bunk stood. I wondered what would happen if I rolled myself sideways. I imagined my body flopping to the floor with a loud thwack, a sharp ache in my head, and an instant gush of blood between my legs. I wondered where the nearest hospital was, if they would need to airlift me, and if they would tell my parents.

The next day after breakfast we met with our groups in the wide, bright light of a northern summer. Natalia had woken up cheerful, more like her usual self than she'd seemed on the plane. I hoped that maybe she'd decided, like me, to leave her troubles back in New Jersey for these weeks we had on the water.

The lake reflected tiny dust particles, dancing like fairies in the air around us. We had to squint through the glare to see one another. Most of us—even the guys—fixed our eyes on the movie star kid. Brendan Taylor was even better dressed than Natalia; in perfectly fitting Gramicci pants and Patagonia fleece. He had tied a kerchief around his neck in a way that could only be described as jaunty. His eyes were robin's-egg blue, so bright and electric that he might have been wearing tinted contacts. He had brown, wavy hair. Not too tall for a guy, about Natalia's height, with a very lean, fit build.

We couldn't look at him directly for too long. Natalia kept elbowing me in the ribs, and we'd giggle and jerk our eyes back toward our feet. On *The New Mill River* Brendan had played someone's cousin visiting from England, an aristocrat with a streak of delinquency. Originally the star of the show had a crush on his character, but then she found out he'd gotten another character pregnant. The next episodes were all about what this girl, Carol Ann, should do about the pregnancy. Of course they never mentioned the *A* word, and eventually Brendan's character was written off the show, along with the girl's. I wondered where that imaginary girl had gone. Where do people in that situation—rejecting abortion and leaving family behind—go?

I turned my attention back to our group. The other two girls seemed to already know each other. They sat together the same way Natalia and I did, giggling and poking each other over Brendan. Their behavior would have made me restrain myself if I thought either of them had any chance of getting his attention. But Meredith was overweight, bespectacled, and baby faced. Poor Lori had short, spiky hair and terrible acne that would definitely not be helped by four weeks camping, no matter how fresh the lake water was.

"I'm voting them off," Natalia whispered. The night before, she had scrubbed her face clean, then dumped all her Bobbi Brown makeup into the trash can by the sink, where some lucky camper would no doubt scoop it up after we left. "I want to do this wilderness thing whole hog," Natalia had said, staring resolutely at her naked face.

Without makeup Natalia didn't look less attractive, only younger and more vulnerable, like all her flaws could finally stop apologizing. Her eyes looked huge and wide set, and the gap between her teeth made her look very European. Sitting in the circle with our makeshift family of the next four weeks, I decided I liked her better this way.

We looked over at the guys. Compared to gorgeous, semi-famous Brendan, our Youth at Risk kid looked like the biggest delinquent who ever lived. He was white, with a shaved head and a tattoo of a scorpion at the base of his skull. There were more tattoos on his arms, not pretty, colorful ones, but green numbers and symbols that looked amateur and vaguely satanic. His name was Mick. Throughout the meeting he drew pictures in the dirt with a stick, an activity that was strangely appealing in its boyishness. Mick was also the only one of us— apart from our counselors Jane and Silas—who didn't seem to notice Brendan. *The New Mill River* came on at nine o'clock on Tuesdays. Probably by that time of night Mick was already out committing crimes.

Both of the other boys in our group were barely taller than me. Charlie looked like this might be his full and final height, and he seemed to be compensating with a lot of bodybuilding. His muscles bulged everywhere—biceps, calves, forearms—in a cartoonish and slightly grotesque way. It was sad, because he had a very handsome face. The last boy, Sam, had that clumsy, puppyish look some boys have just before their big growth spurt. He had blond hair and a chubby face, but his legs were long and spindly, like he'd spend a lot of time tripping over himself.

Last but not least: our fearless leaders. When Jane, the girl counselor, told us she was twenty, Natalia rolled her eyes at me. "She is not," Natalia hissed, hopefully not loud enough for Jane to hear. Jane was tiny and slim. She had long, dark hair, exotic eyes under black bangs, and a faint mustache. If she'd told us she was fourteen, I would have believed her.

Silas, the guy in charge, was enormous. He wore a huge fisherman's sweater that stretched painfully over his belly. He had curly blond hair and a jovial face. He said he was twenty-two. He refused to make eye contact with any of us, just went over the basics of our trip. When he'd finished with his uncomfortable lecture about portaging, and how we'd set up camp the second we landed anywhere, and how we'd all have to learn J strokes and do our share of the cooking, he asked if there were any questions. We all stared back at him in silence.

Silas and Jane pulled out the equipment we would be using on our trip. They showed us the collapsible reflector ovens that we could supposedly use to bake cakes, but I was dubious. The metal oven was full of dents. It looked like something my father would use to store bread in his moth-eaten pantry. Everything at Camp Bell—the cabins, the bathrooms, the equipment— looked about thirty years old. I couldn't help thinking how my mother would snort if she were here. She would say it was just what she'd expect from my dad.

"Okay, then," Silas said. "I'll see you all at the landing at ten a.m." The departure times were staggered, two groups at a time.

Silas and Jane walked away, leaving the eight kids together. We all stared at one another, not sure what to say. Then Mick spat on the ground and walked away. The rest of us watched him go.

"Do you think we should take that personally?" Brendan finally asked.

We all laughed, a little uneasy. "Will there be some kind of weapons check before we get going?" Natalia asked.

"There was one at the airport," said Lori, dead serious. "He couldn't have gotten anything metal onboard the plane. And there's no weapons here."

"He could have stolen a knife from the dining-hall kitchen," Brendan said.

"Or fashioned some kind of shiv from barks and rock," Natalia said, the only one of us confident enough to banter with the movie star. She and Brendan laughed. The other girls looked worried.

"At least we won't have to sleep in the same tent with him," said Lori. "The girls get their own tent, Silas said."

"Yeah," Brendan agreed. "Canvas and zippers are excellent security systems."

He and Natalia laughed again, and I joined in, a little uncomfortable. We'd be traveling in very close quarters with these people for a long time. I thought it would be smarter to forge allegiances than tease them. Lori blushed furiously, probably kicking herself for looking priggish in Brendan's eyes. Truthfully, I couldn't really blame Lori and Meredith for being scared of Mick. So far, he looked like a pretty scary guy. In fact, he looked like the quintessential scary guy, like how you would want someone to look if he were playing a scary guy in a movie about scary guys.

After a little while everyone walked off in pairs—Lori and Meredith, Natalia and me, Charlie and Sam. Only Brendan stayed behind by the water, gorgeous and alone in the bright sunlight.

"Is he following us?" Natalia whispered, as we walked up to the bathrooms.

I looked back over my shoulder. "No," I said.

He just sat there, throwing pebbles into the great, shimmering lake. Even from this distance, he looked kind of sad and lonesome. You'd think someone who had a camp of two hundred people dying to meet him could muster a little more cheerfulness.

"I'm voting everybody off, except for you and Brendan. And maybe Silas. He seems kind of cool, in a big-brother way. You, me, Brendan, and Silas will be the final four."

"Who'll win?"

"Us, of course. You and me."

"Great," I said. I didn't remind her that there could be only one survivor. And these days, I hardly felt that word applied to me. Sometimes I wasn't even sure I wanted it to.

"Cheer up," Natalia said, and patted my belly in an affectionate, probably unconscious gesture of comfort. I pushed her hand away, not wanting her to make a habit of this. "Oh, right," she said. "Sorry."

"It's okay," I said. Suddenly I couldn't wait to get away from base camp, out on the water. Then, I felt sure, I would think of nothing but paddling and portaging for four weeks straight. Bliss.

When we got to the bathroom I lingered inside my stall much longer than I needed. I listened to Natalia pee, wash her hands, and wait for a few minutes before walking back outside. I heard her sigh as her feet touched down outside, a heavy and preoccupied sound.

I felt bad that I wasn't paying more attention to her crisis.

The truth was, I didn't want to think about any crisis at all. I just wanted to sit and focus on the coming weeks. I wanted to appreciate the luxury of a porcelain seat and flushing toilet. Not to mention running water. Finally I stood up and went to the sink. Washing my hands, I stared in the mirror, aware that over the next month I would not be seeing my own face. I studied it closely, making a mental map of my flaws and strong points, not wanting either to grow in my imagination. I looked, too, for changes. I didn't see any. It was only me, staring back, a little more thoughtful than usual, a little more serious.

Remember, I told myself, looking into my own eyes. It would be important to know, when I got back, if anything was different.

chapter six
a motley crew

We had a rocky departure. Of the eight kids in our group, only Charlie and I had ever been in a canoe. Nobody else knew how to steer, and nobody understood how to load the boats so they wouldn't tip over.

Natalia, scrubbed of her makeup, was determined to transform into Wilderness Girl. She waded right into the water with me. "I refuse to be one of those chicks who squeals over spiders and worries about chipping her nails," she told me. We piled our gear plus a share of the communal equipment into the surprisingly sturdy canoe. Natalia strapped a solar-powered lantern on top of our things. All day the lantern would soak up the sun while we rowed, then at camp we could use it to read in our tents. Of course the lamp belonged to Natalia: She and her mother had bought it at Riverside Square with her other new equipment. Camp Bell didn't have anything so modern or snazzy.

I held the boat steady while Natalia climbed into the bow. Then we just sat there, floating, while the rest of the group tried to organize itself. The two other girls barely knew how to step into their canoes. Lori threw one leg over the side too aggressively, sending the bulk of her and Meredith's gear—including sleeping bags—into the lake. I winced when I saw the splash. There was nothing in the world worse than trying to sleep in a wet sleeping bag.

Cody belonged to the group that shared our departure time. Most of them were return campers like Cody, and their expertise made our lameness even more obvious. The male leader from that group slapped Silas on the back and said, "Bummer, dude," not trying to lower his voice or disguise in any way that "bummer" had become another word for us.

In the time it took us to load six canoes and topple one, Cody's group had set off in pairs, athletic and efficient. As his boat floated away, he turned around and waved at me. I waved back, ignoring the chaos around me.

Last night, Cody still hadn't kissed me. But Natalia and I had had the best time, playing football with him and his friends. "Touch football is too wimpy for us," one of his friends had said when we started the game. "But if you two want, touch can count for you."

"No way," I said. "I want to tackle. And I want to be tackled."

"Sydney," said Natalia, her voice full of warning.

I ignored her, not that it made a huge difference. The only guy willing to tackle me was Cody. Because I sucked at football, he got me about a million times, several when I didn't even have the ball. He would run up next to me, put both arms around my waist, and pull me down to the grass. Every time I hit the ground, I would laugh hysterically. But I longed for a more jolting thrash. Cody held me gingerly, mindfully, using his body to break every one of my falls. When the bell rang for bedtime, he held my hand and walked me back to the girls' cabin. "I wish you were in my group," he said.

"Me too." We stood there in the twilight. A mosquito landed on my arm, but I didn't want to swat it away for fear of breaking the mood. When Cody noticed it, he smacked my arm. The mosquito died with a splat.

"Hey," I said, rubbing my arm. "Haven't you hurt me enough for one night?"

"It's all for your own good," he said. Instead of kissing me, he reached out and ruffled my hair, then trotted across the lawn to his cabin.

Now, watching him paddle away, I felt the same sort of delicious, forlorn ache. I wondered if this was how Natalia had felt when she first knew Steve, this combination of comfort and excitement.

"All right," Jane, our leader, finally yelled. "Enough of this bullshit. We're going to assign you partners. Boys in the back of the canoe, girls in the front."

I saw Meredith and Lori exchange terrified looks. Neither of them wanted to end up in a canoe with Mick, who sat at the edge of the dock, running his bare feet back and forth in the water.

Natalia's hand shot up into the air. Jane ignored her, continuing about her business. So Natalia swung her long limbs out of the canoe, splashed through the water, and tapped Jane on the shoulder. Jane turned around and looked up. Natalia towered over her by a good eight inches.

"Your plan doesn't make any sense," Natalia said. "Sydney knows how to steer. So why can't I go in the front of her canoe?"

Silas stood on the dock, unrolling Meredith and Lori's sleeping bags to let them dry out. "She's right," he said to Jane. "There are four people who can do a J stroke. You, me, her"— he pointed to me—"and him"—he pointed to Charlie. Unlike Jane, Silas didn't seem to care if we got off any time today, even though the eleven o'clock groups were starting to gather behind us on the hill. He picked up a bird book and interrupted his reasoning to leaf through it. "I think that's a warbler," he said, pointing in the sort-of direction of a nearby tree. I didn't know who he was talking to, and I didn't see any bird.

"Silas," Jane pleaded, wanting some help.

"Okay," said Silas, snapping out of it. "You." He pointed to Brendan. "She'll teach you how to do a J stroke." At first I thought he meant Jane, but then I saw his finger pointed directly at me. His attention wandered off again, this time to the placement of his guitar in his own canoe, and Jane took over. Brendan waded out toward me, and I paddled to him. We met halfway, in water that hit him just above the knees. I climbed out of the canoe and stood next to him.

"It's pretty easy," I said, willing myself not to be starstruck, or even attracted. Already I felt loyal to Cody. "Just think of a *J*," I told him, "and think of using the water as leverage for the direction you want to go. The person in the bow keeps paddling in straight strokes, and then you use the J stroke to pull the stern around."

Brendan stood close enough that I could feel his breath on my neck. He smelled good, a musky jasmine scent that would draw every mosquito and black fly in Ontario. By now, everyone else had finally teetered into a canoe. Meredith and Lori, looking relieved, sat in the bows of Silas and Jane's canoes. Charlie had Sam, and of course I had Natalia, which left Mick—still sitting on the edge of the dock like he wanted nothing to do with our entire operation.

All of our canoes were painted bright blue. Brendan walked back to the dock, and Natalia splashed her way back to ours. Brendan didn't get into his canoe but pulled it through the water and over to the dock. Like Silas, Brendan had brought along an acoustic guitar—the only oversize item Camp Bell allowed. He had wrapped the case in plastic and tied it carefully to the bar in front of the stern seat, which we now knew—thanks to Jane—was called the aft thwart.

"I guess you're with me," he said to Mick, and then climbed into the stern seat.

Mick shrugged and dropped his pack into the middle of the canoe. His bag looked half-full, and so light that I couldn't imagine it contained a sleeping bag. Which I guess it didn't, because a minute later he threw in another bulky bundle that looked like it was made of cloth, like the old zippered Snoopy blanket I used to bring to slumber parties. It hit Brendan's guitar, striking a muffled chord. I thought about telling Natalia we didn't have to worry about Mick, because he was going to freeze to death during these frigid Canadian nights. But I would have had to speak in a normal voice for her to hear me, and I remembered how sound carried across water.

Mick hopped into the bow of the canoe and took up his paddle. The two boys pushed away from shore. For a second Brendan, the professional actor, looked like he knew what he was doing. He was dressed so exactly right, wearing a khaki Aussie hat with a feather peeking out of the band, Patagonia shorts, and a maroon Harvard Crew T-shirt. But they made it just past the dock before the canoe's bow started drifting back toward shore.

By now our group was already far down the lake. If we didn't hurry, we'd lose them around the first bend. Despite Jane's brief flurry of authority, I didn't quite trust her and Silas to wait for us, or even remember we belonged to their group.

I paddled back to Brendan and Mick. "Maybe for now you guys should just switch sides," I said. "When you want to go left, both of you paddle on the left side. When you want to go right, paddle on the right side. Straight, just paddle on opposite sides."

When Mick looked up, the fury in his eyes startled me. I couldn't tell whether it came from the frustration of trying to canoe, or from being bossed around by me, a girl. But in a few seconds his face rearranged itself, and he followed my directions as if he didn't care—about anything.

A few minutes later, the four of us paddled side by side—the boys with their awkward, semifrantic shifting, and Natalia and me at an even and elegant pace.

We spent the morning in sight of the rest of our group but a good clip behind. It was hard not to feel leisurely on such a bright summer day. A family of mallards floated upstream, the father in the lead and the mother taking up the rear, four ducklings in a fluffy, proud line between them.

"So sweet," Natalia said. Brendan smiled but Mick just kept staring straight ahead, squinting. He was the only person on the water not wearing sunglasses.

"You need shades, man," Brendan said, though he couldn't have seen the squint.

Mick shrugged, then after a minute said, "They're in my pack."

"Want to stop so you can get them?"

"No, it's straight."

We paddled a little farther. And then Mick said—as if that small exchange about sunglasses had spurred his ability to speak, "Shit. Whoa. Am I seeing what I think I'm seeing?"

We were far behind the group, and sun slanted sharply in front of our eyes. But I saw what Mick meant. From where we floated, it looked like Jane had peeled off her shirt. It also looked like she wore nothing underneath.

"Is she just floating down the lake topless?" Mick said.

"No," said Natalia. "She must be wearing a halter, or something like that."

We saw Jane's canoe come to a stop. She stood up in what looked like full, unashamed nakedness and plopped into the water.

"I'm getting closer," Mick said. He started paddling like mad toward the gaggle of canoes up ahead. Brendan struggled to keep up, switching his paddle from one side to the other. Natalia and I laughed, watching them go.

"Ah, nudity," Natalia said, "bringing together all men, everywhere."

"We had Brendan to ourselves for a minute there," I said. "Wait till we tell Kendra and Ashlyn and everybody."

"Maybe you can date him," said Natalia. "After all, here we are, out on this lake. Those two other girls are certainly no competition for you. And I can't, because of Steve."

"Maybe," I said, without much enthusiasm, still thinking of Cody. And then I recognized a hint of condescension in her comment, like being stranded on a remote lake, with no other girls as possibilities, was the only way I could ever hook up with someone like Brendan.

"You can go back home with a movie star boyfriend," Natalia said.

"Sure," I said, but my voice sounded stony. Natalia and I had been friends since kindergarten, and best friends since the seventh grade. In all that time, I couldn't remember feeling so much as annoyance toward her. It was upsetting, now, that every few hours a surge of something like fury welled up toward her.

"We'd better get going," Natalia said, "or they'll leave us behind."

We stepped up our paddling. The others seemed to be waiting for us now, a little blue flotilla up ahead in the sunlight. I dug my paddle deep into the water, curious to see whether Jane actually swam topless, or simply wore the world's most invisible bikini top.

Topless, as it turned out. Our canoe banged lightly into Brendan and Mick's, and as Jane hauled herself back into the canoe we got a perfect view of her breasts, which looked surprisingly heavy for such a small girl, with a complicated network of blue veins. She rested her paddle across the stern and soaked up the sun—like floating half naked among nine strangers was the most normal thing in the world. Everybody looked away from her. In the bow of her canoe, Meredith's plump cheeks glowed bright red. I'd expected Mick to stare frankly, but he kept his eyes glued to the bottom of the boat. Charlie had taken off his sunglasses and squinted straight ahead into the sun, like some sort of stoic cowboy, and Sam looked so panicked and shuffly I felt sure he was trying to hide a giant boner.

"Okay," said Silas. "Onward."

"Hey," Natalia objected. "We just got here. I need to rest my arms."

"That's the penalty for lagging," Jane said, a stern and military stripper. "No rest." She pulled her T-shirt back on, and in a few minutes the other three boats had paddled far ahead of us. Mick splashed his paddle and whooped. "Awesome," he said. "I didn't know this was going to be a topless canoe trip."

"It is not going to be a topless canoe trip," Natalia said. She had pulled her black hair into a high ponytail that sprouted directly from the top of her head. In shorts and a white tank top, I thought she looked much sexier than any topless girl.

"Come on," said Mick. "Our fearless leader took off her shirt. Now you girls have to do the same."

While this should have been threatening coming from someone who looked as thuggish and unfamiliar as Mick, it had exactly the reverse effect. His behavior so exactly mirrored all the guys we knew from home that we couldn't help laughing. Natalia scooped up water with her paddle and splashed it at him.

"Hey," Brendan said, hunching over to protect his gear from the wet invasion. "I'm just an innocent bystander."

Mick peeled off his own shirt. He had the whitest skin I'd ever seen. It looked very wrong amidst the bright blue river and lush green banks, a sudden shock of colorlessness.

"Come on," Mick said. His eyes traveled back and forth between me and Natalia. In a funny way, I appreciated that he included both of us instead of singling out Natalia as the object of his flirtation. "I took off my shirt," he said, "now you take off yours."

"Forget it, thug," Natalia said. I tensed for a minute. But she had said the word with throaty fondness, making it a term of endearment. We all laughed, then paddled to catch up with the rest of the group: suddenly best friends, the new in-crowd, the final four.

We had so much fun talking and splashing water at each other that we held up the entire group. In addition to our laziness, I found myself having to pee at almost hourly intervals. Every time, Natalia and I would paddle over to shore and squat behind trees (she always joined me, as a sign of solidarity). Mick and Brendan would stand guard, promising not to peek and making sure our canoe didn't float away. At the first sign of late afternoon, a slight chill skimming off the water, we paddled up to where our group had already started setting up camp.

"This is way far down from where we were planning to stop," Jane scolded, when we had landed our canoes and walked over for instruction. She had put on a T-shirt, plus a fleece pullover, so we were able to look her straight in the eye. "You four will have hurry tomorrow," she told us.

"Aye, aye, cap'n," Mick said, and gave her a little salute. She gave in, smiling. Silas called us over to show us how to set up the tents.

There were three. One was for Jane and Silas, which of course made us assume they were a couple, even though we hadn't seen anything like affection pass between them. One tent was for the four girls and another for the four guys. "You'll be responsible for setting up your own tent whenever we reach camp," Silas told us. We knelt beside him, watching him plant the stakes and pull the tarp. His fisherman's sweater seemed looser than it had the day before, as if one day of canoeing had cost him significant body fat.

Brendan, Mick, Natalia, and I all labored setting up the same tent. I wondered if that meant we—and not the girls— would be sharing it. Somehow I couldn't imagine topless Jane and distracted Silas insisting on segregating the sexes. I threw my pack inside the tent, then climbed in. After I spread out my sleeping bag in the far corner, I dug through the jumble of clothes for a fleece jacket. Natalia knelt beside me, doing the same. She pulled out a bright white pullover, made of soft fleece that looked like fox fur.

"Natalia," I said, "you can't wear that jacket out here. The mosquitoes will eat you alive."

"No, they won't," she said. "The guy at EMS said bright colors repel mosquitoes."

In the tent's muted evening light, I imagined Natalia and Mrs. Miksa, breezing into EMS and purchasing top-of-the-line everything. Under the most ordinary circumstances, the Miksas hardly ever refused Natalia a thing. Her knowing about Margit probably made them even more eager to please her. They probably dropped thousands in a single shopping trip.

At this very moment, back at the mall in Hackensack, a clerk at EMS was smiling through his retail drudgery, picturing all the mosquitoes that were feasting on Natalia in her

four-hundred-dollar Marmot pullover. At least he hadn't
talked her out of bug spray. She pulled out a little bottle of
Bullfrog, also—unfortunately—deet free. "We'll use lots of
this," she said.

"Don't bother," I said. "We're going to find out who has the
most toxic bug spray and become his best friend." I had barely
finished my sentence when into the tent flew Mick's useless,
childlike sleeping bag. He stuck his bald head in after it.

"Hey, girls," he said. "What's the chatter?"

"Is that some kind of expression?" Natalia said. "'What's the
chatter?' The chatter is, this tent belongs to the girls."

Never mind what she said, her tone could not have been
more inviting. Mick crawled in and spread out his sleeping
bag next to hers. "Come on," he said. "You don't want to
break up our group, do you? Wouldn't you rather share a tent
with Brendan and me than those boring white kids?"

Natalia and I looked at each other, confused. Was this
another expression? Or was Mick just a major weirdo?

"Um," Natalia said. "Don't look now, but we're all white
kids too."

"Shit," said Mick. "You noticed."

Natalia and I burst out laughing. "Hey," Jane's voice called,
from somewhere in the camp. "Everybody needs to look for
sticks. We're roasting hot dogs for dinner."

Surprisingly obedient, Mick climbed out of the tent, leaving
his gear right where he'd put it. While he and Natalia started
searching for sticks ("Not too dry," Jane shouted. "Find one

that's a little green at the tip."), I walked over to Brendan, who stood watching Jane work on the fire.

"Hey," I said to him. "Do you have any bug repellent?"

"Sure," he said. I followed him to his pack, which like everyone else he'd rested against a tree, apparently waiting for our ruling on Mick. He pulled out a huge bottle of Off! Deep Woods Sportsmen—98 percent deet. I could have kissed him.

I closed my eyes tight and shielded them with my hands while he doused me with the poison. It should have been kind of an intimate moment, but Brendan acted more like a mom taking care of me than an interested guy.

"You better save some for Natalia," I said. "She'll probably have a million bites before dinner starts."

"Sure," he said. "I'll hide this in here for us." By "us" I knew he meant him, me, Natalia, and Mick. He stuffed the bottle deep into his pack then carried it over to our tent and tossed it inside—zipping everything tight, to keep out the bugs.

In my mind, Brendan had already faded from movie star to platonic guy-friend. It seemed very normal standing there next to him. We both let our eyes travel across the campsite, to where Mick searched for sticks.

"Interesting guy," Brendan said. "I'm going to really study him, in case I ever have to play someone like that." I tried to picture Brendan dressed up to play someone like Mick—tattoos, shaved head, and all—and thought that the best acting coaches and costume designers in the world wouldn't be able to make it convincing.

Though no one had said a word about his acting, Brendan didn't bother pretending we didn't know exactly who he was. Still, I didn't find him cocky. He just seemed kind of nice and easygoing. And although I got absolutely no vibe of interest toward myself, he also didn't appear to be lusting after Natalia, which struck me as a refreshing change. We could all be just friends, with no messy sex to interfere with alliances.

That night we had a feast around the fire. We sat on logs and roasted hot dog after hot dog on our whittled green sticks. We cooked potatoes on sticks too: They tasted charred and crispy on the outside and firm and green on the inside. We passed around cans of peaches and a roll of cookie dough that Jane didn't feel like baking. No silverware, just sticks and fingers. Everything had a slight tinge of ash, dirt, and bark, but after our day on the water it all tasted delicious.

"We have to eat all the perishables this first week," Jane said. "They won't last much longer in the cooler."

Because Jane had masterminded our entire meal on sticks, there were no dishes or pots to wash. After we'd all gorged ourselves, Brendan brought out his guitar. I had somehow won the spot next to him—Natalia sat next to me, and Mick next to Natalia. Meredith and Lori sat on the other side of the fire with their heads together, their chins in their hands, staring swoonily as Brendan strummed corny old songs like "Leaving on a Jet Plane" and "Kumbaya." He had a sweet, earnest voice and only missed an occasional chord. Silas left his guitar in his tent, and I wondered if that meant he played better or worse than Brendan. Everything seemed companionable enough until it was time to go to bed.

"Hey," Meredith said. "The boys' sleeping bags are in the girls' tent."

Silas and Jane were already heading toward their tent. They stopped and looked at each other. Then Jane gave Silas a look that seemed to say, *Your turn*, which he handled by shrugging and smiling, then following Jane off to bed.

Charlie and Sam stood limply by the fire, waiting for our verdict.

"What are you," Mick said to Meredith, "some kind of prude?"

Natalia surprised me by stepping in. "Look," she said. "They shouldn't have to sleep in the same tent with guys if they don't want to. You should move your sleeping bag."

Her voice sounded more calm and composed than bossy. Mick responded by walking directly to our tent and removing his belongings. I took this as the first sign that he'd already fallen completely in love with her.

Our tent full of girls smelled of acrid sweat and chemical bug spray. Natalia's solar-powered lamp glowed in our corner. It was amazing, that captured ball of sunlight, energy in its most basic state. I thought how my dad would approve.

While Meredith and Lori read paperbacks from their summer reading list, Natalia pulled out a pen and a pad of paper. "I'm going to work on a list of questions for Margit," she said. She planned to send them to her at the two-week point, when we could send and receive mail. We lay down side by side, Natalia pressing a ballpoint pen to a legal pad.

"First question," Natalia said. "Why didn't you have an abortion?"

Meredith and Lori gave no sign that they'd stopped reading and started listening, other than a shift in breathing pattern, but I could hear them absorb our every word.

"Ask her who the father is," I whispered.

Natalia wrote down: *Who is the father?* We had agreed on this language without discussing it, always saying "the father," never "my father" or "your father."

She paused and scratched at a mosquito bite on her wrist. Above the flap in the tent, we could see silhouettes of a thousand bugs—moths, mosquitoes, dragonflies—trying to beat their wings through our canvas fortress.

"What else?" she said.

"I don't know," I said. "But you have two weeks before you send it. We don't have to think of every question right now."

Natalia said, "Every time I get mad at her, I think how scared she must have been."

I paused for a minute, then nodded my agreement. I watched as Natalia wrote in her awkward sideways handwriting: *Were you scared?*

"I have to pee," I said.

I crawled over our tent mates, who hadn't once taken their

eyes off their books. I unzipped carefully and slid out, trying my best not to let in any bugs. But I knew a few slipped by. From where I squatted by the lake, I could see insect shadows joining the girlish ones inside the tent.

No light or shadows came from the counselors' tent, or the boys'. Both stood dark and silent in the camp. Jane had doused the fire with lake water, but the scent of wood smoke and roasted meat lingered. A mist rose off the lake. Mosquitoes buzzed at my ear, then retreated, repelled by Brendan's super-industrial goo.

When I got back to the tent, the solar lantern sat outside. I carried it up the mossy bank and rested it behind a small pine tree. The woods filled with dark sounds, hoots and whistles and twitching. It beckoned and frightened me, like a ghost story.

I stood there a minute, hoping that I wouldn't have to pee until morning. Then I picked up two sticks and made a little cross in front of the pine tree, so I wouldn't forget where I'd left the lantern. The only problem with a solar lamp: There was no way to turn it off, other than hiding it.

chapter seven
newly savage

I learned everything about Meredith and Lori during the night, because it turned out Meredith had a urinary tract infection and needed to pee as often as I did. Every time I crawled over her sleeping bag she would wake up and come along with me. We moved the solar lantern from behind the pine tree so it would light our travels from tent to increasingly damp earth.

Meredith had brought along prescription antibiotics. On our third trip to the tree, she expressed concern for my lack of medication. "You might have an infection too," she said.

"No," I assured her, "just a very small bladder."

"Or maybe you're diabetic," she said. "My cousin is, and that's how they found out. She started needing to pee all the time."

This conversation took place in very early morning, that silent moment between deepest night and the first rays of morning: no longer completely dark, only a hint of light from beneath the horizon. With nocturnal animals finally silent and the daytime ones still sleeping, it was still dark enough that Meredith and I squatted in front of the trees rather than behind them.

"Frequent urination can be a symptom of a lot of medical disorders," she told me.

"I'm really not worried." I hoped my tone sounded final, but I tried not to make it too stern. Without her glasses, Meredith looked like a little girl, pink cheeked and snub nosed, her sandy blond hair endearingly messy.

We stood up and pulled our sweats back up, then headed back toward the tent. We had worked out a complicated system to keep out bugs. It involved unzipping as little as we needed, then sidling under and in quick succession, rezipping between each of our entrances. But when I looked to see if she was ready, she waved her hand and started toward the lake.

"I think I'll stay up and watch the sun rise," she said. I hesitated for a second, almost tempted to join her, but fatigue got the better of me. I climbed over my tent mates and into my sleeping bag. Natalia slept like a log, her hair still in yesterday's ponytail, her mouth closed. She breathed quietly, through her nose, unlike Lori, who snored like an asthmatic.

Lori and Meredith lived in a small town in Ohio, which—Meredith had told me, when she heard that Natalia and I went to private school—had an excellent public school system. The two of them were best friends, and I got the feeling from Meredith's wistful and claustrophobic description that they were also each other's only friend. They had found Camp Bell online and, though they had never done any camping, thought it sounded romantic.

"In the literary sense," Meredith explained pointedly, "not

the sexual." The statement may have proved that her public education was as good as Linden Hill Country Day, but I wasn't totally convinced she and Lori didn't hope to meet guys. I guessed they must be pretty disappointed by the selection: the dreamy but unattainable Brendan, the distinctly undreamy team of Charlie and Sam, and the flat-out frightening Mick. Not to mention the unbeatable competition in the form of Natalia. When I hinted at this, Meredith set me straight.

"No," she said. "We both really needed to get away from the whole guy thing." She told me that in the past year, both Lori and she had lost their virginity to Amish boys who lived in the neighboring town.

"Really?" I said, not able to hide my shock. "How did you meet them?"

"We live near Amish farmland. They're around all the time."

"Wow," I said, not quite able to get my head around this. "Did you date them?"

"We tried to," Meredith said, looking mournful. "But obviously it didn't work out."

"I'm amazed," I told her. "I thought Amish kids weren't allowed to have sex."

"Well," Meredith pointed out, "neither are we."

On our next late-night pee, Meredith told me that Lori was already put off by the overly rustic nature of the trip.

"I don't know what she expected," I said.

"She thought there would at least be Porta Potties at campsites," said Meredith. "And she wasn't expecting to get so wet. Also, her skin is breaking out so badly."

It seemed too mean to point out that Lori's skin had been badly broken out when she got here. So instead I said, "Of course she's going to get wet. We're on a lake."

"I know," Meredith said. "And I kind of like it. I don't mind the water, or peeing outside. I feel so far away from everything. In a good way. You know?"

I definitely did. Lying in my sleeping bag with my eyes shut tight, I could feel the sun outside the tent, rising and widening. Birds started to chirp and sing. The pine branches moved in a silent rustle; I could see their spiraling shadows on the inside of my eyelids. And I sank like a stone into unmoving sleep.

At what must have been midmorning, I stumbled out of the tent in blinding sunlight. Last night around the campfire we had discovered that not a single one of us had brought along a watch. For the next two weeks, at least, we would have to guess how much time had passed on any given day. I squinted into the numberless light, toward the sounds of a much better guitar player than Brendan: Silas, strumming by the campfire. I didn't recognize the tune, a beautiful collection of chords and picking. Silas himself looked strangely beautiful too, unaware that I was watching him, his brows knitted together in concentration. The birds had stopped their hysterical morning chatter, and my own internal sundial struck nine forty-five. Music rose and settled around Silas like daytime stardust, and I wished I knew him better so I could walk over and sit at his feet, listening. That longing, and his distance, felt strangely and sweetly familiar. I walked over to the campfire and sat down on a log next to Natalia.

"Oh no," she said, when I told her what time I thought it was. "I know it's much earlier than that." She sipped black coffee from a tin camping mug. Her hair sat on top of her head in tangled disarray. Her cheeks had creases from the makeshift pillow. Her long lashes were crusted with sleep. But she still managed to look beautiful, hunched in that fuzzy white sweatshirt. On the other side of the campfire Sam and Charlie squinted from either the sunlight or the glamorous reflection of my groggy best friend. I tried to picture the Natalia equivalent at whatever school they went to, and wondered if they felt blessed or intimidated having her along on this trip.

Jane had brewed coffee in a pot that sat directly on the fire, and its strong, charcoal smell competed with the piney woods. I had never gotten around to developing a taste for coffee, and as far as I knew Natalia wasn't used to the sludge either. After every sip she wrinkled her nose in delicate distaste. The one thing I did know about coffee: Pregnant women were supposed to avoid it. I grabbed a mug from the jumble of pots and pans and poured myself a cup. The first sip tasted muddy and acrid, and I almost gagged. But after a while, it felt good to have something warm in my stomach, which felt deeply,

deeply hollow. I put my hand on my belly. It was flat as usual, my fingers resting directly on ribs.

"You look skinny," Natalia said, reading my mind. I frowned at her.

"Don't tell me you're trying to lose weight," Jane said to me. "Last year we had a bulimic on the trip. It was a horrible feeling, going to all this work making food and knowing it would just be yacked up behind a tree. Plus, she had no energy for rowing at all."

"I'm not bulimic," I said.

"Good," said Jane, bustling around the campfire, which was obviously her private domain. She loaded slices of bread into a funny mesh contraption with a long handle, which she held over the fire, shaking it occasionally like old-fashioned popcorn. Like all the equipment that belonged to Camp Bell, the toaster looked like it had been dug out of a time capsule from the 1940s.

"I think I'd rather eat the bread raw," Natalia said.

Jane didn't look up, but frowned quietly. She shook black bangs away from her eyes. Although Natalia had obviously rejected her as any kind of authority, I liked Jane. I thought she looked athletic and unself-conscious, squatting in front of the fire. I thought of her yesterday, peeling off her shirt without any thought as to how we might react. I admired that. I also admired Silas, not paying the slightest bit of attention to any of us, just sitting on a log and picking the prettiest morning music on his battered guitar.

Mick struggled out of the tent and walked over to the fire, where he knelt and rooted through the cooler.

"Are we going to cook this?" he asked Jane, holding up a package of bacon.

"I guess," she said. "We've got to eat all the perishable stuff first. But it's good raw, too."

Mick hesitated, the package still in the air like a question mark.

"We could cook it if you want," she said, "but then you guys would have to scrub the frying pan."

Mick seemed to find that task worth avoiding. He tore the plastic off the bacon and peeled off a long, raw strip, which he rolled into a little ball and then popped into his mouth.

"Hey," Sam said. His voice sounded shrill and boyish. "You can't eat bacon raw."

Mick turned to him and rubbed his belly. "Mmm," he said. Sam's face turned bright pink. Charlie didn't say anything, and it occurred to me that in two days I hadn't heard him speak a word. I had no idea what his voice sounded like.

Mick peeled off another piece of bacon and passed the package to me. My father would have died. If he saw me eating raw bacon straight out of the package—Oscar Mayer, no less—he would have lain down in front of the fire and died. In his world, even grass-fed, organic meat had to be cooked straight through. "You never know what neighboring farmers are up to," he always said. "There's all kinds of ways to contaminate groundwater."

And I don't think I had ever in my entire life seen my mother eat bacon, raw or otherwise. She would definitely have had a lot to say if she knew I was even considering eating raw bacon. But what mattered less than what either of my parents thought? Back at Newark International they had both disappeared into the ether. Since the moment I stepped onto that Air Canada flight, they existed only in theory.

Of course none of that made the food any more appetizing. Aside from being uncooked, the bacon—after an entire sunny day in the cooler—was only slightly refrigerated. But I felt too hungry for my stomach even to growl. The sound it made was more like a knocking, a begging and urgent command. So I peeled off a slice and nibbled the fatty white edge. It tasted salty and fine, a thicker version of the kind of proscuitto Mrs. Miksa wrapped around asparagus spears when she had company. I peeled off another slice to hold in my fingers while I ate the first, then passed the package to Natalia. The truth was, I could easily have sat there and eaten every single slice of that bacon.

Natalia immediately dug into the raw bacon, which surprised me. Usually she was very dainty and picky about her food. About everything, in fact. But last night she hadn't uttered a word of complaint about sleeping on the ground, or using a sleeping bag case stuffed with clothes for a pillow. She seemed committed to diving into every part of this experience, and she dangled the bacon above her lips, then dropped it into her mouth like a strand of spaghetti.

"Yum," she said, her mouth full, only partially joking. Mick sat next to her—not a foot away, like a normal person who'd just met her yesterday, but close enough so that their legs and haunches touched. It was the way a boyfriend would sit next to her, and I expected Natalia to move away, or at least shoot me an incredulous glance. But she just kept laughing and munching on her bacon.

Lori appeared, having just washed her face in the lake. She had her hair back in a headband, and it spiked directly skyward in slightly crazed disarray. Her skin looked red and irritated as she scowled at us.

"Hey," she said. From her tone you would have thought we'd caught and skinned a chipmunk. "That's disgusting. You're all going to get worms."

We looked up at her, our fingers coated in fatty grease. Mick, Natalia, and I burst out laughing. "It's not funny," Lori said. I thought for a minute she might break down and cry. She picked up the soggy bacon package and stared forlornly at the raw slices.

"What are the rest of us supposed to eat?" she said.

Jane stood up, not bothering to point out the war-relic toaster. Clearly Lori's breakfast was not her problem.

"Okay," Jane said. "It's got to be the middle of the morning! And we need to make some serious time today."

Truthfully, I didn't think Jane cared about making serious time any more than we did. She just yelled out these orders because Silas had no interest in them. The occasional shout

of authority seemed like a necessary part of the whole experience, like the guitar music around the fire.

When I was a kid river rafting in Colorado, it used to feel like
visiting another planet. The gray rocks and the red soil, the
jagged river banks and eddies, the lack of man-made sprawl
and motors, the quivering aspens—everything seemed so far
away from suburban New Jersey. Here on Lake Keewaytinook,
the air that surrounded us felt much more familiar. The muddy
banks of the lake and its small colored pebbles matched the
banks of Flat Rock Brook and the creek that ran by the railroad
tracks in Overpeck. The pine and mulch that wafted from the
surrounding woods was the first fragrance I would have thought
of, if someone asked me to describe what Earth smelled like.

But while the broad, blue lake did not suggest interplane-
tary travel, the lack of any other humans made me feel as if
the world had ended. There should have been camps lining
the banks, and other people boating. But we paddled for what
seemed like hours, establishing a rhythm without sound other
than the dipping of our paddles, and without seeing any sign
of life other than ourselves. Even Natalia and I had slowed our
usually nonstop communication. At home we stayed in constant contact: a stream of conversation when we were together,
continued by text message, cell phones, and the Internet when
we were apart. Even in class at school, we would pass notes
to each other. Last year I had Dr. Berman for second-period
algebra, and she had him for fifth-period calculus. We would sit

in the same seat, drawing pictures and writing colorful notes to each other. At the end of the year we snuck into the classroom and screwed the desk off its chair. Natalia had it at home now, nailed to her bedroom wall.

But on the lake, with no cell phones or desktops, we barely communicated. Maybe it was an awareness of how our words would stand out and echo in all this natural quiet. The usual topics—Steve, Greg, our parents—somehow did not seem so pressing, so desperately in need of dissection and analysis. We didn't mention my pregnancy at all, as if in the face of all that had ended—civilization—it didn't matter or exist. Oddly enough, it was this very feel of apocalypse that I liked most: the notion of us ten, the lone tribe left in this glossy green wilderness. It didn't seem to matter that except for Natalia I barely knew any of these people. Rowing along the lake, my arms ached and my heart swelled with illogical fondness. Especially toward Meredith, who rode valiantly in the bow of Sam's canoe, wearing a navy blue tank suit and a gigantic pair of nylon running shorts. Her hair had a pretty sheen, ginger and flaxen intersecting in her long braids, and her perfect skin was bright pink from the exertion. She looked game and earnest. I even noticed that Lori had a good, trim body, and I thought that if the two girls could be combined into one person, using only their good qualities, you would end up with the most beautiful girl in the world.

"I kind of love Meredith," I admitted to Natalia, my first words in what seemed like hours. Natalia nodded, Meredith's opposite in a striped bikini and a frayed denim skirt.

"Then I do too," she said.

I saw her eyes search the water for Brendan and Mick, who had rowed ahead of us, out of sight. I waited for her to amend her Final Four, but she didn't say anything else. Only the second day of our trip, and pop culture had already started to fade away. We could live without the world of pixels and radio waves, we could even immediately forget it, replacing television with campfires, and iPods with old John Denver tunes and Silas's gorgeous, silken picking. I felt something inside me relax for the first time since my dad had told me his post-oil, post-civilization theory. If all the cities in the world shut down tomorrow, we—this group, here now—would be okay, paddling around Lake Keewaytinook. The thought was such a revelation that I shared it with Natalia. At first she nodded in agreement. Then she said, "But of course in that case you'd have to have the baby."

I let my oar drag in the water. The bow of our canoe drifted, barely perceptibly, toward shore. It was weird how Natalia thought about my pregnancy more than I did.

"Think of it," she said. "We'd all be out here, living in our tents, foraging for food. And you'd have this baby, and we'd all take care of it. It would belong to all of us."

The idea was so fanciful, so beyond anything that would actually ever happen, I took a moment to consider it. I pictured the ten of us like some kind of Native American tribe, tending to a baby that we'd take turns carrying around in a little papoose. It would be a very cute baby, with Tommy's glossy hair and my big brown eyes. Maybe we'd eventually run into Cody's group: He, the baby, and I could form a postapocalyptic family. We would be brave and idyllic in the wilderness. There was something beautiful about the scenario. I imagined myself the most necessary member of a family unit. Mother. Wife. *Uxorious.*

Then I pictured myself, nine months pregnant, squatting and screaming in the bushes. "I can't say I like the idea of giving birth out here," I said, happier to mention this image than the brave-new-world version.

Natalia cringed, then nodded. "That would be bad," she said. "And it would get cold in winter."

I started to make a joke about Mick, how if the apocalypse came he would be in charge of running down deer and skinning rabbits for our fur coats. But from up ahead we heard Jane shout that it was time to stop, so we picked up speed again, concentrating on just paddling.

At lunch everyone seemed caught up in the calm and quiet of the day, newly and strangely familiar with one another. Lori even plopped herself down next to Brendan. "I've done a bit of acting myself," she said, in a voice that sounded slightly, suspiciously British.

Everyone stopped talking and stared at the two of them. So far, nobody had mentioned Brendan's acting career. It seemed rude, somehow, like asking Mick about his juvenile record or his tattoos.

But Brendan just smiled and said, "Really?" He seemed very at ease, and very respectful as Lori rattled off the minor roles she had played in school productions of *Our Town* and *Guys and Dolls*.

When she mentioned *The Vagina Monologues*, Mick barked, "Hey! Keep it clean!" Then he, Natalia, and I fell off our log, laughing hysterically. Brendan just reached over and patted Lori's shapely knee. His touch allowed her furious red blush to settle into a smile, and I thought how really nice Brendan was, much nicer than he had to be.

Jane handed out peanut butter sandwiches, and I realized that the three people who didn't know about Brendan's career—her, Silas, and Mick—now only knew about Lori's. So funny, the obvious things we didn't know about one another. I sat next to Charlie, his silence suddenly not seeming peculiar, but stoic and companionable. I liked his Clint Eastwood squint, and the square freckles across his face. Who needed to talk? There was so much to listen to instead, the whole world rustling around us. I thought how much better this was than lifeguarding, my muscles moving instead of lolling, the smell of dirt and algae instead of chlorine and artificial coconut.

By the time we got back on the water the wind had picked up. Natalia, Brendan, Mick, and I paddled together. Brendan was getting better at his J strokes, and this time the four of us manage to pull ahead as the others struggled against the waves.

"I can't believe what a difference this makes," Natalia shouted back to me, her head bent into the wind. Not far behind, with Lori in his bow, Silas yelled that we should continue on straight and hug the shore to keep out of the wind.

The going was tough. We ducked our heads and paddled. As the afternoon wore on, Natalia's slender arms became more and more sinewy before my eyes. At one point we were overtaken by a duck, swimming against the wind with five ducklings behind her.

"Oh," Natalia said, as she had the day before. "So sweet."

It was a beautiful bird, dark with a circle of white on either side of its face, and a crazy plume of feathers on top of its head. It looked like something out of Dr. Seuss. Remembering the bird book, I called back to Silas, "What kind of duck is that?"

"Hooded merganser," he yelled. I could barely hear him over the wind, though his canoe floated less than a yard away.

"Look at that bird," Mick said. "It's making it so easy over the waves. Let's race it."

"No," said Natalia. "You'll frighten her."

Mick had an expression on his face that I had already come to recognize. He looked crazed and intent, possessed by a force inside him, unable to hear what any of us said. Despite cries of protest from every direction, he took off, paddling furiously in the bow. Brendan, for his part, obediently picked up his pace. I couldn't understand why he would listen to Mick, but they seemed to have established a pecking order, if not quite a friendship. It struck me as very odd that Brendan—with all his obvious status—should so instantly go along with Mick.

Natalia and I raced after them, not to join the chase but to try to stop it. We could see the duck's face, eyes wide with determination—recognizing a predator. And we laughed when she did the sensible, intelligent thing when Brendan and Mick caught up with her. She turned around and headed in the other direction, the wind and her ducklings at her back.

Natalia and I watched as the merganser headed toward us, her frantic expression matching the mad professor's shock of feathers on top of her head. Four of the ducklings kept up, but one struggled as it backpedaled over the waves. Soon the canoe stood between the duck and its lost baby.

"Look," Mick yelled. "This one's the slow, fat kid. He can't keep up."

"It's not funny," Natalia screamed. The duck had shepherded her babies close to the bank, into a small inlet. With distinct, rapid nods of her head, she counted them—one, two, three, four. At the lack of number five, her eyes widened in further panic. She squawked at the ducklings, who waddled up on shore. Then she set off after the lost one, whom I now identified in my mind—despite my sudden hatred of Mick—as the slow, fat kid.

"Just don't move," Natalia yelled at Mick. "Just let her get it!"

Mick stopped paddling, suddenly returning to obedience, and stood up in the bow of his canoe. The surge that had driven his chase seemed to be seeping out of him; his face looked calmer but slightly perplexed, as if his actions were as mysterious to him as they were to us. Brendan rested his paddle across his knees, panting, while Silas and Lori floated up beside us and stopped, giving the duck plenty of room to bring her baby back to safety.

I watched Mick. If he could sense the heavy disapproval coming from every direction, he didn't give any sign. He wore faded gym shorts and no shirt, a bandanna tied around his bald head. Maybe he had forgotten sunscreen, because the pale skin across his nose and shoulders had turned a deep pink. The skin around his tattoos looked red, irritated, and I wondered if a tattoo could get infected after it had healed. I noticed for the first time, even from my distance across the sunlit stretch of water, that his eyes were a deep, dark blue, much like the color of the lake itself. He was broad and muscular, with chiseled and regular features that quivered like a hunter's.

Mick, I realized with a start, was hot. Not just hot, but handsome. I wondered why I hadn't noticed it before this second.

The wind seemed to die down as the mother duck and her lost duckling joined the others. Mick sat down and started paddling. We all continued our efforts against the headwinds. My arms and shoulders ached.

"Hey, Mick," Silas said. His canoe was just alongside ours, on the other side of Mick and Brendan. "You're really an asshole, you know?" His voice sounded calm and laid-back as ever, no hint of anger other than the words themselves. "If you ever do anything like that again," Silas said, "I'll kick your ass."

"I'd like to see you try," said Mick, almost but not quite under his breath. He didn't seem to put much heart into the retort.

The wind blew just as he spoke. I could barely hear him, and if Silas registered the words he didn't give any indication.

Mick's shoulders sagged in defeat. He looked as if he knew he'd just exposed himself and been found sorely wanting by all of us—including and maybe especially Natalia. As we paddled on into the afternoon, even though I agreed he'd shown himself to be a complete asshole, I couldn't help it. I felt sorry for him.

That night after dinner, when Silas and Jane had disappeared into their tent, Sam told us that smoking deer moss would make a person sterile.

"A guy at base camp told me," he said. He looked so happy to have all our attention, the youngest kid in the family finding a way to steal the spotlight. "If you smoke deer moss," he told us, "you're sterile for, like, seven years."

"Does it work for just guys, or girls, too?" Natalia asked.

"Both," Sam promised, though he didn't look sure. Everyone but Brendan and I left the fire to scrape the stiff green moss from the rocks. Brendan came around from the opposite side to sit next to me. My stomach lurched. The chicken Jane had roasted in the reflector oven had looked slightly gray before she smothered it with barbecue sauce. I worried that we'd all wake up in the middle of the night with salmonella.

"Is it okay if I keep you company?" Brendan asked. "The smoke keeps getting in my eyes over there." At that very moment the wind shifted and a thick gust of smoke from the fire whipped our faces. We laughed.

"It's your fault," I said. "Smoke follows beauty." I didn't worry that Brendan would take this as a come-on. Since even Lori had tried to flirt with him, this seemed like the new and accepted course of action. Anyway, I already felt firmly sisterly. Brendan's good looks were too overblown, almost caricature: He was so perfect, he couldn't possibly be sexy. All I could think of when I looked at him were my own flaws, my buck teeth and the zits that were no doubt multiplying on my forehead in spite of the Stri-Dex pads. Since waving good-bye to Cody at the dock, I had felt totally unflirtatious. Commenting on Brendan's beauty was more like stating the obvious then delivering a compliment.

Brendan himself didn't sound flirtatious, only diplomatic enough to float the words back to me when he said, "The smoke must be following you, then."

"Yeah, right." I laughed. The interaction was so without sexual tension that it made us friends in a final and comfortable way. We sat quietly for a minute, staring into the fire. Then, because I was tired of nobody directly addressing the other elephant on the lake, I said, "Natalia and I used to watch you on *The New Mill River.*"

"Oh yeah?" he said, as if this were a big surprise.

"You were good," I said. "We totally thought you were English."

"Thanks."

I asked questions about the various actors on *The New Mill River*, whether they were nice or stuck-up. He gave me a little rundown on everybody. The star, he said, was a self-obsessed bitch who spent most of her time primping in front of the mirror and putting other people down. Although she played a very saintly and loving character, this information did not surprise me in the slightest.

"So why are you here?" I said. "Shouldn't you be in Hollywood making a movie or something?"

"I've been trying out for parts since I was four," he said. "I wanted to take a break this summer. Do something outdoors."

Mick's voice broke into our conversation. "We got the stuff," he said, holding up fistfuls of deer moss. The others trailed behind him, each with a mossy little stash. There was some discussion of letting it dry out over a few days, but they decided to go ahead and smoke it wet. Natalia reasoned that if it didn't work, they could always try again. From what we could tell, every rock in the area was covered with a thick blanket of the supposed birth control.

"Wait here," Mick said. "I got rolling papers in my pack." We all wondered, as he crawled into his tent, what else he had stashed in that sparsely packed bag. Within a minute he emerged from the tent and rolled a few deer moss cigarettes, then passed one around in each direction. Everybody puffed and coughed: Charlie, Sam, Lori, and Meredith.

"I wonder who they're planning to have sex with," Natalia whispered. "Do they think they're going to lose their virginity to the movie star?"

I felt tempted to tell her about the Amish guys, but I didn't.

I thought it was kind of touching—the way Lori fluttered around Brendan. Meredith just stood back, as if there were some sort of agreement between the two that Lori was the prettier one. Thinking of this, I felt a stab of indignation on Meredith's behalf, her rosy cheeks and silky braids.

When Brendan passed the cigarette to me I took a deep, lung-filling puff. It crackled as I inhaled, too moist, tasting sweet and ashy. My chest contracted and sputtered in protest. I might have wondered what kind of effect it would have on my pregnancy if I believed for a single second that the deer moss would work.

I coughed out my hit. Brendan thumped me companion-ably on the back. "This stuff probably causes pregnancy more than anything else," I said, "if people really think it works for seven years."

"Never hurts to have a backup," said Mick, inhaling deeply.

Natalia patted my knee, and I grabbed her hand. Ever since the afternoon, I had been waiting for her to say something about the hooded merganser—how that bird was so fiercely devoted to her baby, and here I was, planning to flush mine. I had formulated all these arguments in my head about how the duck had been rescuing a chick, not an egg. Having an abortion wasn't like leaving a chick upstream. It was more like breaking or abandoning an egg, something that ducks probably did all the time. But I didn't have to use any arguments, because Natalia didn't say a word.

Later on we lay inside our tent, working on questions for

Margit by the light of the solar lamp. *Were you the one who named me?* she wrote. *Was the father Jewish? Did you breast-feed me at all, or just hand me straight over to Mom? Did you love the father? Do you know where he is now? Did you plan on ever telling me? Did you ever wish I knew? Wasn't it hard, seeing me all the time with Mom and Dad? Didn't you want to tell me? Were you ever going to tell me?*

I lay next to her in the muted light, blinking at her yellow pad, trying to think of more questions for her to ask.

chapter eight
truth or dare

One night toward the end of our first week, a fishing boat motored past our campsite. Its broad spotlight shone on the water, the largest artificial light we'd seen since leaving base camp. Mick sprang up from his log and ran down to the edge of the lake.

"Hey," he yelled, his hands cupped around his lips. "What time is it?"

The fisherman's voice came echoing back to us across the water, its sound bounding like a skipped rock. "Nine thirty-five," he said, which surprised me. I would have guessed ten thirty, or maybe even eleven.

Mick trotted back. He, Natalia, Brendan, and I had been playing Truth or Dare. Everyone else had gone to sleep. The four of us stared at one another through the smoky darkness, trying to figure out if knowing the time made us feel any different. Earlier today, when we all stopped for lunch, I'd had the distinct impression that it was only about ten o'clock in the morning. Now, in this small moment of knowing, I thought about the meaninglessness of the numbers. Nine thirty-five. Who cared? What was time, anyway, but some random code a bunch of Romans had invented? What did it matter to the likes of us, fearlessly riding our natural rhythms through the North American wilderness?

"Sydney," Mick said, returning to the game. "Truth or dare?"

"Dare," I said.

This was my third turn, and also the third time I'd chosen dare. Usually when I played this game I always chose truth—much less afraid of confessions than failing some fake-dangerous task. But now there was too much I couldn't risk revealing. So far Brendan had made me climb to the top of a scraggy pine tree and Natalia had sent me into the lake wearing all my clothes. Before the fishing boat appeared, I had changed out of my wet things and tied Mick's bandanna around my still damp hair.

Now Mick looked at me with the same tense/excited expression he'd had before chasing after the hooded merganser. "Take off your shirt," he said. I blushed and looked away from his handsome, disturbing face. I had brought a couple of jogging bras on the trip, but they remained buried in my pack in favor of my bikini top—which I'd hung out to dry before dinner.

"Shut up," Natalia said to Mick. "Haven't you seen enough tits for one day?" All week Jane had kept up her topless swims. We never knew when she would peel off her shirt, stand up in the canoe, and dive into the water. Charlie and Sam—not to mention Lori and Meredith—had stopped looking her in the eye altogether, though interestingly, the former two seemed to be puppy-dogging around Jane more than Natalia, which showed what a little nudity could do for a girl. Brendan and Silas were the only guys who seemed completely unaffected by Jane's toplessness. I assumed Silas saw them on an even more regular basis, but I didn't know what Brendan's story was.

"Who said anything about tits?" Mick said. "It's a dare." His eyes looked wide and ultrafocused, like a predator or a sociopath. "I want her to stand topless and let the mosquitoes go at her. One full minute. And you can't slap at them."

"I'll do thirty seconds," I said.

"Sydney," Natalia objected.

"You can't negotiate a dare," said Mick. "You have to just do it."

"Fine."

I stood up and pulled off my fleece jacket. Then I stepped back from the fire, out of the light, and took off my shirt. I twirled it over my head like a lasso, then threw it back into the circle so that it landed on top of Mick's head. He laughed, pulled it off his face, and began a loud, slow countdown from sixty.

What bug repellent I'd applied was on my hands and around my face. The mosquitoes attacked immediately, beginning their stinging, itchy feast. Clear, wintry air closed in around my skin, goose bumps rising along with the bug bites, and I battled the urge to close my eyes. I had a clear view of my three friends, sitting around the fire and peering at me through the smoke. I felt sure that the most they could see was my silhouette, and I liked this image: the gesture of revealing without the exposure. Most of my energy went to not slapping the bugs, which I wanted to do more than I'd ever wanted anything in my life.

"Come on," Natalia said when Mick got to thirty. "That's enough."

"It's all right," I called from the darkness. "I can do it."

"You're such an asshole," Natalia said to Mick, who counted more loudly.

"Looking good, Syd," Mick called. I shivered and hugged myself so that my arms covered my breasts.

"I know you can't see me," I yelled. Mick laughed. By now I'd grown used to his very particular laugh, a mean and sneering bark. It made me hate him, and at the same time, strangely, it made me long for his approval.

Finally the countdown ended. Natalia snatched my T-shirt from Mick and tossed it back to me. I pulled it over my head, then trotted back to the fire, clawing at the hundred welts across my stomach. "I hope somebody brought calamine," I said, struggling back into my jacket. For some perverse reason I sat down next to Mick. He put his arm around me and pulled me close, a friendly attempt to warm me up. It worked: A nice heat pulsed from his skin, the chemistry of testosterone and cheerful cruelty.

Something strange had been happening over the past few days. Although at first I'd been sure he was in love with Natalia, Mick had started alternating between us in his taunts. I thought maybe this meant he didn't know how to communicate with girls, other than by sexual jeering. The fact that he'd barely said a single word to Meredith or Lori either confirmed this theory or showed actual sensitivity. Maybe he realized they were still terrified of him and he was trying to be considerate by keeping his distance. At different times he seemed capable of both or either possibility.

As for Natalia and me, something stopped us from being afraid of him, even when we felt we maybe should. He seemed so clearly eager to be our friend. It was a little like having a wild animal—a wolf or a tiger—for a pet.

"Your turn to choose, Syd," Mick said.

"Mick," I answered.

"Big surprise there," he said.

"Truth or dare?" I asked him.

"Truth."

"That's kind of girly, isn't it?" I said. "Shouldn't a tough guy like you be willing to do a dare?" I had planned to make him unzip Jane and Silas's tent and peek inside. We had a running debate over whether they were having sex in there.

"That depends on the question," said Mick.

I dropped my chin into my hands. Honestly, there was a lot I wanted to know about Mick. He'd told us he came from Pittsburgh and that he lived with his mom—which had been a surprise, because we'd assumed he was a Yout at Risk kid. He'd mentioned a brother, so we knew he had at least one sibling. But that was all we knew. I wondered what he'd done to become a Youth at Risk, if the title referred to his financial status, or the place he lived, or trouble he'd gotten into. I thought of asking whether he'd ever committed a crime, but that seemed too vague. And oddly, I thought it could insult him: not that

I'd assumed he was a criminal, but that it would occur to me he might *not* have committed a crime.

"Come on," Mick said. "Isn't there a time limit on this?"

I decided to avoid the word "crime" altogether. "What's the worst thing you ever did?" I asked him.

"Worst in what way?"

"You know," I said. "Most illegal."

"That's easy," said Mick. He took his arm off my shoulders. Until then, I hadn't realized he'd still been holding me. "I killed a guy."

There was a moment of silence, the pop and crackle of the fire. Then we all burst out laughing. "You are so full of shit," Natalia said. Brendan picked up a stick and turned over some of the reddest embers. We watched a new, thin line of smoke spiral up toward the sky.

"I'm not," Mick said. "It's true. I killed a guy. It was a nigger."

For a moment the world around us halted. Insects stopped buzzing. My mosquito bites stopped itching. None of us moved. We heard no loons, no frogs, no crickets, no sound.

It seems strange to say it. But truthfully, in some weird, instinctive way, Mick's using the *N* word shocked me much more than his confession of murder—maybe because I didn't quite believe the latter. But I had never heard anyone say that word in real life. It was the biggest language taboo I knew, maybe the only one. The word echoed in the dark woods. It hung all around us, marking Mick—one of us only a second ago—a strange and ominous other.

"You shouldn't say that," Natalia whispered. "You shouldn't say *nigger*." She gave the word a shaky, unaccustomed lilt, sounding almost like her parents with their musical, pidgin English.

"Yeah," Mick said. "You're not supposed to kill them either."

"That's not funny," I said.

"Who said it was funny?" Mick asked. Sitting beside him, his elbow hovering next to mine, I wished I could see his face straight on.

"Nobody, man," said Brendan. "Nobody's saying it's funny." I thought his voice sounded a little too cool, like he'd been cast as Best Friend in some gangsta movie. All around us, the night had gone back to its usual chorus of wind and wildlife, but everything had turned surreal, artificial. We were all of us suddenly characters. Mick played the hardened criminal, Natalia the delicately aghast hottie. And me, not needing to pretend I wasn't afraid of Mick—because I wasn't—but pretending as usual to be only myself, one person, sitting there among the others.

Mick told us the story. It had happened at the end of last summer. He was walking through Bedford Dwellings in Pittsburgh, late one night with his brother. They had just bought an ounce of pot—"sticky green bud"—when a man stopped them beneath the Cannon Road underpass.

"There were no streetlights," Mick said. "Totally dark. We could barely see the guy's face, but we knew he must have followed us from the score. It cost us almost three hundred bucks for that weed. We weren't going to part with it easy."

Mick said that the guy grabbed his brother, who had the bag

of pot in the inside pocket of his jacket. He ignored Mick and pressed his brother up against the damp cement wall, holding a knife to his throat.

"My brother kept fighting. I told him to quit it, that it wasn't worth getting killed over pot. But he was crazed, fighting back, protecting the stuff, and I knew he was going to get his throat slit. Meanwhile I was just standing there."

The guy had started beating Mick's brother with his fist, hard blows directly to his face, so Mick sprang forward and jumped onto his back. I could imagine Mick's face perfectly in that moment, the taut, electric predator taking the professional criminal by surprise. "I was riding the guy like a horse," Mick said.

He tried to get the knife away by reaching down over his shoulder, but the guy bucked backward, and the two of them landed on the ground. For a second they were both lying there on the concrete, the wind knocked out of them, face-to-face. "Like we'd been cuddling," he said. Mick got his breath back first. He grabbed the guy's head and smashed it on the ground. It sounded, he said, like he'd dropped a bowling ball. I imagined the loud, jarring *thwack* of it.

"I didn't mean to hit his head that hard," Mick said, his voice suddenly more dreamy than proud. "I guess I didn't know how hard the concrete was. I wasn't really thinking. I was just trying to protect myself and my brother. He still had the knife; I was scared he would stab me if I didn't do something. Then his eyes kind of rolled back, and blood started pouring out of his ear."

For a second it felt like we were all four standing in that dark tunnel with Mick—the kid he'd been last summer. I could see the adrenaline pulsing through his jumpy, sixteen-year-old self as he stood over that not-supposed-to-be-dead body.

"The guy just lay there gurgling," Mick said. "His feet kicked a couple times and then just stopped. My brother and me got out of there fast as we could."

"So you really don't even know that he died," said Brendan.

"Oh, he died." Mick picked a slim stick up off the ground and put it in his mouth like a cigar. He removed it and blew imaginary smoke rings into the air.

"Maybe somebody found him and called an ambulance," Natalia said.

"Yeah," said Mick. "Or maybe he sprouted wings and flew up to nigger heaven."

We had all listened to the cracking head part without flinching, but at the repetition of the *N* word Natalia put her hands over her ears and whispered, "*Shh, shh, shh.*"

"Anyway," Brendan said. "It wasn't your fault. It was obviously self-defense."

Mick shrugged. "I don't lose much sleep over it. Me or him, who else am I supposed to choose?"

Natalia took her hands away from her ears and lay them in her lap. Her cheeks looked red and streaky, almost as if she'd started crying.

"You could have just given him the pot," she said. Her voice sounded shaky and small, not like herself. I felt Mick stiffen beside me. His elbows went tense, and I saw a vein pop in his neck.

"What does that mean?" he said.

"You could have just given it to him, and none of that would have happened."

"But his brother had the pot," I said. I didn't blame Natalia for her reaction. At the same time, I thought she was missing the heroism in the story. Mick could have just run away from that guy, and instead he stepped forward and saved his brother's life. "Mick couldn't have given him the pot even if he'd wanted to," I said.

"And why the fuck should I give him my pot?" Mick said. "My brother and me worked all August washing Mack trucks for Glosky's Construction. Why should we just hand it all over?"

Mick's eyes looked dark and agitated in the firelight. I could feel his bandanna, wrapped tightly around my head, a strange, tingling warmth knowing that it belonged to him, that it usually clung to his own bare skin. He might have been wearing it the night that this happened. If it had really happened at all.

"I'm just saying," Natalia said, "I don't think I would kill someone over a bag of pot."

"Let's just hope you never have to, little sister," Mick growled. He leaned across me, toward Natalia. His tense body crouched over my lap, but he wasn't aware of me any more than the thug in the tunnel had been of him. His nose was inches away from Natalia's, and I could hear her squeaky little intake of breath. In that moment I felt a strange kind of allegiance with Mick.

I was tired of Natalia's Jiminy Cricket routine, and I wished she could learn to keep her self-righteous mouth shut.

But I hated the menacing way Mick—confessed killer—was facing off with her. So I brought up my arm and elbowed him hard in the solar plexus. He pulled back, away from Natalia, and doubled over for a second. And even though he jumped to his knees and drew back his hand as if he wanted to hit me, I felt acutely aware of two things: one, that Mick wouldn't hurt me. Two, that I didn't care if he did.

Be careful. All my life I had heard those words, about everything. From the time I was a little girl: *Be careful, Sydney,* when I tiptoed across the low stone wall surrounding the first farm where my father worked. Leaning too close to the flame when I blew out the candles on my birthday cake. Walking out the door for a date with Greg. *Be careful, be careful, be careful.*

I hadn't realized until just then: I was sick to death of careful.

"You're a fucking animal," Natalia yelled at Mick.

"Me?" Mick yelled back. "She just elbowed me in the gut!"

"She was protecting her friend."

"I was protecting my brother."

We all sat silently for a minute. Then Mick bent down, picked up a palm-sized rock, and threw it at the water. I heard it skitter on the dirt just short of the lake.

"Fuck this," he said. "Fuck all you pansy-ass rich kids. I'm going to sleep."

We sat there, shaky and quiet, watching Mick storm back

to his tent. For reasons I couldn't possibly explain I felt guilty, and exposed—as if I had been the one to make a shocking confession.

Natalia and I walked down to the water to clean up before bed. We washed our faces in silence, splashing water, then brushed our teeth. After spitting out a mouthful of toothpaste, Natalia said, "Your breasts have gotten bigger."

"No, they haven't." I held my toothbrush in one hand and brought the other up to cup my right breast. It felt just the same as always.

"Yes, they have," Natalia said. "I bet your regular bras wouldn't fit you anymore." Her tone was flat, almost accusing. It infuriated me that she would decide to needle me after I'd defended her. Why couldn't she mind her own business?

"I was standing in the dark," I said.

"We could see you perfectly."

My face flushed, and I wondered if Natalia could see my embarrassment, too. A terrible feeling—finding out something you considered secret had been absolutely visible.

"I think you're imagining things," I said. "I feel exactly the same."

"But you're not exactly the same," Natalia said. "You're pregnant."

Mick had returned to the campfire and I could hear him and Brendan, their low voices, without hearing their exact words. Natalia had spoken very quietly, very discreetly, but I couldn't help worrying that they'd heard.

"Please," I said, suddenly feeling vulnerable and defensive. "Can we not talk about it? I'm going to deal with it when I get home."

"Are you?"

"Of course I am." I scratched at a mosquito bite on my arm hard enough that I felt a warm spill of blood puddle underneath my fingernails.

"I was thinking tonight," said Natalia. "It's exactly one month since that night in the park, that first night with Tommy. That means you're probably one month pregnant."

I didn't want to tell her it meant I was six weeks pregnant.

"It seems to me," Natalia said, "that if you really wanted an abortion, you wouldn't be here. You would have found a way to have one. You would have told your mother."

I let out a long, slow breath. Why did everyone talk like desire and action were these two absolute companions? Didn't people do things that went against what they wanted all the time? Like eating a doughnut when you wanted to lose five pounds. Even more often than that, didn't people *not* do things, not say anything? Like Margit not saying she was Natalia's mother, when she must have wanted to a million times. It didn't surprise Natalia that Tommy and I hadn't used a condom. Why was it such a shock that I hadn't grabbed my mom's hand and rushed over to Planned Parenthood?

I zipped my jacket to my chin. Here in Canada, we lived in two seasons. By day, on the lake, we rowed through summer in our shorts and bikini tops. Every morning I traded my sweats for shorts, worried that my stomach would start bulging, straining the buttons, announcing itself to the group. Every day my shorts buttoned easily—maybe even more easily, with all the exercise and rationed camp food.

At night, chilly autumn descended. We bundled up in comforting, protective layers. "Of course I don't want to have an abortion," I said to Natalia. "Who would? But I don't want to be pregnant, either. And there's only one road back to not pregnant."

Natalia reached out and took my hand. Her pretty brows knitted together in sympathy and confusion. I tried to remember that she was my friend, that we loved each other.

"If we keep going in this direction," I told her, "there's no way I can win. First you won't want me to have an abortion because you can't think about Margit aborting you. But then if I don't have an abortion, you won't want me to give it away, because Margit gave you away. You see? You won't be able to forgive me no matter what I do. And how can I have a baby, Natalia? How can I?"

Natalia stepped forward and pulled me into a hug. I hugged her back, my toothbrush still clasped in one hand, a million stars—a trillion stars—decorating the sky above us.

"I don't know what to do," Natalia whispered, her breath warm and minty against my ear. I patted her back consolingly. It seemed perfectly reasonable that she should share in this dilemma. Because it *was* a dilemma, no matter how much I pretended a decision had already been made. We both knew I would carry the possibility of a child until the very last second I lay down on a gynecologist's table.

"I don't care if you have it," Natalia said, testing the words as she spoke them. "Just promise me you'll think about having it."

"Okay," I said, although that thought—that idea—seemed as foreign and impossible as buying drugs on the streets of Pittsburgh, or killing someone, or saying the *N* word.

We packed up our toiletries and walked back up to the tent. It didn't occur to me until I was almost asleep that we hadn't said a single word about Mick's story.

Next morning around the campfire Lori announced that she wanted to go home. Brendan and Mick lay sleeping outside, each with a woolen hat pulled down over his eyes. I could see that Brendan—inside Mick's flimsy cloth bag—also wore a thick down coat, while Mick snoozed away in Brendan's cozy Marmot sleeping bag. Except for Meredith, no one ever got up to greet the dawn, and the rest of us sat waiting for Jane to hand out breakfast in bright sunlight, the ground already warm beneath our bare feet. I tried to guess the time and calculate the day of the week. But it was more than my foggy brain could handle, and I ended up settling for *this morning, right now*, as I stared at poor Lori, her toned and skinny legs shaking slightly at the knees. A few days ago Mick had said he'd be glad to fuck her if only he could put a bag over her head. I'd winced at the cruelty but had to admit that I could see what he meant. Perched on top of her perfect body, Lori's head—the weird, spiky hair and the acne-drenched face—looked perpetually offended by its own unprettiness.

"I'm sorry," Lori said, "but this trip just isn't what I thought it would be. I want to go home."

Jane frowned and poked at the fire while Silas kept strumming his guitar as if he hadn't heard a thing. Lori shifted nervously on her feet, waiting, looking slightly hysterical in her silence. I found myself a little frustrated with Silas. Now would be the time for him to speak up and ask Lori to stay. It would mean that much more because he usually seemed so indifferent. But he didn't say a word, just let his music ripple out all around us.

"Look," Lori accused Jane. "All our equipment is from the Stone Age. And practically the only food you'll cook is coffee and marshmallows."

It was true. To avoid having dishes to wash, Jane tried to feed us almost everything raw. The only thing she'd really cooked had been the chicken, after which she'd made Sam and Charlie scrub out the reflector oven. Now that we ate mostly canned goods, Jane would often rip off the label and heat the food directly in the fire, then pass the can around with a single fork. Lori routinely complained that we would all end up with lead poisoning.

"For example," she said, "what are you planning on giving us for breakfast this morning?"

"I myself planned on peanut butter," said Jane. "But you're welcome to go through the food supply. I'm not the official cook here, you know."

"That's what I'm saying," Lori shrieked. "You never cook anything!"

"That's not really fair," Sam said. We all looked over at him, and he immediately blushed bright red. He looked like he'd grown an inch or two, and I almost expected him to defend Jane on the basis of her awesome boobs.

"If you go home," said Jane, not looking at Lori, "you'll leave us with a one-manned canoe. Someone's going to have to row and portage all alone. It will totally throw us off, having an odd number."

"Meredith's coming with me," Lori said. I snapped my head toward Meredith in surprise, waiting for her to deny this. But she just stared at the ground. I guessed if I could see her eyes they would be filled with tears, and I wished I sat closer to her so I could pat her nice, broad back. I wondered if somehow the two of them had overheard Mick's story last night and decided his delinquency—his dangerousness—was the last straw.

"Fine," Jane said. "Suit yourselves." Lori turned around and ran back to her tent, as if it hurt her feelings that Jane hadn't begged her to stay. Behind Jane, Brendan sat up and rubbed sleep from his eyes. The way he pressed his fists into his lids convinced me that my first impression had been wrong, and that he couldn't possibly be wearing contacts. The bright clear blue of his eyes was natural.

He saw me looking at him and smiled. I smiled back. When he stood up to walk down to the lake, I decided to go along with him. We splashed our faces in the water, then sat down next to each other. A calm day; the lake stood still as a mirror, reflecting the cloudless blue sky.

"Why did you give him your sleeping bag?" I asked Brendan.

Brendan shrugged. He had perfect skin, no signs of a beard along his jawline, unlike Mick, whose stubble was beginning to change into a full-fledged beard.

"He's always freezing," Brendan said. "I tried giving him my down jacket, but it didn't fit him. So I wear the jacket and Mick uses my sleeping bag."

"Every night?" I said. "You must be so cold."

He shrugged again. "It's not so bad," he said. "Mick seemed to have a much more difficult time dealing with the cold. And it'll get warmer as summer goes on."

I wasn't so sure about that, but I didn't say anything. What struck me was Brendan's face, beautifully chiseled and as usual radiating no sexuality whatsoever—at least not toward me.

"That was quite a story he told last night," Brendan said, and I could hear the unlikely tone of admiration.

"Do you believe it?" I said.

"I believe his life is a lot harder than ours." He pulled off his hat and ran a hand through his crumpled, unruly, and luxurious hair. We sat there together, our knees touching ever so slightly. I put my hand on his thigh.

"Brendan," I said softly, "have you told anyone?"

He didn't look at me but kept his gaze out toward the water. "No one here," he said.

"Will you promise me something?" I said.

"Sure."

"Don't tell Mick." I didn't complete the sentence, but two possible phrases could have filled in the blank. *Don't tell Mick you're gay*, would have been one possibility. *Don't tell Mick you're in love with him* was the more important one.

"Not to worry," Brendan said, once again the British boy from TV. "I don't have a death wish, after all."

From behind us and to the right came a thick clattering, something enormous moving through the trees. Brendan and I started at the same time, throwing our arms around each other, his perfectly smooth cheek pressed against my own. I don't know if we were scared of being overheard, or if we were reacting to something more primal—face-to-face with a thousand-pound beast. Because from out of the trees lumbered a moose, its long and comic face staring soulfully at us, the palms of its pale antlers curving fingers toward the motionless sky.

"Shit," Brendan whispered. "My camera is up at the tent."

We clung together, taking in the animal with trembling awe. Brendan and I felt grateful for the unexpected sight of him, and also for being rescued. Because the moose had saved us from moving beyond anything but an unspoken agreement: that whether or not we strictly believed his story, we had greeted this day with a new impression of Mick, our friend, as murderer.

chapter nine
directive

Did I think about telling Brendan my own secret, now that I knew his? Maybe if he could have guessed, in a flash of intuition like I had with him, I would have admitted to being pregnant. But the fact that only Natalia and I knew about my pregnancy protected me, not only from discovery but by making it seem less than real. The moment the information started to spread, it would move from the realm of secret to fact. I couldn't face that transition, not just yet.

It struck me more than once: Human reproduction was just a bad system. Three months for the first trimester didn't seem nearly long enough to process, decide, and act. For example, I couldn't spend time thinking about Natalia's request. How in the world could I seriously consider having a baby? Linden Hill Country Day was not the sort of school where pregnant girls showed up for junior year. Wasn't I already enough of an outsider with my singlemother? Not to mention a father who hailed from the boondocks rather than the 50 percent income bracket.

And what about when the baby was born? Would I give

it away and live my entire life knowing that somewhere out there I had a child? I hated this idea, this secret that would dog me throughout eternity. When I went to college, there would be this huge thing from my past that nobody knew about. Eventually I would have to tell my roommate, and my new boyfriend, and anyone I became close to ever again: this thing about me, this child out there. No one would ever really know me unless I admitted it. On my wedding day I would walk down the aisle with a bouquet of flowers and a white veil, all the while knowing that miles away a little kid lurked, and I was its mother, and I had given it away. Even though I didn't want a child—didn't know if I would ever want a child—the thought of losing one was simply too huge. Not to mention the thought of explaining myself if the kid ever managed to track me down.

Abortion seemed different, the loss of a possibility instead of the loss of a person. If I lost the possibility, I might sometimes remember dates and imagine what life would be like. It would be weird, at twenty-six, to imagine I could have a ten-year-old kid, but that would be a lot different from wondering every day for the rest of my life where it was, how it was, who it was.

I could never be that girl, the one with the huge, gloomy, and tragic past. I only wanted to be me, myself—just normal. God knows it had been hard enough being me *before* this stupid pregnancy. Cross that out and I still had my angry mother and my fixated, distant father. I was still the only one of my friends who didn't have nice clothes or spending money. I still had Greg, my AWOL first love, and his cheerleader.

With an abortion, I could at least return to these normal problems. I could at least stay myself, and this whole thing would just be over with a simple procedure, a sterile metal scrape. The pregnancy would be a temporary layover, a phantom memory. I would remember my time on Lake Keewaytinook in pictures: the clear water, the silent moose, Mick's crazed face in the firelight. In time I would forget almost completely that I'd ever been pregnant.

"You could keep the baby," Natalia said, the day after Truth or Dare. We rowed along the lake, and for once I didn't worry about anyone hearing us. The whole group had rowed ahead, completely out of sight. Mick—either still mad at Natalia and me or freaked out by his confession—had rowed like a madman the minute we set our canoes in the water, taking him and Brendan far out of sight. But Natalia and I knew we were rowing toward the longest portage of the trip, over a mile, and we conserved our energy with slow and measured paddling.

"Natalia," I said. "Please give me a break. I really don't want to be a sixteen-year-old mother."

"You could live with your dad," Natalia said. "It would be a good life for a baby, having all those brothers and sisters."

"Those are *my* brothers and sisters," I said. "They'd be my kid's uncles and aunt."

We laughed, it sounded so preposterous. To me the very idea

just highlighted the obvious, that this baby—this dust speck—could never become a reality.

"But wouldn't it be great," Natalia persisted, "to have someone who was all your own? Who really loved you unconditionally?"

I stopped rowing. On the waveless water the canoe stopped almost instantly, the hull turning gently toward shore. Natalia had taken to tying the halter of her bikini around her back, so her shoulders were a smooth and lineless brown. My daily focal point had become her back, the birdwing shoulder blades, the silky ponytail.

I couldn't understand why she of all people would express this longing for love. Natalia had two doting, smiling parents—grandparents. And Margit had always showered her with affection and gifts. To say nothing of Steve, the boyfriend who loved her with a passion I'd only seen in movies and books. If anyone should be longing for someone to love her completely and unconditionally, it was me. Natalia was the most adored person I'd ever known, and I told her so.

"Really?" She considered this in profile, her eyes staring blankly across the water. "I guess Steve loves me. I know he does. But it's so weird, being away from him. Some days I try to remember what he looks like, and I just draw a blank."

I could have told her. I remembered Steve exactly, his kind blue eyes, his slow and red-lipped smile.

"Maybe we should go home," Natalia said. "Like Lori."

"What do you mean?" I said. This suggestion panicked me even more than her pro-life pressure. I couldn't imagine leaving all this, the outdoors, the wide blue sky, the clear blue lake.

"I mean, maybe we should go home. If all the girls on the trip want to leave, our parents will let us. They'll know it's bad."

"Bad," I said. "Do you think it's bad? I thought you were having fun."

"I think it's bad they have someone like Mick on our trip," said Natalia. "My parents would never have sent me here if they knew I'd be living with a juvenile delinquent."

Somehow I knew in that moment what I'd haltingly suspected was true: Natalia liked Mick too. I wished I could say this surprised me, but of course it didn't. Not at all. I picked up my oar and began rowing cross strokes to right the canoe. Natalia still sat with her oar across her knees, resting. I wondered with a sudden, irrational stab of anger what would have happened if Natalia hadn't come on this trip. Maybe Mick would have fallen in love with me instead. In that instance I couldn't decide whether I'd been cheated or rescued.

"If we go home now," she said, "I can figure out a way to see Steve. You can figure out what to do about the baby."

It drove me insane, the way she insisted on calling it "the baby." Still, my heart went out to her a little bit, thinking how scary it must be to feel herself falling for Mick. Next to him, Steve was an Eagle Scout. If they could catch a single glimpse of Mick, Natalia's parents would beg her to run away with Steve. At the same time I thought of everything we had risked this past year so Natalia could be with Steve. And now she wanted me to give up this last refuge, the canoe trip, because she felt drawn to someone else.

I closed my eyes against the sun and imagined the murdered man lying on the ground, blood trickling out of his ear. I tried to remember if Mick had mentioned how old he was, but only one detail—the ugly word, saying more about Mick than his victim—had lodged in my brain.

"Do you really think it was self-defense?" Natalia asked, though I hadn't said a word. She picked up her paddle and began to row.

"I do," I said, and I meant it. I hated the image, but at the same time I couldn't blame Mick. I even admired him, for doing what needed to be done in order to protect his own world.

We reached the portage at what I guessed was noon. The sun shone strong and bright overhead. So far, the portages on our route had been very brief, but today's stretched more than a mile across a portion of abandoned road that had once led back to Keewaytinook Falls. Summer cabins—long since gone to seed—sagged, forlorn, beside the path. At one point there was a small bit of pavement under our feet. Grass and poison ivy poked up through its cracked median line. It comforted me, somehow, to see nature reclaiming a site so easily.

Jane insisted that we carry everything to the other side before we sat down to eat lunch. Since Natalia and I showed up last onshore, we didn't have a chance to rest before the hike began.

First we had to carry all our gear to the opposite end of the portage. Then we had to return to our canoe, turn it over, and hoist it over our heads. Natalia was taller, so she took the stern. It was slow going. Now that all the boys had learned a passable J stroke, Silas and Jane canoed together. Lori usually went in Charlie's canoe, and Meredith in Sam's, which made Natalia and me the only two-girl canoe. In a way it made me proud of us, forging our own way with no testosterone-fueled muscles. But other times it was incredibly frustrating—the way we always ended up in last place, except for when Brendan and Mick shadowed us for purely social reasons.

The canoe felt awkward over our heads, but at least it shielded us from the sun, which was hot that day. "You okay?" Natalia called to me, and I grunted back that I was fine. She impressed me every day, the way she'd left all her girliness back in New Jersey. Unlike, for example, Lori—who continually whined about hard ground, sore arms, and broken fingernails. I couldn't believe Natalia would seriously consider leaving after all the progress she'd made, and I told her so.

"This place here is neat," she admitted, shrugging one shoulder toward a two-story building that had lost its roof. We could see the structure's innards—its dilapidated stairway and its random division of rooms. An old woodstove stood in the middle of the downstairs, where the kitchen must have been.

"Remember that Robert Frost poem we read in Mr. Lombardi's English class?" Natalia said. "The one about the ghost town? This reminds me of that." I was about to agree when I noticed a fresh explosion of graffiti on the wall just to the left of the stove. In black letters, large enough for me to read from my distance of three yards or so, it read MICK PISSED HERE. Natalia and I both stopped, the canoe suspended over our heads. We stared at the ugly words, not saying anything.

I remembered Mr. Lombardi's lecture about that poem, "Directive." He told us what Robert Frost meant: that you had to lose yourself before you could find yourself. In Mick's world, he had to destroy everything to prove he existed in the first place. I tried to remember the last few lines of "Directive," which had given me chills the first time I read it. But staring through the empty window, my own past as faded and deserted as the ghost town around me, the words wouldn't come.

"Do you have a pen?" I asked Natalia.

"No," she said. "All that stuff is in my gear at the other end." We put down the canoe and walked inside the house. My shoulders felt stiff and unnatural, like the muscles themselves were sunburned. If a smell of urine hung in the air, the stronger scents of dust and pine resin managed to drown it out. Natalia and I pulled nails from the loose floorboards and used them to scrape off Mick's foul graffiti. The wood flaked away easily in damp and moldy strips.

A while later we emerged from the woods onto a sandy, idyllic beach. The water was clear as ever, a deep and gorgeous blue. We dropped the canoe to the ground and headed directly into the lake. Everyone else sat on the sand eating peanut butter sandwiches, their hair wet from swimming. This morning after Lori's outburst, Jane had unashamedly fed us baked beans and canned pineapple, a combination that still sat in my gut so heavily that I wasn't sure I'd be able to eat lunch at all.

Natalia and I dove into the water and swam out till it was deep enough to pedal our feet through the soothing chill. A few loons floated nearby, either so used or unused to people that it didn't occur to them to fly away. We treaded water, staring at the birds, waiting for the trill that made up a fair percentage of our daily sound track. So long Tupac, Incubus, Green Day, and Coldplay. These days a bunch of long-necked and prehistoric birds were the closest thing I knew to rock stars.

We heard a splash in the water, the thunk of a light missile. Natalia and I both raised our arms, shielding our faces. Mick had walked to shore, the bandanna I'd worn the night before returned to his head. He was bare chested in the hot sun. The days of rowing and rations had made him leaner, more muscular, but I'd never found him less attractive. He jittered in a restless, antagonistic way, rocking on the balls of his feet.

He threw another rock. This one landed just shy of the loon closest to us. The bird flapped its wings and squawked—nothing like the musical sound that had become so familiar—then both birds skimmed across the water in clear outrage. Next time they'd know better than to rest so close to humans.

"Hey, you asshole," Silas called. "Don't throw rocks at the loons."

"I'm not," said Mick. "The loons just happen to be there, man." He threw another, this one skipping closer to Natalia and me. I wanted to swim to shore and start eating my lunch, but I couldn't quite figure out the nature of his actions—whiling away the time, or staging an attack.

Silas stood up and walked over to Mick. Since we'd left base camp, Silas had lost weight at an amazing rate, going from burly to slim almost before our eyes. His T-shirts hung off his shoulders, and the drawstring on his shorts grew longer every day. But Silas was still a big guy, taller than Mick and with broader shoulders. He stood over him, hands on his hips, looking down. As a daily presence Silas always seemed bemused but totally uninvolved, which made it all the more remarkable—this pointed confrontation.

"Put the rocks down," he said.

Mick stared up at him, a defiant quiver in his shoulders. He looked taut and ready to spring. Underwater, Natalia's hand bumped into mine. I think it went through both our minds what we now knew Mick to be capable of. It was impossible not to imagine Silas splayed out at his feet.

"Put the fucking rocks down," Silas said. His voice sounded stern but also condescending, as if he considered this standoff the funniest and most pathetic thing in the world.

Mick shrugged like it didn't matter. He didn't exactly put the rocks down, but tossed them lamely to one side. They plopped into the water. Satisfied, Silas turned and went back to his lunch.

Natalia and I swam back to shore. We kept our eyes on the ground, not looking at Mick, but reunited by his assault on us. We shared a PBJ, then joined the rest of our group in filling empty peanut butter jars with the wild blueberries that lined the portage path. We ate as we picked, and talked to everybody, and laughed. Even Lori laughed, and I think Charlie may have spoken—though it was only a mutter, and I couldn't quite make out the words. It was a rare moment of solidarity among each and every one of us—except for Mick, who stayed glowering by the water, throwing imaginary rocks, one after the other, at the escaping wildlife.

When we got to our campsite for the evening, Natalia marched over to Lori as soon as we'd hauled our canoe onshore. "I'm thinking about going home too," she said.

"You are not," I objected.

Lori and Meredith hunched on the ground, pounding tent stakes with rocks. I knelt to help them while Natalia stood by, a glamorous supervisor. Meredith sat back on her haunches. "If Natalia goes," she said, "then maybe I don't have to."

I felt a happy sort of rising in my chest. I knew Meredith didn't want to leave!

"Of course you have to go," Lori said. "My parents won't let me go home if you don't. I am not going to be the wimpy one."

Meredith turned back to pounding stakes. She mumbled something that sounded suspiciously like, "But you *are* the wimpy one."

"I heard that," said Lori, on the brink of tears as usual.

"You can't go home," I told Natalia. I thought suddenly how scary it would be to have her loose in the world, able to tell anyone about my situation. The risk seemed especially high if she returned to her own situation, the spoils of teen pregnancy coming to a sixteen-year head. Better to keep Natalia close, even if it meant facing these constant reminders.

"I'm going home," she said. "And I want you to come with me."

There was something about her tone I didn't like, an unspoken threat—overly aware of all the ways she could blackmail me.

"But I'm not going home," I said. "I don't want to, and I won't."

Natalia rolled her eyes and flounced away from the tent, toward the woods. I followed her. "Look," I said. I felt an angry kind of froth building up inside, the kind of fury I'd only ever felt toward my mother. "I'm going to tell you one thing. If you make me go with you, I'm going to tell my mother I'm pregnant the second I get off the plane. I'll be scheduled for an abortion before our first night at home."

Natalia stopped short and whirled around. My toes bumped into hers, and I took a step back. She put her hands on increasingly slim hips.

"So what?" she said. "That's what you're going to do anyway, right? It's not like if I stay, you'll have the baby."

"What baby?"

We turned our heads at the same time, and there at the edge of the tree line, a bundle of timber under his arm, was Mick. He dropped the wood and walked over to me.

"Syd," he said, with that sadistic mock delight. "You in the family way?"

"Fuck you, Mick," Natalia said. Mick had flattened his palm, and his hand floated toward me as if to touch my stomach. Natalia batted it away.

"How about that." Mick whistled. "Little Sydney's been getting busy. I'd believe it about this one over here"—he pointed a thumb toward Natalia—"but not my sweet, innocent little Syd."

"Please just shut up," Natalia begged. For my part, I stood frozen. I watched Mick retrieve his wood and head back to the fire. I wondered if he would announce the news to everyone. I wondered if Jane and Silas would make me go home.

Natalia touched my shoulder. "Don't worry," she said. "I'll make sure he doesn't tell anyone."

She ran after him. I saw her catch him by the elbow. He took a step closer to her, his forehead practically touching hers. Natalia hesitated the barest fraction of a second, and although I could see her waver between two actions, I couldn't tell which was instinct: stepping toward Mick or stepping away. She decided on the former, allowing his forehead to graze hers and walking her fingers from his elbow to his upper arm, lightly tripping over the misshapen tattoos. Mick's body froze, amazed by this reception, and I could almost see sparks—like metal sawing into metal—flying up around them.

He's so alive, I found myself thinking. Alive and raw and always poised on the brink of something startling. I wondered if it felt as uneasy as it looked.

Natalia as temptress looked so perfectly expert. Her long legs had browned the color of caramel. Her dark hair glinted with impossibly natural threads of gold. She looked like a retouched magazine photo come to life, and I realized that it didn't make any sense to resent her for coming on this trip and taking away all my attention.

I understood that I was pretty in an average kind of way— "pretty enough for all normal purposes." My high school had done *Our Town* too. If Natalia hadn't come along on this trip, there was a good chance that whoever took her place could have just as easily stolen my modest thunder. Whereas Natalia would always be the It girl, wherever she went. No one else in the world could ever be prettier than her.

I saw Mick nod, that trancelike obedience. He looked toward me and held up two fingers. Peace. My chest flooded with something that felt alarmingly like love.

That night around the campfire, Silas sat next to me. It surprised and cheered me, being graced with his nearness. I loved the lanolin scent of his fisherman's sweater. I found myself studying his face so hard—the yellow stubble across his jaw, the small colorless mole at the tip of his nose—that I could feel Jane's hard gaze at me as she knelt over our meal. I looked back down at my hands and asked Silas about his weight loss.

"Normally I'm a skinny guy," he said. "I can gain weight, but I can't keep it on my body. So for months before I leave for Bell, I just eat everything in sight. Big Macs, chocolate cake, everything. That way I won't be a skeleton by the end of summer."

Silas told me he'd been coming to Camp Bell for five years, since he was fourteen. "But doesn't that make you nineteen?" I said. "I thought you were twenty-two."

"Oh right," Silas said. "I meant eight years. Five years as a camper. Three as a counselor."

"Interesting," I said. Though I had never doubted Silas's maturity, I did glance over at Jane, as if he had flubbed her age instead.

"Anyway," he went on, "I've been coming here long enough that I know I need to put on serious weight before the trips begin. You're here four weeks. But at the end of July, I've got four days at base camp and then it's back on the water with a new group."

"Has Jane been coming here eight years too?"

"Not that long. Just a few summers."

He picked up his guitar and started strumming. The sound it made was weird, jarring. Silas lifted it up to his ear and shook it. We heard a clunky, rattling thump.

"A guitar pick?" I asked.

"No," he said. "Too big. This always happens, little pebbles and twigs fall inside when I leave it out."

He loosened the strings and tried to reach around them to locate the offending object, but his hands were too big. I gave it a try, but my fingers kept touching the edge of what felt like a pebble, without quite grasping it. Silas took the guitar from me and in one swift motion ripped the back off of it. Then he gave it a little shake, and the pebble fell out along with some pine needles. He tossed the back of the guitar onto the fire and went back to playing. The music sounded tinny, more open, like an instrument from more ancient times.

I wished I had Silas's ability, to change something so basic and then continue without a backward glance. My body felt worn out from everything it had done that day, not to mention everything that had occupied my mind, and I fought the urge to let my head fall onto his scratchy shoulder. Then, remembering his big hand on top of my head, I thought, *What the hell.* At the moment, in this world, Silas was like the dad. With the intimacy of night and the campfire, snuggling up to Silas seemed a whole lot more natural and easy than snuggling up to my own father. So I did it. I plopped my head right against his upper arm. He didn't acknowledge the gesture in any way, but he didn't rebuff it either. He just kept playing, my head bumping up and down as he moved his fingers along the fret. Jane seemed completely unbothered, working away at the fire.

Before dinner, Natalia, Mick, and I had gathered around Brendan as usual for a spray from his ultra-deet bottle. But now Mick and Natalia huddled up together on the opposite side of the fire, leaving Brendan to Lori and Meredith. Lori sat on one side of him, chatting away about Uta Hagen and

Method acting, while Meredith slumped on the other side, looking embarrassed and apologetic. Brendan nodded politely, and I wished he would try to engage Lori more. Maybe then she would stay.

Not being a schemer, this didn't occur to Brendan. Instead he excused himself to get his guitar and sat down with me and Silas. Silas showed him some new chords, and the two of them played together for a while. We all sat listening, Meredith and Lori up later than usual, Charlie and Sam smoking their deer moss, which had become a major habit. If the sterilization myth proved true, neither of those two would have any hope of ever reproducing. After a while, Mick and Natalia stood up and walked off into the woods hand in hand. I turned toward Brendan, whose eyes were fixed on the pair, sad but maybe also a little relieved.

I had the weirdest, jumpiest feeling in my gut. I wondered if Natalia would have sex with Mick, and if so, would she say that she had done it for me, to keep him quiet. I couldn't bear to think of how responsible this made me, for so many things, not the least of which was this unfaithfulness to Steve. And even though I *did* feel guilty, it also made me kind of furious that I should be put in that position. I hadn't asked Natalia to come on this trip or flirt with Mick. I hadn't asked her to do one damn thing except keep her mouth shut and help me get an abortion—neither of which she'd been willing to do.

An hour or so later, when Natalia and Mick still hadn't returned, Brendan and I walked together to the lake. We washed our faces in water that felt much warmer than the night around us. After all, the sun had been shining on its still surface all day.

"Let's go swimming," Brendan said.

I looked back toward the fire, to where my bikini still hung drying on a low branch. When I looked back to Brendan, he had already pulled off his jacket and shirt. *Why not?* I thought, taking some comfort that even in the strong moonlight I could mostly see only the outline of Brendan's body. Still, I waited until his back was to me—the white glare of his naked butt heading into the water—before I disrobed. Wading into the lake, I placed my hand on my stomach, which still felt flat. I wondered if the pregnancy tests had been wrong. The label claimed the test was 99 percent accurate, but it also said to see a doctor for a blood test. Why would that be necessary if the result was a sure thing? I'd never taken a pregnancy test before. What if I had some weird condition that made my hormones register as pregnant? Or maybe I was just part of that 1 percent, an inaccurate result, a false positive. Never mind what Mick and Natalia might be discussing in the woods, or that if they weren't talking, whatever they did would come back to haunt me. On a night like this, with the stars and moon above me, the peaceful wilderness around me, I felt so young, so untouched and unchanged. How could I feel that way if it weren't just a little bit true?

All I wanted was to float, stare at the sky, doing nothing. Doing nothing, I thought, should only result in nothing. It shouldn't result in a pregnancy, or a baby nine months down the road. It shouldn't result in anything.

The water became deep quickly, my feet floating above the sandy, pebbled bottom. I couldn't believe that another being swam inside me, the way I now swam in this cool, calm lake. I splashed over to Brendan, who treaded water, his head dry. "Are you okay?" I asked him. I hoped my voice didn't travel over the water, back to the campsite. Brendan, either unaware of the acoustics of water or not caring, replied in a normal voice.

"I'm fine," he said. "The truth is that thing last night changed my feelings."

I swam closer. Underwater, our legs moved in and out of each other's. "It was creepy, right?" I said. "Do you think anybody else knows? About the guy he killed?"

"I don't know," said Brendan. "For all we know, he got in trouble for it. Maybe that's why he's here."

I pondered this. It seemed unlikely that Mick could be convicted of manslaughter one summer and go camping with normal kids the next.

"I doubt the kids Mr. Campbell brings on this trip are murderers," I said. "More like drug users and runaways. Don't you think? I mean, he has insurance premiums to pay."

Brendan nodded. He reached out and placed his hands on my waist, then pulled me closer. My chin brushed against his shoulder. The air on our faces felt cold, but his skin under the warmish water felt smooth and good. I wrapped my arms around his neck and snuggled into him, tactfully avoiding his penis, which bobbed limp and harmless in the water.

"Anyway," Brendan said hopefully, "maybe it's not true. It just weirded me out, the *N* word and everything. And how I couldn't be sure it *wasn't* true. It scared me."

"We could pretend to be a couple," I said, tasting the drops of lake water on Brendan's ear. "You and me. That way Mick would never guess about you."

Brendan laughed, as if he wasn't worried enough about Mick to bother with plotting.

"I'm cold," he said, not agreeing to but not rejecting my plan. "Let's go back in."

We toweled off onshore. When we returned to the campfire, bundled up but with dripping hair, Mick and Natalia sat on a log, sharing water from her Nalgene bottle.

"Anyone else awake?" I said.

"No," Mick said. "Just us. Wanna play Truth or Dare?" His voice was a dare itself, full of jeering and menace. I stared at him for a long minute, now accustomed to that spark in his eye—a rabid dog waiting to be baited.

"Thanks," I said. "I think I had enough of that last night."

I turned, heading toward the girls' tent. Behind me I could feel Brendan's discomfort, not knowing whether he was welcome to stay with Natalia and Mick.

"Hey," I said to Brendan, loud enough for the other two to hear. "Want to come in our tent? It looks like Natalia's spending the night with Mick." I waited for Natalia to protest, but she didn't say anything. That wide expanse of butterflies opened again in my gut. I couldn't quite decide whether they represented fear for Natalia or a weird kind of jealousy, or simple sadness—that the closer Natalia got to Mick, the further she would get from me.

"Sure," Brendan said.

I crawled into the tent and over Meredith and Lori, who already snored away. A few minutes later Brendan came in, dragging Mick's crappy sleeping bag. Unfamiliar with our system, he let in a cloud of mosquitoes.

"Hey," I whispered. "You let the bugs in. Don't you guys have a system in your tent?"

"Yeah," he whispered back, settling between me and the far wall. "Give me your flashlight."

He turned it on and shone the light at the wall. As mosquitoes gathered in the beam, we smashed them one by one. As we missed, he moved the beam from side to side. We smashed and missed, smashed and hit, cracking up between every blow.

"Come on, girls," Lori moaned. "I need to sleep."

We laughed again, then turned off the light. I moved my sleeping bag closer to Brendan and threw my arm over him—hoping the closeness of my body might make up for his flimsy sleeping bag. Within a few minutes, the zipper to the tent opened, and Natalia crept over Lori (more moaning protests) and Meredith. "Move over," Natalia whispered, yanking her tangled sleeping bag out from under me.

"What happened?" I whispered, and Natalia whispered back, fierce and offended:

"Nothing. Of course, nothing."

I listened to the sound of her breathing, almost expecting a sob, or a whimper—some indication of a torn and restless heart. But all I heard was silence, barely even a breath, until she announced, "I love Steve."

This must have sounded as incriminating to her as it did to me, because after a minute she added, in a more honest voice, "It's weird. He can be so sweet." Two faces floated in my memory, the two boys. And though one seemed to me distinctly sweet and the other distinctly not, I didn't have to ask Natalia which one she meant.

The next morning, after Brendan left the tent, Natalia stuck her head out and called to Meredith, who sat by the water having her usual dawn communion with the loons. It may have been the first time Natalia had spoken to her directly, and Meredith responded with immediate obedience, trotting back to the tent at the fiercest clip I'd seen from her.

"Listen," Natalia said, in a low and definite voice. Sleep crusted her lashes, and her face looked puffy and creased, but she couldn't have commanded more authority if she'd been standing at a podium. "I've decided definitely. I'm going home, and so is Sydney."

"What?" Sunlight cast moving pixels into the tent, blurring everyone's face. I sat up, adrenaline pumping. "I never said that," I said. "I am not leaving."

I could feel Natalia go pale, even if I couldn't quite see her.

On the other side of the tent, Meredith gained courage from my defiance. "I'm not leaving either," she said.

Lori burst into tears. Natalia sighed, exasperated, but her voice was also laced with tears as she issued the request that was clearly a command: "Could you two please leave us alone for a minute?"

Meredith and Lori scuffled out of the tent with no hesitation. I sat up, still zipped into my sleeping bag below the waist.

"I am not asking you," Natalia said, her voice shaking with the unshed tears. "I am begging you. I need to go home. I need to see Steve. I need to get out of here. My parents won't let me come home if you don't also. They'll think I just want to see Steve."

"I can't," I said, surprised at the coldness in my voice. "I can't leave."

"You won't leave," Natalia said, "because you're in denial."

"This isn't about me," I said. "This is about you wanting to cheat on Steve." A cloud passed overhead, graying the light around us. Natalia's face looked less wounded than concentrated. I could see the panicked strategizing.

"I had this thought," she said, "that if you had the baby, I could take it."

I couldn't help it. I burst out laughing. "You?" I said. "How can you take it any more than I can?"

"I have more money," she said. And although her statement was obvious, I felt somehow that I'd been punched in the gut. Natalia had everything. *Everything.* She had every guy on the face of the planet panting after her. She had Steve, and now she had Mick. She had two smiling, glamorous parents who doted on and adored her, and she had a sister who adored her just as much. So what if the family configuration had turned out to be a giant lie? At least the truth of the matter remained: a giant, daily lovefest. While I was threatened with a crappy public school, she would be outfitted in a fur-lined parka and sent off to the slopes in Switzerland.

Natalia had come to the lake on the basis of a simple request, and in the space of three days had been outfitted with the most expensive equipment possible. I had borrowed equipment from the Stone Age and would spend August working on a farm to pay for July. Natalia had everything, and now she wanted my baby, too.

"You don't have any money," I hissed. "Your parents have the money." I found myself returning to the name by which I'd always known them—by which I still thought of them. "Your parents aren't going to support you and my baby. How would you live?"

"Oh, so you're worried about its well-being but you don't mind killing it."

I paused, shaken and confused. Not so much about what Natalia had said but about why it would bother me so much to hand something over that I didn't even want.

"My baby," Natalia persisted. "You just said those words, my baby."

"That's because you said it," I whispered. And then, because

I couldn't think of anything else to say, and I didn't want to continue like this, I said, "I'm not leaving."

Natalia's tears stood up and made themselves known, pooling in her eyes but not quite falling. "Everything that happens next is your fault," she said. "It's your fault for not using a condom. It's your fault for getting sent on this stupid trip and not deciding what you're going to do. It's your fault for wanting to kill your own damn baby."

Her voice had risen to a high, clear crescendo. She escaped the tent noisily, leaving the zipper wide open and flapping. I crawled out behind her tentatively. The cloud still hung over camp, so gray that I could barely make out the smoke wafting from the fire. But I could make out the faces of everyone who sat around waiting for breakfast: Charlie and Sam, playing Spit with a soggy deck of cards; Jane and Lori, locked in their own fierce conversation while Silas and Brendan strummed their guitars, the music loud enough to drown out the words—if not the tone—of our battle; Meredith, miserably chewing on an ancient piece of beef jerky. Only one set of eyes looked at me knowingly, and because they were strangely full of understanding and forgiveness, I walked toward them.

"It's going to be okay," Mick said, as I sat down next to him. He put his arm around my shoulders. It felt strong and brotherly, like he had faced worse dilemmas than mine and lived to tell the tale. "It's going to be okay, Syd," he said again. And for that brief moment, knowing my secret was mostly still safe, I could almost believe him.

*   *   *

As we ate breakfast (marshmallows and Wattie's baked beans), Jane made two announcements. One, that because we had been such lazy rowers (she eyed Natalia and me), we were two days behind schedule. We would have to step it up over the next five days if we wanted to arrive at our supply pickup on time. Two, when we got to the supply pickup, Lori would be going home, but Meredith would be staying.

We all looked over at Lori, who stared ferociously at the ground—next to Meredith but several feet away. Her poor skin looked red, ravaged, and inflamed from days of sun and sweat. Jane's visible disgust at Lori's weakness made my own sympathy flare. Poor Lori couldn't stomach the canned food, and she seemed particularly allergic to the Canadian mosquitoes. While the rest of us suffered bites that swelled and itched for half an hour or so, Lori tossed and turned all night, itching. The one thing that appealed to her on this trip was Brendan, and he not only didn't return her crush, he wouldn't even take her seriously as an aspiring actress. She had come to Camp Bell for adventure, to discover something new about herself and the world. What she had discovered was this: She hated the wilderness.

Jane clearly found all of this hateful and inconvenient. She said again that Lori's departure would give us an odd number of campers, so somebody would have to row alone. Portages would be even more difficult. "Maybe somebody from one of the other groups will be going home too," Jane said. "Then we can take somebody new, or send somebody over."

"I would go to a different group," Charlie volunteered. It might have been the first time I'd heard him do anything but mutter. His voice sounded surprisingly adult, deep and gravelly. I don't know why I should have assumed that his silence meant he was content instead of miserable. Here I'd wanted to believe that except for Lori we were a happy tribe, rowing through our peaceful, postapocalyptic world. Now I realized we'd been more like a school cafeteria, with one group laughing at the elite table, and everybody else on the fringe. And now the elite table (Natalia on the other side of Mick, unwilling to meet my eyes) had started to break apart as well.

"Maybe Lori will change her mind," I volunteered out loud. "Maybe we'll have so much fun in the next five days, she'll feel like she just has to stay."

First Lori raised her eyes and looked at me, then everyone else did: as if they'd only realized at that exact moment that I was completely insane.

If it hadn't happened naturally, Jane probably would have insisted on it. But that day Brendan and I went in one canoe, Natalia and Mick in another. To preserve Brendan's manliness, he took the stern. He'd actually become fairly good at steering, and the two of us immediately power stroked to the front of the group. Natalia and Mick didn't fare as well, since neither had learned how to steer. Jane had to keep rowing back to them, shouting instructions. Still, we made great time and reached the place they'd planned to camp by lunch. Jane and Silas were overjoyed, confident that we'd reach our drop-off point on schedule. In three days we'd be eating raw bacon and reading mail from home.

As we headed toward our lunch spot, we passed a fishing boat anchored in the middle of the lake. Two burly, overdressed men ate lunch, taking time out between bites to yell at a small butterscotch pit bull who cowered on the bow. As we floated past, Sam interrupted them. "What time is it?" he yelled up.

"Three o'clock," the one wearing the baseball cap called back, after consulting his watch.

Jane looked deflated for a second, then perked up. "We still have hours of daylight left," she said. "We'll have a quick lunch and then get back to rowing." As we floated toward a sandy, pine-lined campsite, Jane called out to us cheerfully, "Look at this place. Isn't it beautiful?"

Lori must have been made brave by her impending departure, because she said, "It looks exactly the same as the last campground. Everything on this lake looks exactly the same."

"That's because you have a bad attitude!" Jane barked back at her.

We pulled our canoes ashore and walked to the fire pit. Not that we'd be cooking anything. As Jane lay out the lunch supplies—the last of the whole wheat bread and the jam she'd made the night before by adding sugar to mashed wild blueberries—Natalia walked over to me.

"Hey," she whispered, as if our earlier argument had never taken place. "What happened with you and Brendan last night?"

I stared at her, not quite willing to accept this olive branch. Her forehead scrunched up, uncharacteristically troubled, and I couldn't help but cave. "Nothing," I said, in a perfectly normal voice. "We just went swimming."

She stood, her face sweaty and dusty and difficult to read. In ten days we had rinsed off in the lake regularly, but we had barely washed our hair or soaped up our bodies. Despite liberal application of sunscreen, we were both several shades darker than when we'd begun. With her black hair and dark eyes, Natalia looked almost Native American. Her new sinewy muscles and the lack of makeup made it hard for me to decide whether she looked older or younger. I tried to remember my own face in the mirror, back at base camp. All I'd seen of myself since then was a murky reflection in the water. Sometimes I felt about my face the way Natalia felt about Steve's. I could barely remember what I looked like.

From the water, the two fishermen continued yelling at the dog. We heard a yelp; maybe it had been kicked. One of the men laughed. Ordinarily this would have been something for Natalia and me to discuss, to object to, to exclaim over. But she was too busy waiting for me to ask about what happened between her and Mick. "Nothing happened with Mick and me," she finally said, as if this must be something I'd been desperate to know. "It wouldn't have anyway. But I've got my period."

"TMI," I said.

Natalia blinked back at me, clearly hurt. When had there ever been that possibility, too much information between the two of us? "God, Sydney," she said. "Please don't be mad at me."

I sighed. In the past week, Natalia had deserted my abortion plans when I desperately needed her on board in order to carry them out. By pointing out my inferior financial status, she had broken a taboo that had existed between us since the dawn of time. She had betrayed her boyfriend, the dramatic love of her life. And there was so much more that I didn't even want to be able to put into words.

So maybe to avoid that effort, I lied. "Okay," I said. "I won't be mad."

Natalia reached out and touched my arm. "Good," she said. Then we parted—she into the woods to pee, and me to eat my blueberry sandwich. As I sat down to eat, Silas stood up. The men on the fishing boat continued their haranguing of the poor dog. Silas rooted around in his canoe and then pulled a wad of bills from his pack. He splashed out into the water, holding the money above his head.

"Hey," he yelled to the fishermen. "I'll give you a hundred bucks for that dog."

There was a brief moment of silence. Then the one with the hat stood up, picked up the dog, and tossed him into the water. Silas threw the money into the boat. The dog swam past him, toward the shore, without looking back once.

By the time Silas got back to us, Meredith had already fed the dog two pieces of bread. The fishermen had motored off, perhaps worried that Silas would change his mind. I patted my knees, and the dog wiggled his way over to me. I gave him the rest of my sandwich and scratched his head. He seemed like a nice dog, with a big grin, not affected by the previous abuse other than being very happy to have escaped it. When Natalia emerged from the woods she sat down next to me. The dog thrust his fat nose directly into her crotch. She pushed him away, holding his face firmly in her hands.

"What did I miss?" she said.

"I'm in love," I told her, loud enough for everyone to hear.

We both laughed. Jane frowned across from us—either unhappy with the new addition to our crew or assuming that I meant Silas and not the dog.

chapter ten
the drop-off point

We reached our drop-off point at dusk, rowing through a light rain. It felt like reaching Avalon, with mist and twilight all around us, the dog perched and wagging in the bow of Jane's canoe. We had all taken turns carrying the dog in our boats, but he seemed to know who had masterminded his rescue. Given a choice he hopped in with Silas every time, and shadowed him closely whenever we reached camp. Two nights before, after much discussion, Silas had christened the dog Bucket Head.

"That's a terrible name," I said.

"He's a terrible dog," Silas said, which was true enough. Bucket Head had so far proved himself sweet but stupid. His first night camping with us, he had ripped into the food bag and eaten the last of our bread and marshmallows. Whereas before we had packed up our food halfheartedly, not quite believing in the need to protect it from bears, we now had an inside threat and made sure we sealed the cooler, even though we had almost nothing left but a sad assortment of dented cans.

The two other groups who shared our drop-off point had already arrived. Almost immediately, the three Youth at Risk found one another, which surprised me a little because one of them was African-American. Mick and the other two guys gathered by the edge of the lake, laughing and telling stories. I saw him gesture toward Natalia and then lean in close to whisper something. Three big guffaws erupted jarringly. If Natalia noticed, she didn't say anything. For the past two days she and I had wandered together through an unnaturally silent truce. She had stuck physically close to me in an obvious effort to avoid being alone with Mick, but I think we both felt like any sort of real conversation would just lead back to an argument.

Now we explored the other campsites, looking for the friends we'd met at base camp. I hoped I might find Cody, but no such luck. We roamed among the other kids, everyone looking more or less the same in our unwashed shorts and dirty raincoats. The main thing we learned from brief and passing conversation: the mail and food had not arrived yet, and all the other group leaders had been preparing much more elaborate meals in their reflector ovens. One group we visited was in the middle of devouring a pineapple upside-down cake. They gave us a piece, which Natalia and I immediately took into the woods, not wanting to split it more than two ways.

"I'm glad the mail hasn't come yet," Natalia said, between glorious sugary bites. "It gives me another night to work on my letter to Margit. Will you help me?"

"Sure," I said. We licked the last of the cake off our fingers and went back to our tent. Meredith and Lori were off somewhere else, so we had it to ourselves.

Natalia stared at her sheet of paper. "It's not really a letter at all," she said. "Just a list of questions. How can I send her this?"

"We could redo it," I said. "Write a little introduction, then the questions."

She lifted her pen as if to add a question, then pressed it to the paper and drew a large X. It struck me as a meaningless gesture—the words on the paper still visible, nothing really ruined.

"You know what I wonder most," Natalia said. "I wonder what my father was like."

"Your father," I said, carefully testing the new possessive pronoun.

"Yes, my father. I wonder if he was kind of a delinquent, kind of a loser. Like Mick or Steve."

I didn't like hearing these words attached to Steve, whose only claim to loserdom was public school and some very minor teenage brushes with the law. If I really went to Bulgar County High in the fall, maybe Natalia would start referring to me as a loser too.

"Steve's not a delinquent," I said. "He's not a loser."

"Oh, but Mick is?"

"You're the one who said it," I pointed out. I didn't remind her that Mick had already admitted to the biggest crime a person could commit.

She relaxed her shoulders. "Did you see how those three

guys found each other the second we landed our boats?" she said. "It's like they're from the same tribe or something. What I'm thinking is, maybe my father was like Mick and Steve, some goy from a crappy family. And that's why I'm drawn to these guys, because of my genetic makeup. My DNA. Like, if you had your baby, it would grow up to cruise Overpeck for boys exactly like Tommy."

I ignored this unpleasant vision of the future and thought of Margit's standard-issue husband—handsome, successful, from a good family. Margit had always seemed like such a prim and obedient person. I couldn't imagine her straying too far from the fold in terms of mate selection. "The father was probably someone from Linden Hill Country Day," I said. "It was probably her high school sweetheart, a perfectly nice guy."

Natalia looked down at her list of questions and drew another line through it. "I never heard of her having a high school sweetheart," she said. "I keep trying to think of her, remember what I know about her. Like, it seems like five minutes ago I would have said we were so close. Now all I think is I don't know her. I don't know her at all." She pressed down hard with the pen, but still didn't do much damage to the overall legibility.

"It's just weird," she said, "expecting them to tell me the truth now, when all they've ever told me is lies." A large tear dribbled to the end of her nose, then plopped onto the paper. I gently eased the pad out of her hands and ripped off the top sheet.

"Dear Margit," I wrote, on a fresh piece of paper.

"She knows that's not my handwriting," Natalia said.

"So she'll know you dictated it," I said. Natalia stared off for a minute, then wiped her eyes with the back of her hand. She sat up straight.

"Dear Margit," she said. "As you probably know, I found out that you are not my sister, but my mother. Obviously we have a lot to talk about, and I want you to be prepared. Here is a list of questions. I hope you will answer each one truthfully when we see each other again. I really think that at this point everybody owes me some serious truth."

She paused, waiting for me to catch up. My penmanship was nowhere near as good as hers, so I took pains to write clearly, if not prettily.

"In the meantime," she said when my pen stopped moving, "I want you to know that I understand you had a choice, and that I'm grateful you decided to have me. I'm thankful for this life I have, and I deeply respect your courageous decision."

I stopped writing. Outside the tent, shadows and voices milled, new people getting to know one another. Rain fell on the roof, not hard enough to make noise, but creating strange shadows, dark lines that rolled across Natalia's face. I put the pad back in her hands.

"Here," I said. "Write it yourself."

I climbed out of the tent and zipped it shut behind me. Silas and Jane had built a fire, which struggled to stay alive in the gathering dampness. The two of them reunited with the other counselors, talking and laughing. Bucket Head stuck close to

Silas. I could see Mick and his shady friends down by the water, but Brendan was nowhere to be found. Only Meredith and Lori sat by the fire, eating the wild blueberry mash with their fingers. I walked over and joined them. "Is that all the food we have left?" I said. My body had quickly digested the pineapple upside-down cake, and now my stomach grumbled furiously for more food. Jane, socializing fifty feet beyond, didn't look like she planned to cook us anything.

"There's a couple cans of hash left," Meredith said. I opened one of them and settled it into the smoldering embers in an attempt to warm it up.

"So," I said to Lori, who crouched miserably underneath the rain. "Do you think you'll change your mind?"

"I'm getting out of here the very first second I can," Lori said. Meredith looked at me and shrugged apologetically. I smiled at her.

By the time I fished the hash out of the fire, the two of them had crawled into the tent to get out of the rain. A few minutes later Natalia sat down next to me. The food had heated up surprisingly well, and after a few bites I handed the can to her. She tasted it daintily, then scrunched up her nose and handed it back to me. The meat had an old, metallic taste, and the tiny potatoes tasted slimy and dense. But I couldn't stop eating. Sensing Natalia's eyes on me, I thought my gestures were too ravenous and put the food down. Bucket Head appeared immediately, sitting up at attention and wagging his tail. I picked up the can, in case someone else wanted the food.

"You might as well give it to him," Natalia said. "He's got to eat too."

I removed the fork and handed the can to the dog. His nose disappeared as he greedily lapped up the last of it. One second he'd jam his nose deep into the can, and the next second he'd paw at it frantically, trying to work it off his nose. Natalia and I laughed, and for a second I thought we could leave the weirdness of the tent behind. But then she said, "Mick says you're going to hell."

A cold wave of fury washed over me. Part of me could understand why Natalia had gone haywire. However screwed up my own family was, at least I knew where I came from. I had never been lied to, never had the entire world shift around me and my identity. I got why she had a hard time with the idea of my abortion, even though it completely screwed up my ability to get one. But still.

"Mick says *I'm* going to hell?" My voice shook too much to rise above a whisper.

"For having an abortion," she said. The can empty, Bucket Head trotted back to Silas. Natalia picked up a stick and poked at the dying embers. I could hardly see her face, half-hidden by her neon pink rain hood. I wondered why I didn't feel like crying. Weren't my hormones supposed to be going crazy? Shouldn't I want to cry at the slightest provocation? But I didn't want to cry. I just felt cold and tired and strangely dead inside. I wished, for the thousandth time, that I'd never met Tommy, or at the very least that I'd spoken up and insisted on stopping before it came to this. It was all so unfair. The mistakes I'd made weeks ago had taken up the most insignificant, fleeting moments. And here I sat, still paying for them. If things kept progressing at this rate, I might be paying the rest of my life.

"Don't you worry about it?" said Natalia. "Don't you worry that you'll go to hell if you have the abortion?"

"Why are you suddenly talking about hell?" I said. "I thought Jewish people didn't believe in hell."

"How do I know I'm even Jewish?" Natalia said. "I could be Catholic or Muslim or Buddhist. I could be someone who believes in hell. How am I supposed to know?"

"I thought it only mattered if your mother was Jewish."

"If that were true," she said, "then why all the hysteria about dating Jewish boys? The father matters. Believe me. He matters big-time."

I had seen Natalia cry before, many times, and in the past I had held her hand and rubbed her back and helped her find solutions. But now I did something new. I stood up and walked away from her. As I left, she ratcheted up her sobs, so clearly for my sake that I only moved faster. My hood slid off, exposing my hair to the come-and-go rain.

I found Mick by the lake with his friends. They sat on land in one of the empty canoes, passing a deer moss joint. When Mick saw me coming he blew out a stream of smoke and stepped out of the canoe. "Hey, Syd," he said. His raised his eyebrows, taunting and suggestive, then held the makeshift cigarette out toward me. I shook my head.

"I guess it's a little late for you, huh?" he said.

"I guess so."

"So what can I do for you?"

"Nothing," I said. "I hear you're a Catholic now."

Mick laughed, a thin stream of smoke tracing the exhale of his breath. "Born and bred," he said. "Don't take it personal, Sydney. I'm just looking out for your immortal soul."

In the darkness I saw Mick's chiseled, restless face—a caged animal waiting to spring from his own skin. I knew he didn't believe in hell any more than he believed in the world where we now stood, the close woods and the vast lake and the hundreds of animals living out their lives, unseen, all around us. He had only been baiting Natalia, trying to get closer by placing a wedge between her and me, and of course by agreeing that I shouldn't have an abortion.

I wanted to ask him not to tell anybody, but knew this would be exactly like telling him to spread the word. The less he knew about my fears, the less he could exploit them. For now, Natalia had told him to keep quiet. I would have to trust in this motivation, protecting me, to please her.

"I could always help you out, you know," Mick said. He leaned into me, his bright blue eyes inches from mine. He put one hand on my shoulder and drew the other back in a fist. He pulled back his elbow, then pressed the fist into my belly in a broad, frightening pantomime.

I stepped back, out of his grasp. I could feel my breath, quickening as if he actually had pressed the wind out of me.

He laughed again, a jeering burst. "Just let me know if you change your mind," he said. "I'm here for you." He ruffled my damp hair like a well-meaning big brother, then jogged back to his friends in the canoe.

The rain picked up. I could feel it gather in my hair, flattening the curls, water streaming down my face. My view of the three Youth at Risk, their own little rainbow coalition, blurred. Part of me wanted to run back to Mick and beg him, insist that he ram his fist as hard as he possibly could into my stomach and end this whole nightmare. Because who cared what happened to me? All I cared about was having this thing, this extra being, gone. At the same time, a more primal part of me brought my hands to my belly, terrified that his simple touch had done damage there. An ancient instinct, contrary to everything I knew about myself, cupping my hands like a mother. A mother! The one thing in the world I knew I didn't want to be, not now, possibly not ever.

I ran into the woods, through the rain, scratching my shoulders against trees, my sneakers squishing and squeaking over the wet leaf litter. And I wished for bears to come out of hiding, to maul me and harm me until my body expelled its invader. I wished to fall, a hard, bruising tumble that would bring days of fever and pain. I wished to get lost and starving in the woods, alone and hungry, nowhere near enough food to sustain one life, let alone two.

The bears stayed quiet. My feet planted themselves frantically but firmly. And no matter how far I ran, I could hear the voices from camp bouncing off trees; teenage voices in their swirl of festivity and petty drama, not one of them understanding the life-and-death struggle I had no way of escaping.

By the time I got back to our tent, Meredith, Lori, and Natalia were already asleep. I crawled over them and peeled off my soaking clothes, then climbed naked into my sleeping bag. In the darkness, my heart pounded from running and from the memory of Mick's fist against my stomach. For the first time in my life, I seriously considered the idea of hell.

Neither of my parents was particularly religious. My father brought his new family to a Presbyterian church one or two Sundays a month, but he saved his fire and brimstone for social and environmental matters. My mother had been raised Catholic, but I'd never seen anyone in her family pay attention to anything Christian besides Christmas, which involved presents and roast turkey but no midnight Mass. I'd never heard my mother mention the word "hell," and if she knew I was pregnant she would deliver me to an abortion clinic faster than you could say Hail Mary. But still. What if hell did exist? And what if abortion earned me a one-way ticket? I tried to imagine a world with devils and pitchforks and never-ending flames. But none of it felt as frightening as a huge pregnant belly, or childbirth, or finding myself a mother at sixteen.

In the tent the other girls snoozed beside me, dreaming their simple dreams, unaware how lucky they were, to house one single soul.

chapter eleven
my life, not flashing
before my eyes

Every night we burned our garbage in the fire. When the girls got their periods, throughout the day they would collect their tampons in a brown paper bag, which they would toss into the flames with the rest of the trash. Spared this ritual myself, I would watch the witchy smoke climb high into the Canadian night, its spell not powerful enough to make my body join in.

The night after we left our drop-off point, Natalia burned her last bag of tampons. I sat next to her as she used the flare of light to read her letter from home for the thousandth time. She and I had forged another strained truce, maybe because we couldn't avoid each other, or maybe because we felt so sorry for each other.

The letter from Natalia's parents didn't mention anything they'd revealed before she left. It was just chatty news and loving words. No mention of Steve or Switzerland or even Margit—other than that she sent her love. Natalia pored over it again and again, trying to find something between the lines that clarified her new, strange situation. Finally, giving up, she tossed it into the fire. "At least you have something to throw," I told her.

She patted my knee. "Maybe she didn't get hers out in time," she said.

All I'd got in the mail was a single postcard, written by Kerry and signed by her and "Dad," not an actual signature, but in Kerry's handwriting. When Mr. Campbell handed out the mail, we'd all crowded around him, waiting for our names to be called. I stood there as all the letters were handed out, not realizing how much I wanted to hear from my mother until it became crystal clear she hadn't written. Now, sitting next to the fire, this seemed so frankly mean that it brought tears to my eyes. What had I done that was so bad? What, beyond my inconvenient existence, had earned me such a hostile rejection? Before being left almost empty-handed and clearly waiting in the midst of all the other kids waving their letters from home, I had almost begun working up my resolve to tell her about the pregnancy. I knew that she would take everything finally and completely out of my hands. But now, all I could think of was how she would find the pregnancy proof of me as all-around bad kid. I thought I would almost rather have the baby than let her rescue me—in all her self-righteous fury—from my reckless teenage self.

We'd left our drop-off point plus one dog, minus two people. Lori motored off in Mr. Campbell's boat, waving happily, the first time I'd seen her smile in the two weeks I'd known her. I stood on the shore with Meredith, waving as if we'd been friends, wishing her clear skin and feather pillows for the rest of the summer.

Charlie motored out on the same boat but didn't bother waving. He sat in the front seat, on his way to join a group who'd lost a camper to acute appendicitis (the kid had been airlifted out in the first week, to the hospital in Keewaytinook Falls). I wondered how, without cell phones, they had managed to contact a helicopter. Maybe Silas had an emergency one, stashed in his pouch with the surprise wads of cash. But when I asked him, he just laughed. "There's no reception here, kemo sabe," he said. "No cell towers hidden in the trees. Your modern technology's no good on Lake Keewaytinook."

That first night after the drop-off point, the letter from home burnt along with the last of her tampons, Natalia allowed Mick to claim a tent for them. Silas and Jane had already gone to bed, and Mick stood up and pulled back a flap, letting mosquitoes buzz inside by the hundreds.

"Not so fast, little man," he said to Sam, who knelt to throw his sleeping bag inside. "Tonight this is for the lady and me."

Sam scurried away like a frightened puppy. I watched Natalia, waiting for her to make some sort of snotty refusal. At the drop-off camp she had avoided Mick, repelled by his rowdy association with the two token thugs. But now she only paused for a second, then shrugged and followed him into the bug-filled tent.

Brendan, Meredith, Sam, and I climbed into the other tent.

I pulled the down of my sleeping bag up around my ears to drown out any sounds that might drift in. Condoms had not been an item on Camp Bell's list of necessities; they hadn't even made the suggestion column. I hoped that if nothing else, my current state would operate as a cautionary tale and keep them from actually having intercourse. Not that I felt superconfident Mick would allow Natalia to refuse him, if he wanted to have full-on sex.

The thought made me pull the sleeping bag away from my ears. What if Natalia yelled out for help? I needed to be on the alert, so that I could rush to her rescue if she needed me. And if there wasn't much I could do on my own, I would at least be able to wake Silas. Tall and leaner by the day, with his hero's disposition, Silas would come rushing to Natalia's aid without a second thought.

I lay awake, imagining different scenarios where Silas would protect each of us from Mick. He would stop Mick from punching me in the gut and causing a miscarriage. He would stop Mick from cracking Brendan's head open upon discovering he was gay. He would stop Mick from grabbing Jane's naked breasts in an uncontrolled, animal moment. Before I fell asleep, I imagined Silas in that underpass in Pittsburgh, how he would step between the mugger and Mick's brother. He would step between Mick and his victim, stopping the whole thing with one careful shove—so that nobody would wind up on the ground, bleeding. Nobody would end up dying.

At the mail drop-off, Mick had grumbled when we found

out our parents weren't allowed to send packages. His mother had promised to send him two boxes of Crunch Berries. I pictured Mick at home, shoveling pink and yellow cereal into his mouth, the box with its cartoon picture of Cap'n Crunch at his elbow. With this image in my head, it was hard to feel seriously frightened of him. Falling asleep, hearing no sounds at all from the other tent, I had one last and fleeting thought: that Mick would never hurt Natalia or do anything she didn't want, for the simple reason that he loved her. For all my other fears, this last seemed like the truest realization, so much so that I immediately drifted off to sleep.

I slept late the next morning, stirring and then drifting back off as the others left the tent one by one. I could hear the conversation by the morning fire and smell the by-now appealing aroma of coffee. But sleep glued me to the sandy ground, even as I heard Jane calling my name every five minutes.

"It's late, Sydney," she kept saying, though of course she had no idea what time it was. We had all proved ourselves completely pathetic when it came to reading the summer sky. Finally Mick poked his bandanna-covered head into the tent. "Rise and shine, Syd!" he shouted, like an overenthusiastic drill sergeant. I could tell from his face—drawn and agitated—that this morning would star the bad Mick rather than the good, and it frightened me to be alone with him in an enclosed space. I sat up with a groggy and startled squint, waiting to see what meanness he would inflict.

"Jesus, Syd," he said, loud enough for everyone to hear. "You are butt ugly in the morning."

He let the flap fall closed, and I brought my fingers up to touch my face—outlining the puffy area around my lips and eyes, trying to recall the exact contours. I felt so convinced that what he said was true, I couldn't bear to leave the tent, showing my butt-ugly face to the group. I changed into my clothes inside the tent and packed up my things. I could see the shadow of my crazy, unruly hair, curling in every direction. Outside, I could hear everyone else at work, taking camp apart.

Finally Brendan poked his head into the tent and handed me a cup of coffee. "You'd better get going," he said. "We need to take the tent down. And don't listen to Mick. You look adorable."

I sipped the coffee, grateful for the reassurance but worried that if Mick heard Brendan use the word "adorable," the jig would be up for at least one of us.

It's funny, how your relationship with your own looks changes when you go weeks without seeing yourself. None of us really knows what we look like, after all. In that nanosecond it takes for a mirror to give our faces back to us, our mind has already done all sorts of perverse rearranging. I've known too many girls—beautiful girls, skinny girls—who respond to their own reflections with "yuck"s and starvation diets. So I always tried not to overreact to what I saw in the mirror. A zit here, a lack of symmetry there. I seemed to be living the life of a passably pretty girl, so I tried to leave it at that.

But of course insecurities will arise. On the river—with no guys of interest, other than unattainable and heroic Silas—this seemed to happen less. Every night Natalia and I dutifully splashed water on our faces, then went over them with a Stri-Dex pad that became completely black on first contact. We washed our hair once or twice a week (I don't think Jane or Meredith had washed theirs at all since the trip began). Then we twisted it into ponytails, pulled on our filthy shorts, and went on with the day.

Mick's comment, though, had done what he'd meant it to do. It cut me down to size, making me feel blue and worthless for the rest of the day. I rowed with Brendan, disliking this recent reduction to girl status, riding in the bow. My bikini top felt tight; the straps cut into my shoulders. Meredith's mother had snuck a thin tin of butterscotch candies into her letter, and I could smell them on her tongue no matter how far away from me she paddled. The scent went straight through my sinuses, not so much unpleasant as bizarre in its intensity. If I hadn't liked Meredith so much, and been so against littering, I would have found that tin and tossed it into the middle of the lake.

At midafternoon we rowed up beside a waterfall that bordered our next portage. Silas shouted to us at the mouth of the vortex, and we all made a sharp turn just before we could be sucked into the fall's undertow. After we'd hauled our canoes ashore, we stood for a while, watching the blue water. There were two currents. One ended in a perfectly calm blue pool. The other ended in the kind of steep, dramatic drop-off that Lara Croft herself would be unlikely to survive.

"It's a great slide," Jane said. "You just have to make sure you turn out of it before the drop-off." She pulled off her shirt and dove in, letting the current take her down toward the drop-off, then gracefully riding the currents to the right, into the gentle pool. I watched her plunge down under the water, then come shooting up for air, her tan, naked breasts bobbing in the water.

We all lined up and rode the current, one at a time, as if it were an amusement park ride. The activity seemed to bridge the various gaps between us. I watched Meredith fly down the current, with her thick, chubby body and her unwashed braids. She laughed, her round face bright and happy. Meredith loved it here so much. Nobody at school would ever call her pretty, but I thought she was beautiful. The sight of her, along with the good water, washed Mick's comment out of my head. I forgot the awful *U* word and returned to my animal self. My body, because it could do what I told it, was good. In this week after our supplies had been replenished we ate well—plenty of fresh protein still stored in the cooler. My well-fed and well-used muscles let the water carry me down its natural slide. Then I swam over to the appropriate fork at just the right moment. On the rock ledge that divided the two courses of water, Mick and Silas sat sunning themselves in a rare moment of peace.

Both shirtless, Mick looked as muscular and imposing as Silas did lanky and meatless. At first Bucket Head had objected to our trips down the lesser waterfall, running alongside us and barking dire warnings. But now, exhausted, he resigned himself to lying down on the rocks and panting.

I climbed out of the water, then walked upstream for one more slide. My legs felt slightly shaky as I eased myself in, but I wasn't quite ready to give up the sensation. I floated into the eddy, letting the current take me down, down. And I don't think I'll ever be able to say for sure, whether that second I missed the turn was a flash of conscious decision or simple tiredness, or the sun blocking my vision at just the wrong time. But suddenly I found myself drifting to the left of that rocky ledge where two men and a dog rested.

I didn't have time to call out. Instead I tried to turn my body around and swim upstream, a useless effort that immediately backfired: The eddy dragged me under, and the more I tried to claw up out of the water, the deeper the current pulled me down. I could feel it as surely as if a pair of hands dragged me by the heels. At first there was a definite sense of fighting and pulling and clawing. But as I saw bubbles rising in that underwater world, rocks scraping the bottom of my feet and the back of my shoulders as I tumbled by, I felt myself go calm. I knew that the drop-off was fast approaching. I could see it, if not concretely, somewhere inside of myself. Soon I would be plunging over the waterfall, going down, all possibility of air and breath lost forever.

And a feeling of peace and insight came over me, as if death were not something to fear but simply an answer to a question that had loomed over me ever since I first understood that I wouldn't live forever.

This, I thought. *This is how it ends.*

But in the very second before I plunged down into the rapids, a hand reached into the water and closed around the top of my arm. It dragged me out of the currents like a mother cat retrieving her kitten—a simple and no-nonsense gesture. I knew Silas had saved me, and despite my previous calm the most profound adoration and gratitude swept over me.

Onshore, I coughed out a minute's worth of missed breath, then opened my eyes into the hot summer sun. Silas sat on the rocks, his long legs stretched out in front of him, his hands behind his back, propping himself up. Apparently he hadn't even seen my almost drowning. I thought about calling out to him but wasn't sure exactly what I would say. Bucket Head danced around me, celebrating my rescue with short, excited yaps. And standing in front of me, a happy sort of smirk across his face, stood my rescuer: Mick, cocking his head to one side, looking no more or less pleased with himself than usual.

Mick gave my stomach two short, staccato pats. "Okay then, Syd," he said. "I guess your soul belongs to me now." He laughed and sat back down on the rocks. Exhausted, I sat down next to him, panting along with the dog, who covered my face with relieved kisses. Mick on one side, Bucket

Head on the other—the only two who knew I'd almost died, and only one of them seemed to consider it a reason for celebration. But then, after a minute, Mick's hand came down on my knee. It was wet and comforting, the least threatening gesture I could imagine. "You gotta be careful, Sydney," he said.

I nodded and let my head rest against his strong, sunburned shoulder. "Thank you," I said. "Thank you, Mick."

Back on the water, I had the oddest sensation, one that I could only describe—however reluctantly—as a craving. I wanted a glass of lemonade. Not just any glass of lemonade, but Paul Newman lemonade, poured over exactly four ice cubes in one of the big Ball canning jars that Kerry used. I wanted it so badly I almost found myself whimpering as I rowed, and I prayed that this was not a symptom of pregnancy but a reaction to almost dying and wanting to experience some of the good the world still had to offer.

It was so weird. Facing death, my life had not flashed before me like a movie, the way it was supposed to, so over the next few hours—portaging and then rowing—I tried to reconstruct it for myself. What were the important events? Which people had meant something to me? What had I done to make the world a better place?

The last question was sadly easy to answer: NOTHING. As my father would probably sum it up, I had always been a consumer, never a contributor. And I certainly knew that my mother considered me nothing but a drain of resources. Quite probably the reason she hadn't written was that she didn't want to break the news yet of my reassignment to public school.

I placed my paddle in the water over and over again, the wood biting into my increasingly calloused hands. Whenever I hiked with my dad, we always waited for the moment when we'd established what he called a trail rhythm—a consistent walk, conducive to observing nature and getting lost in our own particular thoughts. The same held true for these days on the lake. After a while our arms moved in a traceable, consistent rhythm. Some days we chatted. Others we all fell into private daydreams.

I thought about my old boyfriend Greg. A year ago he had seemed like my whole world. Now I didn't even know what he was doing this summer. He could be trekking in the Himalayas, he could be starring on *The Real World*, he could be doing anything for all I knew. Way back when, the loss of him had been painful, but I had survived it. Today, faced with my own mortality, the memory of Greg registered as a tiny, faraway blip.

The bigger people: Mom, Dad, Natalia. All of them had their issues, particularly these days. But rowing that afternoon— my life a sudden luxury—my mouth watered for a drink that was weeks away, and I kept coming back to that last question: What had I done to make the world a better place?

Certainly I had never done anything on the order of Silas's rescue of Bucket Head. As if on cue, the dog jumped out of Silas's canoe and paddled in the water beside it. His tongue lolled out and his tail wagged happily in the water, an off-kilter rudder. If Silas had not been with us on that day, none of us would have saved him. The dog would have gone on in his unhappy life, never experiencing this free, frolicking happiness of shared raw bacon and endless tummy rubs.

And if Mick hadn't been along today, sitting on those rocks, or if, say, he'd been caught for the murder he'd committed last summer and sent to jail, maybe I and the small being inside me would have gone flying over those rocks, down the waterfall, my oxygen supply cut off. I imagined the umbilical cord squeezed tight, a thrashing and a gasping within my deepest regions. How strange, the small amount of space I took up: Within the small circle of my waist, an entire person was spinning into being.

I tried for one minute to imagine that person, if that could be my contribution. I tried to imagine myself giving birth, and changing diapers, and carrying my own baby around in a BabyBjörn the way I carried Rebecca. All these images seemed just only impossible, like science fiction, like trying to imagine walking on the moon.

I looked across the water at Mick. Although he would never admit it, would never even boast about it, I knew he felt proud of my rescue. I could tell by the way he paddled, and the way he looked at me—shy and then triumphant, then looking away. As much as Mick could still be a jerk—an insensitive, unfeeling, and downright frightening jerk—he also had these moments of touching vulnerability, even sweetness. Sometimes it made me think of that story we'd read in ninth-grade English,

"Flowers for Algernon." It was as if this trip, being with all of us, had made Mick a better and nicer person. But then we would get these glimpses of the person he had once been and would always become again. Two Micks, and I pictured the good one floating and falling over the waterfall, disappearing forever like I had almost done. So sad.

But maybe saving my life would be a moment he could actually carry away with him. Maybe it could almost be redemption for what he had done, really through no fault of his own, last summer. And it struck me: Almost dying was the closest thing to altruistic that I'd ever done.

Unless, of course, I decided to have the baby.

At camp that night, Natalia came over to help me as I set up our tent. I had just dumped the contents from the carry bag onto the sand. She knelt down and started to fish out the stakes.

"Oh," I said, surprised. "Does this mean you're staying with us tonight?"

She looked up at me, and I noticed her eyes were red-rimmed, either with exhaustion or from crying. I knelt down to help her look for the stakes, so she could whisper to me.

"I don't know," was all she said.

I stood up and started locking the poles together. Brendan came over to help us. He stood on the other side of the tent as I threaded the center pole through. When Mick sauntered past, carrying the other tent, he looked over at Natalia.

"Hey, Brendan," he called, his voice booming through the

campground. "You picked the right girl. How was I supposed to know the mousy one would be the goer?"

Natalia threw the stakes down and marched over to Mick. She followed him past the fire pit, over an embankment, where he apparently planned on setting up the tent—as far away from the rest of us as possible. For a second I wondered if the rest of the trip would see five of us in one tent and Mick all alone in the other. This division seemed clear and sad to me, but quickly faded as I watched Natalia and Mick at the edge of the woods, standing toe to toe as they exchanged intense words. On the one hand, I felt relieved to know that Natalia had not had sex with him. On the other hand, they had never so clearly and obviously looked like a couple. Brendan walked over to me and put his arm around my shoulders. "Are you okay?" he asked. I nodded.

"You know the weird thing?" he said. "Sometimes I feel like every day I know Mick I hate him a little bit more. And yet I'm still very attracted to him. Isn't that sick?"

"No," I said quickly. "I know what you mean." I felt like I should say more, instead of cutting off the conversation by agreeing so quickly. It made me feel guilty, and sick to death of not being able to return Brendan's confidence.

It was exhausting, to always feel so confused and conflicted: about Mick, about Natalia, about Mick and Natalia. About myself and my future. I kept thinking about that morning, and how I'd almost died, and how in that moment I felt calm and powerless, almost accepting. And then, through no fault of my own, a hand had reached into the water and plucked me back into life.

Life. Not so long ago I'd had the clearest picture of my own life: school, and friends, and one day college. Now everything was all screwed up. I tried for a second to think of Tommy as something besides a troublemaker. For the first time it occurred to me how rude I'd been at the keg party, running away from him like that. Sure he was drunk, but he was also so happy to see me. *Hey, baby*, he had said. Like a boyfriend. Maybe if I went home and told him, he *would* come up with some kind of solution. Maybe he'd marry me. I wondered for a second what our life together would be like. I would have a husband, and sort of a cute one at that. Maybe we could live the way my dad and Kerry did, borrowing a house on somebody's farm. I tried to picture my days, what they would look like, and all I could see was Kerry, standing in the kitchen rolling out pie crust. I saw a mountain of diapers. I tried to picture the baby, but the image very stubbornly would not come to me. All I could conjure was an image of Rebecca, and Kerry somewhere in the background, waiting to take her from me if she started screaming.

And then a very clear aftermath presented itself. Because really Kerry wouldn't be there, and after a few years neither would Tommy. It would be just me and a little kid, alone in a ratty apartment—me resentful all the time about everything I'd missed.

There was no way to tell what might come from doing

nothing. Weeks ago I hadn't said no, or insisted on a condom, and now I was pregnant. I hadn't done anything to end the pregnancy, and now I was on this canoe trip. I hadn't fought for my life in the water, and here I sat—alive and rowing on a summer day in Canada. And all I could do was wonder what would happen next, because pretty soon doing nothing would lead to the biggest something I could ever imagine. A baby.

Unless I found a way to change my strategy.

chapter twelve
the biggest
delinquent
who ever lived

Now that Natalia rowed with Mick, she and I communicated even less than before. I rowed in the front of Brendan's canoe, wishing for my phone so I could text her. It was
impossible to talk to her alone, and I couldn't tell whether Mick
shadowed her so constantly because of devotion or because he
wanted to keep her away from everybody else.

Today, though, felt a little bit like old times, the four of us
floating along together—this time at the front of the group.
Natalia looked tan and weary in her red bikini, yawning between
oar strokes, her hair escaping from its ponytail. I closed my eyes
and tried to remember the girl I knew from home—her hand-
me-down designer shoes, her made-up face and manicured
nails, her hair carefully tousled with Catwalk styling cream (of
course at my house, we used Suave). But by now Lake Keewaytinook Natalia seemed like the real Natalia, the only one who'd
ever existed. It was like the lake had stripped away everything
extra—clothes, makeup, Steve, her parents/grandparents and

sister/mother—and left this sad, muscular, Indian princess of a girl in the old one's place.

Mick's loud voice startled my eyes open. "What time is it?" he shouted to a canoe coming around the bend. Dark blue like ours, the pair steering it looked vaguely familiar. Another identical canoe followed it, and I heard Silas somewhere behind us shout a greeting. The next thing I knew we had all come to rest together, floating on the water, suddenly nine canoes instead of four.

"Hey, stranger," a voice said, as another blue canoe smashed into ours. It took me a second, as if it had been years rather than weeks. But I found myself smiling back into Cody's long-lashed hazel eyes.

We set up camp not far from where we all met, the two groups together. Cody and I walked down to the water for a swim. I waded out and then plunged in headfirst, wishing for a pier so I could show off the swan dive I'd spent eight sum-mers perfecting. Cody splashed in after me. I noticed that he, like everyone at Camp Bell, had improved in some ways and deteriorated in others. He had gained a tan and signi-ficant muscle on his upper body. But his hair was wild and matted, his jaw scruffy and unshaved. Despite all the time we spent in the lake every day, none of us had been using much soap. Instead of individual body odor, we all seemed to travel under a collective musk, part lake-floor moss and part weeks-old sweat.

"You look good," Cody said, treading water next to me. "You look cleaner than everyone else, somehow."

"It's the hair," I said, tugging on a thick, unruly curl. "Even water won't tamp it down, so it doesn't get all stringy like everyone else's."

"So," he said, "I see you're riding in the movie star's canoe."

"We're just friends." The words, escaping from my mouth too quickly, sounded like an admission. My face instantly burned red, giving even more away.

Cody reached under the water and grabbed my hand. I could feel my blush fading away. Of course every second Cody had suspected that Brendan and I were together, his interest in me skyrocketed, and I was fairly certain the interest had been substantial to begin with.

I could feel our legs, kicking near each other underwater. It was nothing like swimming with Brendan. The cool water felt charged with sexual currents. The waves that lapped against my shoulder sent tingles down my spine, along my arms and legs. I avoided looking directly at Cody and splashed backward, away from him.

"I'll race you back to shore," I said, and started in on the crawl—my specialty event. I knew that for at least a few minutes I would look graceful and competent. But I had no hope of beating Cody, an athlete *and* a guy. When I got back to shore he was already waiting for me, holding a towel open. I stepped into it and he wrapped it around me, half hugging my shoulders, half drying them off. I had a vague memory of my mom doing the same thing for me when I was little after a swimming lesson.

"Hey," Mick called to Cody, as we walked up from the water. His face had that look, taut and predatory. I could tell that Natalia had just done something to piss him off, and I was about to pay for it. I braced myself as he said, "You don't have to bother with the Galahad moves, dude. She's a goer."

Of course my heart dropped, and my stomach sank in embarrassment. At the same time, just the other day Mick had saved my life. I couldn't ignore my debt for that long enough to worry about his corrupting Cody. So instead I rolled my eyes and brought my finger up near my ear, twirling it in the universal symbol for *cuckoo*.

Cody laughed. "That's too bad," he said. "Ours is pretty cool. His name's Jesse. The whole reason we were backtracking this way is he heard there's a package store called Backwater Jack's on the water."

"Really?" I had a hard time believing this. In three weeks we hadn't seen one commercial building, only scattered summer homes and camps. The one liquor store I'd seen had been way back in North Bay, and its sign had said it was run by a government agency.

"I guess it serves fishermen and summer people," said Cody. "It's on one of the counselors' maps. We're going to try to find it tonight after our counselors go to bed. Want to come along?"

"Sure," I said. In my head I started calculating, trying to figure out ways to leave Mick out of this particular adventure.

*   *   *

But by afternoon Mick and Jesse had bonded like the tribesmen they were, and Mick had transformed into the co-mastermind of the plot. He decided we should go while it was still light instead of waiting for dark. Mick, Jesse, Cody, Natalia, and I gathered at the water. The counselors were so involved with one another they would barely notice if we got back in time for dinner. And for all we knew, they'd be elated if we returned with beer. I considered asking Silas to pitch in money, but Mick quickly shot this idea down.

"No way," he said. "It's not necessary, anyway."

"Why?" I asked. "Do you have money?" My father had given me a twenty-dollar bill at the airport, and it still lay rolled up and untouched in the front pocket of my pack.

"I've got enough," he said, using the tone I'd come to know well, the one so sure that its speaker knew everything in the world.

"How are we going to buy liquor, anyway?" said Natalia, pulling her boat out into the water.

"The drinking age is nineteen in Ontario," Jesse said.

Natalia and I looked at each other. Considering that the oldest of us was seventeen, the drinking age might as well have been forty. Jesse shrugged. "I'm guessing they don't card much out here," he said.

Natalia and Mick rowed in one canoe. Cody and I rowed the other, while Jesse sat in the middle and read the map. I had taken a quick look before we set off, and it struck me as an unreadable document—little islets with pine trees, and winding portages along the shore, everything looking exactly the same. But Jesse seemed confident, and within half an hour we floated up to a tiny island, most of it taken up by a small wooden building with a small, barely readable sign: BACKWATER JACK'S. It didn't have glass windows, just mosquito screens, and the wood boards were gray and damp. There were no lights on inside, or any other signs of life.

"It looks closed," Natalia said. We rowed our canoes up and pulled them ashore. Mick trotted up to the flimsy screen door and pulled it open. He poked his head in and whistled.

"Hellooo?" he called, in a mocking, high-pitched voice. "Anybody home?" We watched him disappear into the store. In another minute he emerged, carrying a case of Molson. He trotted down the embankment and dumped it in the canoe.

"Oh," said Natalia. "There must be a clerk there after all." As Mick headed back in, she followed him. I knew she was probably hoping the store sold chocolate as well as beer. I walked up the hill and through the door after Natalia. The store consisted of a single room, its walls lined with shelves stocked mostly with Molson and Moosehead. A few boxes of Nestlé bars sat in front of the cash register, behind which were various fishing supplies—nets, bait, lures, and line. What the little store lacked was any kind of cashier, which didn't stop Mick from helping himself to another case and heading toward the door.

"Hey," Natalia said. "We can't just *take* it." I shuffled in agreement. It was one thing to borrow her mother's car without asking, or steal a couple of paltry plastic rum bottles from an airline company. But taking all that beer from this quaint, family-owned operation seemed not just illegal, but flat-out mean. Besides, what if we got caught? On the wall behind the cash register hung a dusty framed certificate with the initials LBCO. It was the only sign of law or government I'd seen in more than two weeks, and I wondered what Lake Keewayti-nook's version of police officers might be.

"Who's going to stop us?" Mick said.

Natalia and I stood there, watching him elbow his way out the door. Neither of us were angels, it was true, but robbing a liquor store seemed a little extreme. Even Steve had never com-mitted anything so close to a felony. I watched Natalia's face, a little blue vein bulging gently on her forehead. I couldn't tell whether she felt anxiety or excitement at crossing this new line.

"We could leave money," I said. She turned and looked at me, startled, as if she'd forgotten I was there. I walked over behind the cash register. Not electronic, it had round keys with numbers. It looked like something that might have been at the Linden Hill Children's Museum when we were little, donated by an old business that had finally upgraded to computers. I pressed the No Sale button, and a tinny bell chimed as the drawer heaved open with a spastic click.

Backwater Jack's had no hours posted on the door. The LBCO certificate and a neon Molson sign, unplugged or broken, were practically the only indications to non-natives that the house was anything more than someone's raggedy summer cabin. But apparently it did a brisk enough business: ones, fives, tens, and twenties were piled in the till. I stood there, staring at the money, which just lay there, taunting me with its possibilities.

The pile of twenties was thick and green. I imagined the time it had spent on the lake, damp air curling its edges and sharpening its mossy money smell. It looked to me like salvation, like the answer to all my worries. I thought that I wouldn't take any more than I needed. I would carefully ease the stack out and count out three hundred dollars. Three hundred dollars should be enough, I thought. And if not, I would be three hundred dollars closer.

I heard Natalia's soft and resolute voice. "Don't do it," she said. I didn't know if she meant *Don't take the money*, or *Don't have the abortion*. Or both.

I heard Mick coming up the steps and slammed the drawer shut. Stealing the money seemed so flatly unheroic. What chance did I have of saving Mick if I helped myself to the money in this till? On the other hand, what other choice did I have?

"Anything in there?" Mick said, jutting his chin toward the cash register.

"No," I said. "It's empty." He hesitated, not sure if he believed me. Then he went back to pilfering cases of beer.

Natalia stepped forward and patted me on the shoulder. "We'll find another way," she said quietly. "If that's what you decide you want." She reached across the counter and helped herself to a small stack of chocolate bars. Then she reached into her pocket and took out two twenty-dollar bills. I put mine on top, and we weighted them down with a small stapler.

We rowed back to camp with three cases of Molson. Mick and Jesse didn't bother hiding the beer from either the counselors or the campers: Everyone but Meredith greeted us like conquering heroes, even Silas and Jane cheered at the sight of the beer, and Bucket Head added his rusty bark to the general happiness. It was almost like the counselors had handed out the information—the lone, floating package store—so that we would go out and get beer for them, no questions asked and no answers offered. Maybe they did this every year.

Back home, we would have opened the warm beer on the spot and started swilling immediately. But our time on the lake had taught us to be patient and resourceful. We unloaded the cases from the canoes and plunged the bottles, one by one, into the sandy bottom. As everyone else headed up to the fire to check on dinner, Mick and I knelt knee-deep in the water, arranging rocks to keep the beers in and create a kind of makeshift refrigerator. We worked together silently, occasionally offering each other suggestions on rock size and markers.

"I bet they'll be cold enough for us to split one by the time we're through," Mick said. I didn't look up at him, just kept stacking rocks. Late-afternoon sun beat down on my bare back, but my legs, toes, and fingers felt deliciously chilly from the water.

"So how are you feeling, anyway?" Mick asked. I stopped working and looked up at him. I could tell from his expression, full of unlikely concern, that he meant my pregnant state. It was the first time he'd mentioned it without jeering.

"I feel fine," I said. "I'm dying for a glass of lemonade, but except for that I feel totally normal."

"That's weird," he said. "When my aunt was pregnant, she couldn't go an hour without puking. She was always clutching her stomach and running to the toilet."

"My stepmother was like that," I said. "But not me. I feel fine."

I hadn't been around much when Kerry was pregnant with the twins, which was during my nightmare-induced exile. But often during these last weeks I had thought about her pregnant with Rebecca, how she would stretch out across the sofa eating Saltines while the twins rode Big Wheels around the living room. Her skin had taken on a perpetually green cast, and I'd thought that if I ever wanted children I would seriously consider adoption. Maybe my own symptomlessness had something to do with my frame of mind. My body, I thought, must be listening to my intentions. Maybe people like Kerry and Mick's aunt experienced nausea and exhaustion because of the looming, awesome, and terrible responsibility of parenthood.

"You know," Mick said, "I know someone in Pittsburgh who could help you out. All you'd need is a ride there, and she'd only charge you, like, fifty bucks. I had a girlfriend who went to her once. She just feeds you this cocktail of herbs and cleaning fluid, and then in, like, three days the thing's gone."

I sat back on my haunches, submerging my shorts in the water. Mick looked at me, his face relaxed and normal. His hair had grown out a tiny bit, enough so that I could tell which direction it would flop across his forehead. In his bathing suit, minus the bandanna, his blue eyes looked uncharacteristically calm—as if the afternoon's heist had satisfied his hunger for excitement. He seemed very close to normal. As if he had no idea that what he was offering could end up killing me.

What would my mother think if she could hear this conversation? How ridiculous would it be if a girl like me—educated, with parents she should be able to turn to—ended up doing what Mick suggested? Except that really, if my physical well-being were the most important thing to me, I would have told my mother immediately. I remembered what she said that night in our living room. *I don't know why such a smart girl does such stupid things.* And I knew she meant in terms of my health, my future—which never seemed quite real to me, quite important. The future was so far away, it might as well be happening to a different person. And my health was a matter of course. What mattered to me was just myself, this me inside—away from her—and she always had to stomp that down. A part of me wanted to protect that self and keep it from her, even if it meant drinking some underground abortionist's toxic brew, or going ahead with a pregnancy that no part of me wanted.

"Maybe," I said. "Thanks, Mick."

"Sure." He reached out to pat my head. He looked pleased that I would consider accepting his help. We stood up and walked together to the campfire. Anybody watching would have assumed we were the best of friends.

Just before and then during dinner, before the beers were opened, Cody and I began a strange kind of dance, keeping mostly to our own groups. Cody milled about with his friends, talking and laughing, at one point even putting his arm around one of the girls. But then at regular intervals he would look back at me, not necessarily smiling or even acknowledging the glance, but paying enough attention that I knew before long he would sit next to me, hand me a lake-chilled beer, and the physical side of our romance would begin.

"My girlfriend," Brendan lamented, as we spooned peanut butter out of a jar. One of the other group's leaders was busy preparing some sort of elaborate hash—not heated in the can, but pan-fried and seasoned—but for us Jane had put out an assortment of condiments, including the last of our wild blueberry preserves, which—when we opened it—turned out to be completely fermented. So as a prelude to our beer party, we passed around makeshift blueberry wine. After I took my first, nose-squinching sip, Brendan handed me the peanut butter and said, "I'm losing my girlfriend to an outsider hottie."

"You think he's a hottie?" I asked, wanting my own opinion seconded.

"I definitely do," he said. He lowered his voice to a whisper. "I've got a couple condoms in my pack, if you need them."

"You *do*?" I said. Brendan shrugged, nonchalant.

"Sure," he said. "You never know."

I absorbed this for a second. Then I had a thought. What if Cody and I had sex tonight, and then in two weeks I got in touch and told him I was pregnant? The timing would be exactly right, and it would give me just enough time to get my abortion in under the wire. Getting the money would suddenly be his responsibility. He wouldn't even have to come get me; Natalia and I could take care of that. I could always turn to one of my other friends if Natalia didn't want to help.

I shook my head sharply, remembering my hand hovering over that cash register. First an almost thief, and now an almost con artist. What was happening to me?

The sun began to dip, the evening slowly turning to mauve. I thought of what Lori had said, about everything on the lake looking the same, a statement that was equal parts true and preposterous. The sunset, for example—every night its color came up with a subtle surprise, the last bit of sunlight reflected off the lake from a different angle. I thought of those twenty-dollar bills, abandoned in the till. Maybe tonight I would blow Cody off and sneak away in a canoe. Help myself to the twenties and rescue myself from all this uncertainty and indecision. However rotten that scheme, it sat better with me than lying to innocent Cody.

The blueberry wine came my way again. I took another sip and it spread, sweet and spoiled, inside my chest. My head began to buzz, and from across the fire I could see Cody, eating his more elaborate meal. He caught my eye, and instead of looking away he grinned. My stomach dropped a little.

The problem was, I couldn't figure out a solution that didn't bring at least a little shame. If stealing money and tricking Cody was out of the question, no other option—abortion, adoption, giving up my own life for all eternity—seemed any less terrible.

People began floating down to the lake and fishing out beers. Although most of them had Swiss army knives, and we had two can openers with church keys on the handles, the guys all tried to open the bottles without tools. Nobody except Mick could actually do it. He would rest the bottle against a boulder and then tap the cap off with the flat of his palm.

When Brendan stood up and headed down to the lake for a beer, Cody took only a minute to take his seat beside me. No show-off, he opened two bottles of beer with the can opener Jane had left next to the fire pit, and handed one to me. Then he gave me a plate of corned beef hash.

"Oh," I said. "Thanks."

"Your dinner looked pretty lame," he said.

"But look," I said, picking up the nearly empty preserve jar. "At least we have fine wine."

Cody leaned over and took a sniff, then exhaled—half coughing, half laughing. "No thanks," he said. "I think I'll stick to this Canadian vintage."

"Good choice," I said. "I'm sure last month was a very good year."

I looked back down toward the lake. Brendan was talking to a tall, muscular guy from Cody's group. I wondered if they knew each other from base camp.

"So," Cody said, trying to sound casual, "you and the movie star have become pretty tight, huh."

"Didn't we already have this conversation?" I said, flattered that he was still jealous.

Cody smiled, his lips still damp from his last sip of beer. "Just checking," he said.

I jutted my chin toward the lake, and Brendan. "We're good friends," I said. "But the truth is, he would be more interested in that guy there than in me."

I felt an instant stab of guilt, sacrificing Brendan's secret in the name of getting closer to Cody, who just nodded and said, "He might actually have some luck with Roger."

"Don't tell anybody," I said.

"I won't." He let his knee move a little bit, pressing against mine. We could hear laughter and splashing: the drunken skinny-dipping had begun.

"You feel like going for a swim?" he said.

"Sure." We stood up, carrying our beers, and I followed him down toward the water. Darkness closed in around us, along with the first hints of chill. I thought about running back to the tent to grab my jacket—it would be freezing when we got out of the lake—but I didn't want to run into anyone.

Just at the mouth of the water, where everyone else had gathered, Cody grabbed two more beers and then took a turn into the woods. I could see Natalia, her head bobbing out on the water, watching us disappear behind the trees. As Cody and I walked down the sandy path, stepping over roots and rocks, he reached his hand back to me. I grabbed it and kept following. His white T-shirt shone through the darkness. BREWSTER FLATS, it read, in big, bold letters.

"I love the way guys dress," I said. The blueberry wine and surprisingly cold beer had gone to my head. "All the T-shirts. You can't tell much about a girl from her clothes, about her history anyway. But with guys, it's like a record of everywhere they've been and everything they like."

"That's cool," said Cody. "I never thought of it that way." We emerged from the trail onto a beautiful beach. Our groups should have camped here. The great expanse of sand, two fire pits, and the opening of trees made way for a steady stream of moonlight.

"Wow," I said. "Did you know this place was here?"

"I did a little scouting earlier," Cody said. He pulled his T-shirt over his head and let it drop to the sand. Then he took off his shorts. It felt too personal, too intrusive, to look at him, so I busied myself taking off my own clothes. By the time I'd undressed, Cody was already treading water, waiting for me.

I felt very conscious of the moonlight as I walked, naked, down to the water. Cody had left the extra beers with his clothes. I took the last swig of mine and carried the extra bottles down to the water with me, to chill while we swam. I wondered if what Natalia said was true, that my breasts had gotten bigger. My hair felt wild on my shoulders. My muscles felt taut and strong. It felt unbearably sexy, sauntering naked through this wilderness, the hiss of cicadas and the coo of the loons pulsing all around us.

I dove in headfirst and swam underwater—like a fish—in Cody's direction. When I came up for air I realized I had gone in the wrong direction. He had to swim to catch up with me. We were both sputtering and laughing by the time his hands found my naked hips.

I could tell as his fingers straddled my waist that everything there was slim—if not slimmer than it had been before. We faced each other in the moonlight, chilling ourselves in the same lake water we'd used for a refrigerator. I let some of it lap into my mouth, trying to clear my suddenly fuzzy head. And then we fell on each other. His hands moved from my waist to my bare butt, and I wrapped my legs around his waist. We kissed and kissed, drinking each other like we'd been lost in the desert these past three weeks, Cody kicking his legs to keep us afloat. The physics of the water kept our activity to just that—kissing, kissing, beneath the insistent and all-encompassing moon.

By the time we paddled ashore, we were practically paralyzed by the cold water and the delicious, tingling frustration that might be satisfied at any moment. There was no question of continuing our makeout session on the sand—it was much too cold. Instead we shivered into our clothes, nowhere near what we needed to stay warm, retrieved our beer from the water, and headed back to camp.

The party still raged, now mostly centered around the fire. I could hear Silas's and Brendan's guitars, and drunken choruses of "Leaving on a Jet Plane." Peering through the smoke, I saw that Roger sat next to Brendan, leaning into him slightly as he played. Meredith was on the other side of Brendan, singing away in a sweet contralto, and I realized that even she was drunk. I took a quick inventory of the crowd and felt relieved that Mick was nowhere nearby.

Cody and I separated to go to our tents and bundle into warm clothes. "Get your sleeping bag," he whispered, squeezing my hand and planting a kiss somewhere between my lips and nose. I squeezed back. Five minutes later I met him by the lake, bundled into my fleece jacket and wool cap, and of course carrying my sleeping bag—ever obedient. We grabbed a few more beers from the lake and headed back down our path.

The perfect beach waited for us under the perfect moon. Cody zipped our sleeping bags together, and for a while we sat on top of them, talking and drinking. The noise from the party mixed seamlessly with the buzz from the forest. We swatted mosquitoes and linked elbows, talking about swimming, school, and hometowns. Close as I felt to him, I didn't say a word about any of the things that had been most pressing on my mind. Not Natalia and Mick. Of course not my pregnancy. After a while we crawled into the sleeping bags. Cody's hand, still chilly, found its way under my shirt. His tongue traveled into my mouth. His hand warmed up, squeezing one breast, then the other. My head fogged and buzzed deliciously, with the beer and the blueberries and the night. The woods and the boy.

It all felt so good, so good. Nothing like Tommy, or even Greg. I could see that full moon over his shoulder. I couldn't care less about the bugs. His hips pressed into mine. That I could reveal everything to him—my body, my desire—and not let on what I carried inside me made it all the more unreal. Cody pushed up my coat and let his tongue wind around my nipple. I closed my hands into his hair and moaned.

Cody moaned too. He slid one hand into my jeans, and then unzipped them. I realized he wasn't wearing any pants. When had he taken off his pants? I realized that through all of this night, I hadn't made a single move to stop him from doing anything. Shouldn't I have at least pretended to protest? I remembered Mick's words, which must, no matter how much he liked me, be echoing in Cody's mind: *She's a goer.*

Maybe it was true. My jeans were around my ankles. My breath panted so close to Cody's ear, so loud and exposing, I thought I would die from wanting him inside me. I could sense him gearing up to make that plunge—his face so close to my own—and suddenly I couldn't breathe at all. My short, encouraging breaths had somehow morphed into long and shuddering ones.

"Get off me," I heaved. "Please. I can't breathe."

I started struggling against him, as if he and the sleeping

bag combined to make a straitjacket. Cody pulled back immediately. I clawed at the zipper. He calmly reached over and
unzipped from the other side, then threw the top bag off of me.
I jumped up, pulled my jeans back on, and ran toward the lake,
hyperventilating.

It was not a windy night. Cold air settled gently around my
bare legs. I realized that my shirt and jacket were still bunched
up above my breasts, and I pulled them down with a desperate
yank. I stared out across the water, wondering if my frantic,
honking breaths could be heard back at the party.

I could hear Cody behind me, approaching cautiously. He
stood next to me and placed a hand on each shoulder. "Here,"
he said. "Sit down."

I lowered myself to the ground. Cody moved his hand to
the back of my head and slowly pressed it down between my
knees. Then he rubbed the place between my shoulder blades
in light, comforting circles. "Just take it in calm," he said. "Out
with the bad, in with the good. One breath at a time. Let it
slow down. You're all right."

Gradually my breathing went back to normal. One or two
cycles of oxygen was all it took for mortification to set in. "Oh
my God," I said in a squeaky, despondent voice.

"It's okay," said Cody, and I started to cry.

"I can't," I sobbed. "I'm so sorry. I really, really want to, but
I just can't."

"You don't have to," Cody whispered. "You don't have to."

He put his arm around me and held me close. We stared

together out across the water. After a while I stopped crying, but we didn't say anything more. We just sat there, until there was nothing left to do but zip ourselves back into the sleeping bags and cling together until the moon melted into morning sunlight, and the cool night air transfigured into dew.

chapter thirteen
cliff diving

After Silas and Jane had rowed a canoe full of empties to leave on Backwater Jack's doorstep. After we had eaten the last can of baked beans for breakfast, and pulled down our tents, and made our bleary, hungover way to our canoes. After Cody and I had said a sheepish and awkward good-bye, letting our fingers part from each other slowly, and I had watched him row away with a pretty blond girl in the front of his canoe. After all that, we set out on our own way, back toward base camp, exactly five more days to spend on the water.

It was the hottest day yet, and I felt terrible. Physically wrecked, a hangover like I'd never experienced. My body trembled from someplace beneath my skin, a tremor that rocked my nerve endings. I tried to row from my shoulders, but my hand kept slipping off the butt of my oar. Poor Brendan, in only slightly better shape, had to propel the canoe almost entirely on his own. In the morning I had seen him and Roger come out of the same tent, with pale faces and messed-up hair. Clearly Brendan had used those condoms himself and was definitely the worse for wear.

But Brendan wasn't pregnant. And for the first time in six weeks, I had to completely, entirely admit that I was. The smell of Meredith's damn butterscotch ripped through my respiratory system like a chemical weapon. I couldn't get that glass of lemonade out of my head. My stomach heaved with the remains of the beer and the disgusting blueberry wine. I felt like I'd developed an allergy to my own body. I felt like dying.

We stopped for lunch after only a couple of slow hours on the water, at a flat stretch of sand girded by rocky cliffs. I guessed we'd rowed barely three miles from last night's party, but that may have just been my sudden and all-consuming pessimism warping my perception. Brendan and I dragged our canoe onto shore.

Mick and Natalia pulled up just behind us. Natalia jumped out of the canoe without looking at me and walked purposefully toward the fire. I could tell she was furious about my obvious hangover, and I braced myself for her lecture on fetal alcohol syndrome. As Mick came toward us, I also braced myself for his remarks about my behavior last night. But instead he walked over and thumped Brendan on the back.

"Dude," he said. "Have an interesting night last night?"

Brendan and I froze. I reached out and grabbed his hand, as if the pose of us as couple could still protect him. Mick laughed. "Give it up, you two," he said. "The cat's out." He smiled and rumpled Brendan's perfect hair with what could almost be called fondness. Brendan and I looked at each other, then back at Mick.

"We thought it might bother you," I said to Mick. I tossed the words out softly, like a hand grenade, not sure how strongly they would be lobbed back at me.

But Mick just shrugged. "I'm cool with it," he said. "My brother's a fag."

And then he walked up toward the fire, his bare shoulders looking less red, less freckled. Natalia must be putting sunscreen on him in the morning, I thought. Brendan and I stood for a second, still holding hands, watching him go. And I would have bet that Brendan also replayed that vision in his head, Mick killing the guy in the tunnel to save his brother. His brother the fag.

"Did you ever notice," Brendan said, "that whenever Mick talks about home it's always his family? My brother, my sister, my mother, my aunt. It's cute. Sweet. It all sounds so cozy."

"Yes," I said. And then, "He surprises me."

"You and me both, honey," Brendan said. "You and me both."

At the fire pit, Jane dug through our food bag and empty cooler. All we had left were canned pineapple, a bag of flour, some severely dented cans of tuna, and a sack of brown rice. Natalia suggested using the flour to make tortillas. She held up the little Camp Bell cookbook, a battered and stapled pamphlet stuffed in with the food supplies.

"It will make such a terrible mess." Jane sighed. "Maybe we can do it later in the week, if it comes to that." She sent us down to the water to search for freshwater clams. "We can just boil them," Jane said, "and then dump out the water." I'd seen the clams all along the trip, clinging to rocks and roots, but never imagined they were edible.

"Do you think these are safe?" Natalia asked. We stood thigh-deep in water, collecting the clams in our T-shirts. They were small and smooth, about half the size of the steamers my mother sometimes ordered at seafood restaurants. They made a musical noise, clanging together like muffled bells as I plopped them in, one after another.

"It doesn't matter to me," I said. "I'm not eating these. I can't eat anything. I feel like hell."

Natalia knelt to pick up another clam. She looked cool and perfect, not shaky at all, and I wondered if she'd had anything to drink last night. Without looking at me, she dropped a clam into her T-shirt and said, "Morning sickness?"

"No," I said sharply. "Not morning sickness. Hungover. I have a hangover."

"Oh," said Natalia. She faced me now, her eyes flatly sarcastic. "Right. It couldn't be morning sickness. You're not pregnant, right?"

I felt a surge of fury, along with a desperate need to change the subject. "What about you, Natalia? Has Mick inseminated you yet?" I almost added something crueler, about Margit becoming a grandmother, or her parents inheriting a new child. But the meanness of that one remark already made my head hurt. And anyway, Natalia looked completely steeled to anything I might have to say.

"A lot you'd care," she said. "You haven't asked once about me and Mick."

"That's because I really don't want to hear about it," I said. "If you must know, it makes me sick how fast you turned on Steve."

"I'd think you'd be overjoyed," Natalia said. "We'll be home soon enough, and then Steve will be all yours."

My already shaky insides went pale: that she would see something so faint within me when I hadn't admitted even in my own mind that it was true. "You don't know what you're talking about," I whispered.

"Don't I?" she said. She shook one hand dry, and I noticed for the first time that she'd stopped wearing the tinny Irish wedding ring Steve had given her. She walked out of the water, cradling the clams in her shirt. As she brushed by me she whispered, "Little slut."

I stood there in the bright sun, the water all around me, watching her walk up to the fire pit. Steam rose from the pot of boiling water, and Natalia dumped the clams straight in from her T-shirt. I followed after her and did the same. She refused to return my glance, which—she might have been surprised to know—was more wounded than angry.

Is that really what you think? I wanted to say. *Little slut.* Little slut.

I pictured Cody rowing along, not far away, on this hot and sparkling lake. And I prayed that whatever he was thinking, it did not include that pair of words, their rhythm (little slut, little slut) guiding his oar through his own foggy, hungover mind.

*   *   *

I managed to choke down a single clam. Afterward I escaped under the shadow of the cliffs for a nap. I'd been asleep maybe ten minutes when Mick's voice woke me, goading Sam to jump off into the hopefully deep water below.

"If it's so easy," Sam's shaky voice said, "why don't you do it?"

Good boy, I thought to myself. This might have been the first time I'd heard Sam talk to Mick at all, let alone stand up to him.

"Okay, you little pussy," said Mick. "I'll do it."

The next thing I knew, a fine spray of water hit my face. Mick had catapulted from fifty feet above. "Hi," he said, treading water. I scrambled to my feet.

"Hi," I said. "How was that?"

"Fucking awesome."

I followed him as he climbed back up to the top of the cliff. My hands still shook as I grabbed rocks and roots, shakily pulling myself to the jagged top. Sam stood there, looking miserable. Now he would have to jump, and he obviously didn't want to.

I stepped forward and grabbed Sam's hand. "Come on," I said. "I'll go with you."

We walked together to the very edge. The water looked a long way down. The view was wonderful—what seemed like the entire pristine lake, the pine trees and the white cedars' leaves camouflaging every campsite and building. The only house I could see had to be Backwater Jack's—floating farther away than I would have guessed, a glint of what might be sunlight from our empty beer bottles twinkling like a star from another galaxy. From up here, the illusion of the lake as uninhabited disappeared. We could see fishing boats and Windsurfers, and groups of canoes that might have been from Camp Bell, making their slow way back to base camp.

"Are you ready?" I whispered to Sam. He made an uncertain grunting noise, and I reached out and grabbed his hand. It felt chubby, childlike, and it struck me that if I ran into him five years from now I might not recognize him.

"I'm going to count," I said. We took another small step closer to the edge. One more move and we'd be heading toward the water. "One . . . two . . . three!"

We jumped.

A long, long way down. The wind took our hair straight up. A single moment when it felt like our stomachs stayed behind us, up on the rock, and then that intense sensation as they rushed to catch up to us. Our heels smashed through the water with a sharp slice, and we let go of each other's hands as our faces plunged beneath the water, bubbles rising all around us.

We surfaced to cheers. Meredith, Silas, Natalia, Brendan, and Jane stood at the bottom. Natalia was the only one not smiling. When I emerged from the water and walked past her, dripping wet, she turned away to avoid catching my eye.

I climbed back up to the top, everyone else following. One by one, they each took the plunge. Even Meredith jumped, her braids flying straight up into the air like Pippi Longstocking. Sam went again, this time on his own. Bucket Head, beside himself, ran from the bottom of the cliffs to the top about three hundred times, barking in a panicked way that sounded like he meant, *Stop, stop, stop it right now!*

When everyone else had gathered on the beach below, I walked to the very edge. My toes gripped the rocks. I raised my arms over my head, wove my fingers together, and pointed them outward in the prayerful position that was second nature to me only when diving. I had never prayed for anything in my life. I rocked once, twice, off the balls of my feet.

"Bullshit." At first I thought it was Mick's voice, but then I realized Silas had spoken. I stifled a smile over what he was about to see.

"Sydney, don't!" Natalia screamed.

I didn't listen. Instead I rocked right onto my toes and threw my body into its practiced arc. I felt myself flying. My insides stayed behind me, on the cliff, watching me go, and I wished they would stay there forever. I realized at just the right moment that if I flattened my body—let myself fall belly first—it might solve all my problems, the mess of my life expressing itself into the cool, clear water.

My mind wanted to do it, but my body would not listen. It ignored my orders and turned downward into a swan dive. My hands were no longer a prayer but an arrow. They led my body in a swift rush, wind whipping up from the water, and suddenly I was plunging, deep and then deeper. The tips of my fingers touched the lake's silty bottom, and then I turned and rushed up to the surface.

Nobody cheered this time. Even the dog quieted. Everyone just stood, staring in disbelief. I treaded water, staring back at them, my hair for once flattened like an otter's around my face.

I walked out of the water, my skin cold and dripping, every hair on my body standing up, electric. My hand did not tremble as I reached for the towel Meredith handed me. My head felt clear. My stomach felt empty but settled.

My hangover was gone.

Our group rowed close to one another that afternoon, all four canoes in a tandem cluster on the water. After a long, quiet while, Natalia announced that it was Meredith's birthday. Meredith, in the front of Sam's canoe, jerked her head around in surprise.

"I know I said I wouldn't tell," Natalia said. This singsong may have sounded believable to the rest of them, but I knew her well enough to know that not only was it nowhere near Meredith's birthday, but this was the first Meredith had heard of it. "You know how shy and humble she is," Natalia said, "but I feel that a birthday absolutely deserves a cake. Don't you think so, Jane? There's a recipe in the reflector oven cookbook for a blueberry cake. I'm going to make it tonight, for Meredith's sweet sixteen."

The muscles in Jane's neck looked stiff, but even she had to agree to washing a dish or two in honor of Meredith's birthday.

When we got to camp, we all set out with our tin camping cups to collect wild blueberries. I'd just found a bush and begun plunking them into my cup when I felt a hand on my shoulder. I looked up. Natalia stood over me, her face serious and remorseful.

"Can we talk?" she said.

"Sure." I stood and followed her up a mossy embankment. When we got to the woods, we faced each other. Natalia put her hands on her hips.

"I have a couple things," she said. "First off, I'm sorry. I shouldn't have called you a slut. You know I don't think that."

I didn't say anything, didn't nod or give her any indication that I accepted the apology. She went on, not noticing or caring. "No matter how you feel about me," she said, "I have one thing to say to you, Sydney. No matter if we're friends or not." Her eyes looked wide and round and glassy, and I couldn't help feeling sorry for her. For some reason, when I looked at Natalia I filled up with sympathy instead of anger. At the same time, I did not want to hear what she had to say.

"I'm not interested, Natalia. You're treating me like I'm Margit, but I'm not. This baby, this thing that's not going to be a baby. It's not you. It's not anybody, because I can't have it."

"Then why didn't you get an abortion right away?" she said. "Why didn't you tell your mom and be done with it?"

"It's not because I'm confused," I said. "I know what I want."

"Listen to me, Sydney," Natalia said. Her voice trembled, and I could see that the finger she held up in front of me also shook.

"You can hook up with a million more guys like Cody. You can spend the next twenty years looking for the love of your life. But the real, true love of your life, it's this. Right here."

She stepped forward and put her hands flat on my bare stomach. The warmth of her palms pulsed through my skin. I had started this trip thin, and the weeks of exercise and Jane's stingy meals had made me thinner still. The distance between my spine to the skin of my belly felt very slight. Nothing going on in there but an insistent cry for food; I'd eaten nothing but one puny clam since breakfast.

I pushed Natalia's hands away. "Stop it," I hissed. "This isn't about love. And it isn't about you. You were supposed to help me."

"You better know right now I'm not going to."

Panic swirled around me. I knew she and I had been growing further and further apart, but I couldn't believe that when it came down to it, Natalia wouldn't step up to the plate and rescue me. I did a quick mental inventory of friends who might take her place: Kendra, or Ashlyn, or even Greg. I would have to contact them the second I got home. I couldn't fool around much longer.

I looked at Natalia, prepared to face an enemy. But she didn't look like an enemy. She looked like my best friend in the world, her face drawn into the deepest kind of concern. She pressed her hand back against my belly. *The love of my life.*

My gut lurched with a new nausea. I wanted that lemonade. I knew I was pregnant, and I knew—strangely, unwillingly—that

if I had the baby I would love it more than I'd ever loved anything in my entire life.

It was terrifying.

"Sydney," Natalia whispered. "Just promise me you'll have it,
and I promise you I'll find a way to make everything okay."

"All right," I whispered.

Her eyes widened, like she couldn't trust herself to believe it.
"All right what?" she said.

"I'll have the baby," I said.

Natalia stepped forward and drew me into a tight, body-
clasping hug. I stared over her shoulder, into the darkening
woods, not believing in the promise I'd just made.

We had no milk and no eggs. Natalia baked Meredith's fake
birthday cake with flour, sugar, and vegetable oil. It came
out dusty and charred. We set a twig on fire, stuck it in the
middle of the cake, and sang "Happy Birthday" while Silas
and Brendan smashed out chords on their guitars. Meredith
blew on the twig mightily, not extinguishing the flame at all,
then plucked it out and tossed it in the fire. The cake tasted
like wild blueberry Play-Doh, but we were starved enough
for sugar to choke down every last piece. We ate with our
hands, of course—Jane not willing to dirty forks. Afterward
we lay around the fire, staring stupefied into the flames while
Silas sang us his own original songs. My favorite was called
"Evelina," about a girl he used to love but didn't anymore. Silas
had a scratchy, lonesome voice, and I wondered what it would

feel like to lose someone like him. I watched Jane listen to him play and imagined that Silas would be the most distant and unknowable boyfriend. Losing him would probably feel a lot like having him. Listening to his songs made me feel sad in the best, sleepiest way. I could almost forget my promise to Natalia—the decision I'd made, and everything it meant for my future.

On the way back to camp Natalia had formulated a plan. We would come home from Keewaytinook and act as if everything were normal. I would go on pretending not to be pregnant and hide it from my mother as long as possible. When I got past the point where abortion would be an option, and I couldn't fit into regular clothes anymore, I'd tell the guidance counselor at school—whichever school I went to—and the guidance counselor would help me tell my parents. If neither one of them wanted to support my decision, I would go live with Natalia— or Margit, if Natalia's parents refused.

"I mean, how can Margit say no, right?" Natalia said. "Who's going to understand better than her?"

I listened like a robot, or an obedient child. Everything was finally out of my hands. The decision had been made. The embryo would become a baby. All I had to do was absolutely nothing.

When Silas put aside his guitar, Jane piled the dirty dishes in the lake. "Maybe the fish will eat them clean," she said. Then she and Silas headed to their tent. They walked at that same confusing distance from each other, three feet between them.

I tried to imagine what happened when they zipped the tent closed—whether they fell on each other hungrily or maintained the distance, sleeping back to platonic back.

Natalia couldn't bear to part with me, either because it elated her to have my friendship again or because she worried I would change my mind if she left me alone. So she, Mick, Brendan, and I all piled into the same tent. I lay down, staring at the ceiling. On one side of me, Brendan snored gently. On the other, I could hear Natalia and Mick, kissing and snuggling. Occasionally Mick would make a noise that sounded almost like a giggle, and I had to stifle my own laugh at the tough guy making such a sweet and girlish noise. After a while Natalia whispered a very pointed good night. Mick groaned, but I could tell that it was less a complaint than a nightly ritual. I felt sure that what I'd overheard was exactly what had been happening night after night: kisses, cuddles, and then a frustrated shutting down.

I waited until everyone was asleep. Then I did what I'd been dying to do almost every night for the last two weeks. I crawled over my sleeping tent mates and out into the night. Bucket Head lay curled up in a tight ball by the fire, and he thumped his tail sleepily as I rooted through the cooler. He sat up at attention when I settled by the fire with the small plastic bottle of ranch dressing. I spent an hour dribbling the dressing onto my fingers and licking them off. Every once in a while I would dribble on my left hand and share with the dog.

Somehow I thought that giving in to this bizarre urge

would make me cross a line in my head. It would make me face my current state, and what it meant for my future. But the only thing I faced was a relieved kind of gladness at being Natalia's friend again. When I tried to look at the future I couldn't get past the fall, and whether I'd be at Linden Hill or Bulgar County High. I couldn't get past *me*, the girl sitting in the pine and wood-smoke forest, the one protected by distance and an endless firmament of stars. The one who'd be lost forever if I kept my promise to Natalia.

chapter fourteen
the rescue

J ane's fish-as-dishwasher plan didn't work, and it ruined everyone's day. We spent nearly an hour scouring plates and cake pans with Dr. Brauners. Far into the afternoon, Jane complained about the chore and the time we'd lost. When we reached our campsite that night, she quickly sifted through our food supply, and I hoped she wouldn't notice the missing ranch dressing. She didn't seem to, and finally decided on the industrial-sized tin of tuna fish and a squeeze or two of the remaining mustard.

"Is that okay?" I asked Jane, pointing to the severely dented and misshapen side of the tuna fish can.

She turned it over, shrugged, and said, "What's the worst that could happen?" Everybody sat around watching Jane squat over the can, mixing the tuna and mustard together. She refused to use a bowl and seemed to be losing quite a bit of fish as she mashed it into the tin with a fork. The smell assaulted me so hard I practically doubled over. It went through my nose and attacked my entire body, a nausea so brutal and complete I could feel it in my elbows and toes.

"You don't look so good," said Jane, looking up.

"I feel sick," I whispered.

"You haven't eaten anything all day," said Jane. "Here." She held out the can, and I shook my head violently.

"Is there anything else you want?" she asked, sounding annoyed and maybe even a little accused.

I had the usual vision: a glass of lemonade, so cold that a film of condensation melted under my fingertips as I closed my hand around it. Ice clinking, and a sprig of fresh mint. Both my parents grew mint in the summer. Funny to think so randomly of a small thing—besides me—that they kept in common.

The only thing in the whole world I could possibly stand to put in my body was that glass of minty lemonade. Anything else, I knew, would make me sicker than I already felt. "I'm going to go lie down in the tent," I said to Jane.

I knelt in front of the flap, my fingers shaking as I pulled down the zipper, and crawled into the tent on my hands and knees. Tonight Natalia had decided to return to her private tent with Mick. Brendan, Sam, and Meredith had already laid out their sleeping bags in the other one. The material felt smooth and cool under my palms. I used the last piece of energy I had to pull my sleeping bag out of its stuff sack. Then I collapsed on top of it, dead to everything.

Hours later I awoke to darkness—both inside my mind and outside, in the world. I had been sleeping so deeply, so dreamlessly, that my body still felt paralyzed. It took several seconds to remember where and even who I was. Somewhere in the near distance I could hear a strange retching sound. At first I thought it might have been me; my stomach felt brutalized and scarred by hunger. I curved my hand across my belly, which finally seemed to be swollen with hopeful cramps. I heard myself moan, a soft, painful sound, and realized that the other sound had come from outside the tent.

"Are you getting sick too?" Meredith whispered. I pushed myself up on one elbow and looked at her.

"What do you mean?" I said.

"Did you sleep through it?" she asked. "We've all been puking the last hour or so. First me, then Brendan and Sam. I think Natalia and Mick are out there too."

She put her hand over her mouth, then bolted out of her sleeping bag. She ripped down the tent zipper and scrambled outside, abandoning our careful system and letting in a million mosquitoes. A new tone of retching joined the other, closer and more pained.

I crawled out of the tent and walked into the bushes. I squatted to pee, leaning forward to examine my underwear. No blood. The pain in my belly must be hunger, I decided, and nothing more.

I walked over to the food box, sealed tight against bears and Bucket Head. It opened with an airtight *whoosh*, and I dug through the cans. I couldn't imagine waiting long enough to find a can opener to pry one of them open. On the other side of the fire, I could see Mick and Natalia's tent—the flap open, the light from her solar lamp shining meekly. I walked over and crawled inside.

Disciplined hoarder that she was, Natalia still had two chocolate bars from Jack's in the front pocket of her pack. They were both misshapen, having melted and hardened many times over the hot days and chilly nights. I ripped one open and shoved a piece into my mouth. As soon as one square began melting on my tongue, I shoved another one in. When I was finished, I sat there for a minute, mosquitoes and black flies buzzing around my head. I breathed heavily while my stomach gurgled, as if the mini feast had been a marathon run.

I put the other chocolate bar in the pocket of my coat and climbed out of the tent. I didn't feel guilty about stealing it. If Natalia wanted the responsibility of making me have a baby, she could also have the responsibility of feeding me. I looked around the campsite, trying to locate her, and realized that all three tents were open, flaps rattling in the breeze, letting in every bug on the lake. I could see Meredith, crouched on all fours next to our tent, her braids hanging toward the ground. Looking at her silhouette, arched in the dark, I noticed for the first time that she'd lost a lot of weight over the past few weeks.

"Natalia?" I called. The sound barely traveled, a near whimper in the darkness. When all I heard for reply was a low, miserable moan, I felt gripped by the most eerie kind of fear. I walked toward the sound, up to the tree line, where Natalia sat, rocking back and forth and holding on to her stomach. Mick lay a few feet away, splayed out on his back. I crouched next to Natalia and lightly touched her shoulder.

"Natalia," I said, "what's happening?"

She opened her mouth, I thought to answer me, but she leaned forward and threw up. I stroked her head and saw Sam lying not far from Mick. It was awful, like some kind of psycho killer had crept into the camp and attacked everyone but me.

From the fire pit, Jane came walking toward me, doubled over, clutching her stomach.

"Sydney," she panted. "You have to go with Silas. Everybody's sick. Really sick. The tuna. You didn't eat the tuna. You have to go for help."

I ran down to the lake to meet Silas, thinking maybe he'd been spared too. But I found him puking into the water. Bucket Head stood next to him, worriedly wagging his tail. The dog looked fine—either he hadn't eaten any tuna or his doggy stomach worked better than ours.

"Jesus," I said to Silas. "Where are we supposed to get help?"

"We're only a couple days from base camp," he said. His voice sounded croaky and alien. "There should be other camps not far from here. Or a house with a phone, or a boat that can take us to the hospital."

"But look at you," I said. "How the hell are you supposed to row?"

He was barely in better shape than the rest of them, but there was no way I'd go by myself. I took the stern while Silas climbed into the bow and picked up his oar like it weighed a thousand pounds. He had become so skinny that I could see his collarbone sticking out above his thick fisherman's sweater. The smell of unwashed lanolin—soaked with these weeks of camp-fire smoke—managed to drown out the vomit. Bucket Head tried to jump into the canoe with us but I pushed him out, not wanting the extra weight. As we pulled away, the dog splashed into the water, paddling after us madly. I couldn't worry about him, could only trust him to give up and return to shore with a resigned doggy sigh. The only thing I could do was lift my arms and row.

And row, and row. We rowed in the dark for what seemed like hours, Silas's oar practically useless in the water, the waning moon doing the best it could to light our way. I rowed faster than I had in three weeks, with more purpose and concentration than I'd ever known. It seemed like every fifteen minutes or so, Silas would lean over the bow and puke. I would row harder.

It all felt so unreal. The urgency of the puking friends we'd left behind, the deep sleep from which I'd awoken, the promise I'd made to Natalia. I couldn't imagine anything that came next; I felt like Silas and I would just be out on this lake, rowing for-ever in the darkness. It seemed impossible that we would find any sign of civilization advanced enough to come to our rescue. It seemed impossible that my friends—the young and healthy athletes—could be in any kind of real danger. It seemed most impossible of all that I'd agreed to become a mother.

I'm sixteen years old, I thought, as I spiked my oar into the pure, cold water. *I'm sixteen years old.* The great horned owls hooted like omens. The loons trilled, alternately sounding like fates laughing or babies crying. I could do nothing to stop either sound.

Finally we came to a sign on the water: LAKE KEEWAYTI-NOOK ADVENTURE TRIPS. A motorboat floated beside a small pier. I rowed ashore and pulled the canoe, with Silas nodding off in the bow, onto the sand. No matter how skinny he'd become, he was still a full-grown man, and I don't know where I got the strength to haul both him and that canoe. As the muscles in my back crackled and snapped, I thought I could also hear the adrenaline, bubbling up beneath them.

Walking between the trees on what I hoped was a path, I wished I'd thought to bring along Natalia's lantern. Complete darkness settled around me. After a few steps my eyes adjusted enough to see a small wood cabin. The door was closed, and I couldn't see any sign of life but a pair of dirty socks drying on the porch rail and a fire pit that smelled as if it had been drenched with lake water within the last few hours. I walked up the steps and knocked. No answer. I tried the doorknob and found it unlocked, so I eased the door open, thinking that if nobody was home I could use the phone. I wondered if 911 worked in Canada. I wondered if I would be able to give rescuers the vaguest idea of our campsite's location.

"Who's there?" a voice said, as I fumbled around for a light switch. My eyes settled on a bedroom doorway, where a man stood, his hairy belly bloated over boxer shorts, his crazy gray hair pointing toward the ceiling in sleepy disarray. As an over-head light flickered on, I saw the double barrel of a shotgun, aimed straight at me.

I raised my hands in the air. "It's me, Sydney," I said lamely. The man lowered the weapon, peering into the darkness with instant sympathy. Under the bare lightbulb, standing on crooked floorboards, my face must have been a study in need, fear, and helplessness. I could see the man recognize me for exactly what I was: a very young girl in trouble.

"You need help," he said, and I broke down and wept at the kindness in his voice.

His name was Mr. Dickerson, and he drove Silas and me back to our campsite in his motorboat. He radioed a neighbor from down the lake, Mrs. Potter, and she followed behind us. Silas lay collapsed on the floor of the boat, so when we reached camp I jumped down and started to round up our fallen troops. The campsite looked and smelled like a massacre had taken place— our campfire still smoking, the smell of vomit hanging heavily in the air, everyone lying on the ground, moaning.

"How many are there?" Mr. Dickerson called to me.

"Six," I said. We roused them one by one. Natalia got weakly to her feet and draped herself across my shoulders. It amazed me that such a slim girl—all bones and skin and muscle— could feel so heavy on my back. We limped together toward Mrs. Potter's boat. Mrs. Potter stood in the bow, shining a spot-light down on us. Then she leaned over to offer us a hand up.

"You want me to help you puke?" she said, the concern on her face as clear as her snaggled teeth. "I got long fingers." She held one up to illustrate.

"No, thank you," Natalia and I said—a chorus of singsong politeness that tripped over the still waters of the lake, where we would not row again any time soon.

The lights of the hospital in Keewaytinook Falls shone very bright after our weeks on the water. By the time we reached its sterile halls, I was too exhausted to announce myself as the only one who didn't need treatment. The nurses shuffled me with the rest of them into one big recovery room. Silas, Jane, Mick, Sam, Natalia, Meredith, and Brendan lay across their cots, moaning and puking into triangular tin trays. I sat up on the end of mine while a flurry of nurses and PAs attended to the others. A blond doctor who looked younger than Margit inspected us one by one. She wore a girlish ponytail and burgundy scrubs.

"So," she said, when she got to me. "You're feeling better than the rest?" She shone a light into one eye, and then the other.

"I'm fine," I said. "I didn't eat any tuna."

"Oh." She snapped the light off and put it in the breast pocket of her scrubs. "Smart girl," she said. "Your friends here are all going to have their stomachs pumped."

"It looked like that was pretty much taken care of back at the campsite," I said.

She smiled wearily. "Well, we're going in for the rest of it. Then they'll have to be on intravenous fluids. I'd say they have a good two days here, at least. Is there somewhere you can stay?"

The doctor placed a flat, cool hand on my forehead, and something in my stomach lurched at a memory from this motherly touch: the days of someone taking care of me. She had pale brown eyes with long lashes, like a deer. She looked like one of my best friends grown up and responsible. I wanted to ask if I could stay with her.

"I guess the camp we're from, Camp Bell," I said. "Somebody from there could come and take me to the base camp."

"Okay," she said. "Give the nurse that number and we'll take care of it."

"I don't know the number. I don't even know if they have a phone."

She smiled at me. "We'll take care of it," she said, and started to turn away.

I understood, in that moment, that I had choices. I could choose to watch her walk out that door. I could choose to let her forget, within minutes, that she'd ever seen me. I could follow my usual MO and do nothing. I could let the rest of my life roll out in directions I'd never wanted to travel, not for a single minute.

Or else I could summon the same strength I'd used to row for help. I could reach out and grab the hem of her top as she turned away with a swish of that girlish ponytail. What surged up in me at that moment—as my hand reached out for her— felt more like survival than choice. It felt like gulping down a glass of water when you're dying of dehydration.

"Yes?" she said, looking back at me. "What is it?"

"Doctor," I whispered. I looked at her name tag. "Dr. Colwin."

"Yes?"

It had been so long since I said it out loud. And then I wondered if I had *ever* said it out loud. Natalia, after all, had been with me when I took the test. And of course I'd never told Tommy, or Cody, or anyone else. So it sounded so foreign, so incorrect, when I opened my mouth and whispered, in a tone that was more question than statement, "I'm pregnant?"

Dr. Colwin cocked her head. I saw her examining my features the way I'd examined hers.

"What's your name?" she said.

"Sydney Biggs," I whispered.

She scribbled it across her pad without looking down. "And how old are you, sweetheart?"

"Sixteen," I said.

She smiled a sad, closed-lip kind of smile and called over her shoulder to a nurse. "Betty?" she said. "Will you please bring Sydney to curtain five?"

I waited behind curtain five on the other side of the ER. A nurse had brought me there and drawn blood. Then I sat, very still, for a long, long time. Finally Dr. Colwin pulled the curtain aside. She smiled at me again and put on a pair of rubber gloves.

"So, Sydney," she said. "Do you want to tell me about this situation?"

"There's not much to tell," I said. "There was this guy, and now I'm pregnant. I took a test before I left for camp."

"And when was that?"

"Almost six weeks ago."

"Okay," she said. "And do you know what you want to do about this?"

I paused, staring at the wall behind us. "Did you test my blood?" I asked her. "Am I really pregnant?"

"Yes, sweetheart. You're really pregnant."

Until that second, throughout everything, I had held on to the shred of possibility that the whole thing was a giant mistake. Even though I had known it wasn't, known it in my heart for all these weeks, hearing the words made the world fall away from underneath me. Bright fluorescent lights, civilization—so much less real than the world of lakeside forests we had left behind. I wished I could go back there and just continue as if none of this had ever happened.

"I can't tell my mother," I whispered. "And I don't have any money."

"Money for what?" said Dr. Colwin.

"An abortion."

"You don't need money," she said. "You've got the Canada Health Act. Abortion is a medically required procedure. If that's what you want."

"A medically required procedure," I whispered. The words sounded so absolving. I could almost push away Natalia's phrase, *the love of your life*, echoing ominously inside my exhausted head.

I leaned back on the table while Dr. Colwin examined me. Her fingers probed gently, tenderly. I felt so tired, I could almost have fallen asleep with my feet in the stirrups. All I wanted, finally, was for this to be out of my hands.

Outside the window, morning had started with a slow, gray light. "Okay," Dr. Colwin said. "You're under twelve weeks. We can schedule you for an abortion this afternoon, if that's what you want."

Before I had a chance to nod, the nurse—Betty—stuck her head into the curtain. Dr. Colwin stepped outside with her, and I could hear them talking in low voices. Then their footsteps moved away, soft soles over linoleum, and I could feel a new kind of fear burbling up inside me. I could tell there was some sort of a problem, and I cursed myself for believing that one single thing in the world would ever go easy for me, ever go right. It felt like hours before Dr. Colwin returned. Her cheeks looked mottled and flushed, almost like she'd been crying.

"Sydney," she said, "we have a problem."

"What?" I said. "What?" I had been so close. My life, so close to returning to its correct track. How could I go back, in that other direction, when I'd been so close?

"I didn't realize you're not Canadian," she said. "You don't have a health card. I can't schedule the procedure without a health card unless you can pay for it."

"How much does it cost?" I asked, even though I didn't have a penny. I guess I felt, after everything, I should at least find out how much it would cost to solve this problem.

"Three hundred and fifty dollars," Dr. Colwin said. It sounded like such a ridiculous amount, piddling and impossible at the same time.

"But listen," I said. "All the other kids, my friends, they're American too. You're treating them. They don't have health cards."

"The camp's going to pay for their treatment," said Dr. Colwin. "They can get reimbursed by their insurance company. But American insurance doesn't cover abortion, unless it's medically necessary."

Medically necessary. As easily as those words had been given to me, now they were taken away. I stared at the sympathetic doctor, not knowing what to do.

"You didn't tell anyone at the camp, did you?" I said.

"No, I sure didn't," she said. "And I sure won't, no matter what you decide. But Sydney, you are going to have to make some decisions here."

"I don't have any money," I whispered.

"I know," Dr. Colwin said. She had that look again, like she might start crying, and I thought that maybe if I just sat there, not saying a word, she would offer to pay for it herself. Or maybe she could take up a collection from the nurses and other doctors. Ten dollars here, twenty dollars there, and we would have the money in no time.

We sat awhile in silence, and I could almost see the possibilities running through her head while they ran through mine. My stomach grumbled, and my muscles ached from the long, hard row. And before long I realized that I knew two things, definitely and without a doubt. The first: My abortion was not Dr. Colwin's responsibility. It was mine. The second: After having come this far—this close—there was no way on earth I could walk out of this hospital still pregnant.

Betty brought me a cordless phone. First I called my mother's work number, but she wasn't there. Probably she had spent a long early morning on the phone with my father, and people from Camp Bell, hearing about what had happened.

There was no answer at home, either, so I called her cell. She answered on the first ring. Her voice sounded breathless and oddly young.

"Mom," I said, "it's Sydney."

"Sydney." Her voice cracked in a way that made me want to cry. "Sydney, where are you? Are you all right?"

I knew how worried she must have been since getting that late-night call. I knew the words she wanted to hear most in the world: *Yes, Mom, I'm fine.* But I also knew if I said that, I wouldn't be able to continue on and tell her the truth.

"Mom," I said. "Mom, I'm pregnant."

I could hear her breath suck in. "Oh, Syd," she said. "Oh, honey. When? How?"

I ignored that last, obvious question and said, "A little while before I left."

I waited for her to ask why I hadn't told her, but she didn't say anything. I guessed in that moment she knew exactly why

I hadn't told her, because the quiet on the other end sounded more sad than angry.

"Mom," I said. "I want an abortion."

"Honey," she said, in that same watery and sympathetic voice. "Of course you do. Of course."

I hate to say it: It broke my heart a little, hearing her say that. Like, what other thing could you possibly want, faced with the nightmare of having a child?

But then there was this little pause, and I could tell she was about to speak, and I knew exactly what she would say. Something she used to say when I was little but hadn't said in a long, long time.

"Sydney," she said. "You're my whole heart. You know that, don't you?"

I nodded at the phone. Because I did know it, as well as I knew that I myself wasn't anywhere near ready—to have my whole heart outside my body, walking around in the world. Someday, maybe. But right now, I needed it for myself. I needed this to be over.

And by evening it was. I lay in a recovery room—far away from my fallen tribe—coming out of the anesthesia from my D & C. Dr. Colwin didn't perform the procedure, but afterward she came in and sat with me awhile. She even held my hand. Before she left, she leaned over and whispered in my ear.

"Good-bye, Sydney," she said. "I'm glad to have met you."

"Thank you," I said, never in my life meaning the words so completely. "Thank you."

chapter fifteen
whole again

The next night found me alone at base camp while the rest of my group still recovered at the Keewaytinook Falls hospital. Mr. Dickerson and Mrs. Potter had motored Bucket Head and all our equipment back there. The dog had been waiting for me at the pier, and my pack had been waiting for me on a bunk in the cabin closest to the dining hall. Meredith's and Natalia's packs sat on the bottom bunks next to me. I moved Natalia's to the far end of the cabin, then walked to the dining hall to eat dinner with the camp secretary and the camp cook and a few maintenance men. They thumped me on the back and smiled as I piled one plate of cold cuts for me and another for Bucket Head.

After dinner, I carried the day's worth of hospital-quality sanitary napkins in a paper bag down to the fire pit by the lake. There was nobody to stop me from building a fire—me, feeling like the lone surviving camper from Group Four. I used the foolproof technique that Jane had shown us, a small tepee of twigs followed by slightly thicker sticks, and then—once the embers had taken—a small log. When the flames climbed and crackled toward the sky, I placed the bag on top of it, participating just this once in the ritual—though there were plenty of clean, unused trash cans I could have used instead.

Earlier, in the bathroom mirror, my face had stared back at me, weirdly unfamiliar. My eyes in a deeply tanned face seemed paler and not as large. My hair curled more crazily and hopelessly than I could ever have remembered, and streaks of blond shot through the dark, unruly mass. My white T-shirt had gone gray, stained with blueberries and dirt. I looked like some kind of girl Tarzan. Who could guess what she'd been through, that primitive girl in the mirror, after all those years in the jungle?

Now I sat on a log with the dog at my feet. I watched the smoke climb into the sky. Carrying so much away with it. Carrying possibility and sorrow, I couldn't deny. But at the same time, carrying my life—my future, my self—back home to me.

I stood up and walked to the water. It was a clear, starry night. I heard loons and crickets. Mosquitoes feasted on my bare arms, but I barely even felt them anymore. The lake lapped the shore, soaking my sneakers, and I knelt down to fill my palms with water. I splashed it on my face, then filled my palms again and drank in a deep slurp. The dirt on my hands made the water taste gritty, salty.

In a few minutes I would douse the fire. I would walk up to the bathroom and shower away the grime and oil of three and a half weeks. The blood of more weeks than that would spiral down the drain, as it now spiraled in the smoke, climbing back up toward the sky.

In the light of the fire, I took off my clothes and walked into the water. The lake gathered around my body in a clingy, delicious chill—crisp and heavy enough to bring me down, if only I weren't so strong: strong enough to reclaim my life, and stay afloat.

I remembered then the last lines of that Robert Frost poem, the one that Natalia had tried to recall back at the abandoned village. And the words—about what's discovered after losing your way—filled me up with the greatest finality, and the most complete relief. I closed my eyes and let myself sink just under the surface, while the last lines of the poem surrounded me as entirely as the lake. I lunged up, out of the water, and after I took in a deep, soul-cleansing breath, I spoke the words out loud.

"'Here are your waters and your watering place,'" I called up to the starlit sky. "'Drink and be whole again beyond confusion.'"

chapter sixteen
northern lights

For the other campers, the return to base camp felt like a celebration. Everyone was so happy—to have toilets and beds, and showers, and hot meals served indoors, with no plates or pans to scrub in the lake. By afternoon the camp was full of campers, freshly showered but still wearing their filthy clothes.

Group Four arrived by motorboat somewhere near evening. I walked down to the launching pier to greet them. They looked amazingly healthy, considering the pumped stomachs and intravenous fluids. The hospital staff had done laundry for them, so they were the only campers wearing clean clothes. They all had thick gauze bandages on each arm. They stepped off the boat one at a time and gave me a hug. They smelled like the strangest combination of antiseptic and campfire smoke.

Mick got off the boat before Natalia. He swept me into a bear hug that cracked the back of my ribs. I hugged him back, thinking how familiar his scent had become to me—the faraway but lingering odor of Tide, the acrid scent of Brendan's Off!, and his own indefinable sweat, a very personal fingerprint.

I waited for a second after he let go. Natalia stood in front of me, her hair pulled off her face by a cloth headband. She had her hands in the back pockets of her denim skirt. "Guess what?" she said in her old cafeteria voice.

"What?"

"I looked at Jane's chart," she said. "She's only seventeen."

"No way."

"Born exactly ten months before me," Natalia said. "I knew it. I knew she was no kind of adult."

"Did you look at Silas's chart?"

"Yup. Nineteen years old."

"Now if you could just tell me if they've been having sex," I said, and Natalia laughed. Then she caved in and hugged me. "Go for a walk?" she said.

"Sure."

We'd had such good weather. All summer the sky had been kind to us, offering few days of rowing against headwinds, or sleeping and traveling under rain. Today was no exception. Mrs. Potter had told me that the canoe trails around Lake Keewaytinook were established over thousands of years by the Teme-Augama Anishnabai: the Deep Water People. Their ancient path, where Natalia and I now walked, was dappled with sunlight, a lovely warmth beating on the back of our necks, along with a cooling breeze. We couldn't see a single cloud above us, not the barest wisp of white, only a clear blue sky. Tomorrow would be August. The air felt a little crisper, a little colder. Fall would come early here in the north.

"Silas says we might see the northern lights tonight," said Natalia. "Sometimes people do, in between trips, when it's colder."

I didn't answer, just looked up at the sky as if the spectacle had already begun. "So," Natalia said after a while. "Have you thought any more about what you're going to do?"

We stopped walking and faced each other. Of course the question itself indicated that something had changed. After the days indoors at the hospital, Natalia's skin had begun to peel a little; I could see a fresh pink layer underneath her eyes. Strange, very strange, that my secret had gone from being pregnant to not being pregnant. Strange, again, that such a huge event could take place—in my body and my heart and my mind—and still not be visible to the naked eye.

"I want you to know," Natalia said, "that I will still take this baby. I will take care of it, and I will love it just exactly as if it were my own."

She looked so earnest, and I wanted to love her for the offer. I wished for a cloud to float by and give us a little shade, a little darkness, to match the news I was about to deliver.

"Natalia," I said quietly, "there's no more baby."

She stood blinking at me for a long moment. Then she said, "The hospital?"

I nodded.

"I thought so," she said.

I opened my mouth to say I was sorry, but thought better of

it. Because I wasn't sorry. I couldn't be. In the end I had chosen hope when hope presented itself. I had chosen me, and a life beyond that fleeting craziness two months before. I had chosen this new wisdom and resignation over months and years of uncertainty and trouble.

"I don't know if I can talk to you for a while," Natalia said.

"I get that," I told her. She reached out her hand and I took it. We stood there for a few minutes. And then she let go and walked away.

Soon Natalia would be home. She would face Margit as her mother for the very first time. And maybe after that, she would see that whatever I had done—whatever I had given up—it had never for a single second been her.

I saw Cody that night at dinner. I was sitting at a table by the window with Meredith. I saw him cross the dining hall and stop to talk to Mick and Natalia. Natalia pointed me out with a casual toss of her head. I hadn't realized before that she'd noticed where I was sitting.

"Hey," Cody said, sliding in next to me, his tray piled high with sandwiches. "I heard what happened. I was worried about you."

My heart stopped for a moment, and then I realized he meant the food poisoning. "Sydney was the only one you didn't have to be worried about," Meredith said.

Cody sat down across the table from us. I nodded toward his food. "Hungry much?"

"Man," he said, "I am starving. Absolutely starving."

"Me too," I said. I reached over and slid one of the sandwiches off his plate. We sat there, eating together. Meredith and I filled him in on the tainted tuna and our dramatic rescue. "Sydney paddled for miles," said Meredith, "to find us help."

"Well, it wasn't miles," I said, though I knew it had been. "And Silas was with me."

"Puking all the way," Meredith said.

"It wasn't pretty," I admitted.

Cody reached under the table and placed one warm, oar-calloused hand on my knee. I could feel his skin through my worn jeans. "You're my hero," he said. I smiled at him. Across the room, Jane and Silas ate with the other counselors, Bucket Head wagging his tail at Silas's feet.

Hero: For the first time in my life, despite everything, I felt strangely deserving of the word. My mother had promised not to tell my father about the abortion, and I knew how proud he must be of my midnight rescue mission.

"A bunch of us are going to sleep outside tonight," Cody said, "to see if the northern lights come out. Want to join us?" He was asking Meredith, too, but he looked pointedly at me.

"I still feel a little weak," Meredith said. "I'm going to bed early, inside."

I could see Mick and Natalia, clearing their trays. At another table, Sam had reunited with Charlie, and I saw Brendan saunter out the door with Roger. Our little tribe had already disbanded.

"Sure," I told Cody. "I'd love to see the northern lights."

*　　*　　*

The sun had just begun to set when I retrieved my sleeping bag from the bunkhouse. I had to grab my pack, too, and stopped by the bathroom to change pads. My stomach still cramped every few hours, and the doctor had said to be alert to body temperature changes. Every once in a while I brought my hand to my forehead, which felt cool and normal. I wondered if it would be best to just join Meredith inside, but I couldn't bear to miss the northern lights, or one last night with Cody, even though I couldn't imagine letting myself so much as kiss him.

When I came out of the bathroom Mick was standing outside, leaning against a pine tree. I looked around for Natalia and saw from his steady gaze that he wasn't waiting for her, but for me.

"Syd," Mick said. I walked over to him, and he put his hand on my shoulder. "Natalia told me what happened," he said.

It seemed funny, somehow, her name on his lips—though of course I'd heard him say it a hundred times before. But in that moment the word sounded so elegant, and he pronounced it as if nothing could be more natural. It was as if he really had been changed by his association with her. With us.

"You did the right thing, Syd," Mick said. "She'll realize that before too long."

"Thank you," I said, meaning this more than I could possibly express. His hand still sat, heavily, on my shoulder. I thought with a surge of happiness that it wouldn't be like "Flowers for Algernon" at all. Mick would keep becoming his better self, growing into his potential more and more with every day that passed.

"Mick," I said, "do you ever think about that guy? Under the tunnel? Do you ever feel guilty about it?"

He frowned for a second, unsure what I was talking about. Then he remembered and took his hand off my shoulder. He waved it, pushing the question out of the air—dismissing it as ridiculous.

"No way," he said. "That was like a time of war. Him or us. I did what I had to do."

He cocked his head and smiled at me, and I nodded gravely. "Are you going to see if the northern lights come out?" I said.

"Wouldn't miss it," Mick told me.

I took a step back, a little awkwardly. Then I raised my hand and waggled my fingers to say so long. As I turned and headed down the hill, my sleeping bag under my arm and my pack over my shoulder, Mick called out to me.

"Keep it in your pants tonight, Syd," he yelled. "No point starting in right where you left off."

"Shut up," I yelled back. Leaves and mud squished under my feet, and my chest swelled with love. Still. If I never saw Mick again in my whole entire life, those last words—from both of us—would be completely perfect.

I met Cody down by the water, with a gaggle of other campers that included Meredith. Apparently she'd changed her mind about sleeping indoors, and I felt glad. Somebody who had been so disciplined about watching the dawn deserved, more than any of us, the aurora borealis.

"Want to go for one last swim?" Cody asked.

"I can't," I said. When he cocked his head in question, I said, "It's too cold."

We walked away from the others to find a place to lay down our sleeping bags. It was rockier than our last spot, on a small slope. As we settled down next to each other, the sky growing darker above us, I decided to level with him.

"Cody," I said, "I can't sleep with you tonight. I can't have sex, I mean."

He moved a little closer and put his arm around me. "That's okay," he said. "I figured you wouldn't want to, after last time."

I let my head drop onto his shoulder, feeling grateful and amazingly comfortable.

"Are you a virgin?" he asked.

"No," I said. And then, because he seemed like such a nice guy, and because from the start it had been so easy just to be with him, I told him the truth. "Two nights ago I had an abortion."

"No way."

The sky grew dark, then darker still. The lights in all the outbuildings had been turned off, and the stars gathered above in a thousand layers. The stars. How I would miss all those stars. Back home would feel like a more distant planet with its overhang of pollution and spattering of one star here, a moving airplane there. Here, on the lake, we hung flat out into the solar system, right in the thick of every world.

Cody still didn't speak. "It's not what you think," I said. "I've only slept with two people in my entire life." Even as I defended myself, I realized that at sixteen two people might be exactly two too many.

I waited for him to take his arm away, but he let it stay there, insistent and even a little protective. "So," he said. "That night, when we were together. You were pregnant?"

I nodded. He might not have been able to see me, but he would feel the top of my head brush against his chin. "Intense," he said. I nodded again. He squeezed me a little closer. Up above, just behind or just in front of the stars, I saw a little flash of green. It flickered, then bowed. Something inside me contracted, and I reached for Cody's hand.

"Look," I said.

We lay back on our sleeping bags, holding hands. Above us the sky moved and roiled. It danced and flickered, like an ocean tide from a faraway galaxy. After a while it got colder, so we crawled into our separate bags. We didn't hold hands again, but lay next to each other, staring up at that gently explosive sky.

We could have said something about how beautiful it all was, and how lucky we were to be watching it. But what words could match the spectacle up there above our heads? How could we describe it in a way that would do justice rather than make it smaller? So we kept quiet, our limbs lying against one another, touching through layers of down and Gore-Tex.

Tomorrow we would return to civilization. But right now everything—the white pine and the wildlife and the thousands of trails forged by the Deep Water People—lay around us in a pulsing hush of ancient wilderness. The two of us, so new in comparison. We were like babies, safe somehow in the forest. We were the newest creatures on Earth, with nothing to do but move forward into the world, starting fresh.

epilogue
a time made simple

August in New Jersey. Hot, humid, muggy, and buggy. I'm living at my dad's house. Every morning he wakes me up just before dawn—which comes much too early on these long summer days. I climb from the tangle of my sleeping brothers and pull on clothes that are almost as grimy as the ones I wore on Lake Keewaytinook. Then I go downstairs and eat breakfast with my father in the dusky kitchen. No one else is awake, not Kerry or the kids, so it's just the two of us. My dad and me. We don't talk much—some mornings we don't talk at all. I'd like to say I feel closer to him, but some days the air just hangs with everything I can't say. The silence doesn't seem to bother him. He's content to leave things between us just as they've always been, and I'm learning not to want any more from him than he's capable of giving.

It's strangely companionable, the two of us eating the freshly laid eggs that he scrambles with unpasteurized butter and sprigs of basil from his garden. After breakfast he drives off in his truck. I put on a wide, floppy straw hat and pedal Kerry's one-speed cruiser three miles down the road to Campbell's farm.

My only day off is Monday. The rest of the week I spend half the day in the fields, weeding and picking ripe produce. Then in the afternoon I sit out at the roadside stand, my face streaked with farm soil and my arms sunburnt and sore. I sell summer squash and corn, fresh tomatoes and blueberries. There are no checks or credit cards; the Campbells trust me with the folded cash and jingling coins, and although I am not getting paid for my work—I'm paying for my month on the lake—I have never pocketed a single penny. It feels good to be trusted.

I pedal home in the afternoon and get there an hour earlier than Dad. I run upstairs to take a long, steaming shower before he's there to remind me of the ten-minute rule and lecture me on precious resources. Kerry doesn't tell. She's grateful to have me there watching the kids. Some afternoons she naps, sometimes she goes for long walks. She looks like she's lost a little weight.

Rebecca can stand up on her own now. She teeters to her feet and wobbles in every direction. She beams so proudly, it's like her smile is what keeps her balance. The other day she was sitting in the high chair and Kerry asked, "Where's Sydney?" Rebecca lifted up her chubby arm and pointed right at me. It was the weirdest thing, like suddenly receiving direct communication from a houseplant.

My mother saw Rebecca for the first time when she dropped me off here after my plane came in from Toronto. She even held her for a few minutes while Dad carried my pack into the laundry room. Mom said Rebecca looked just like me when I was a baby. Dad seemed surprised, as if he'd forgotten I hadn't sprung up from the ground sixteen years ago, exactly the way I am today.

Two weeks ago we were quite a spectacle, the campers from Lake Keewaytinook, coming back to civilization. When we got off our chartered plane, everyone in the Toronto airport stared at us. We looked fresh from some major trauma, most of us in filthy clothes and all of us with deep, native tans. A few motherly-looking women actually came up and asked why we were all so dirty.

Natalia and I said good-bye to Meredith, Brendan, Sam, and Mick. We all stood together under the airport security lights, the five of them with their hospital-washed clothes and me in the T-shirt and jeans that had been worn for almost thirty days straight without seeing a drop of soap. We took turns hugging one another and writing down e-mail addresses and cell phone numbers. But I think we all knew these good-byes were the most final we'd ever known. There would never be another time like the month on the lake, the six of us together. Not even if we decided to come back next year, as Meredith was already plotting.

Mick seemed the saddest of anyone. He even hugged Brendan and Sam. When he hugged me he pressed his hand into the small of my back, a fierce but strangely gentlemanly gesture. "I'm happy for you, Syd," he whispered in my ear, and I had to fight back the urge to say that I loved him. It was still Mick, after all, and of course he would take it the wrong way and turn it into a lewd joke. So I just said thank you and kissed him on the cheek. I'm pretty sure I tasted a salty tear.

We all headed to our gates and let Mick and Natalia say good-bye privately. I was already settled into my seat on the plane when she came walking down the aisle. She paused and looked at her ticket—of course since we'd sat together on the plane ride to Toronto, we were assigned seats next to each other for the ride home.

"Do you want to switch with someone?" I asked her.

"No." She sighed and sank down into the seat beside me. "Let's not talk, though."

I agreed, but I don't think she let a minute pass before saying, "It feels like a million years since we were last on this plane."

"It does," I said.

"Everything's different," she said. "Every little thing in the world is different."

"I know."

"But you know one thing that's the same?"

"What?" I asked.

"You and me. Sitting here together."

I dropped my hand into her lap and she scooped it up, clasping it tightly. She didn't let go of my hand for the entire flight, not even when she drank her Coke—not spiked this time: How could we even consider ruining our first taste of Coke in four weeks? We didn't say another word until the plane touched down in Newark. Natalia finally let go of my hand and said, "That was the best summer of my entire life."

I knew then that Steve would get some sad news when he tried to contact Natalia. Picturing Mick—his stubbly head and his sunburned shoulders—I couldn't help feeling happy. I knew I would do whatever they wanted, Mick and Natalia, if they needed help finding a way to see each other again.

When I walked through the security gate, my mom stood there waiting for me. Her hair was a little longer. I walked toward her slowly, tentatively, and then she opened up her arms. I threw myself into them. She held me fierce and tight, like she would never let me go anywhere again. Her hair smelled like honey and Ivory soap. Just underneath her skin—soft and familiar—there was that sixth sense we shared, not a scent exactly, but something deeper and more difficult to define. Something I'd known my whole life, that whatever happened I could identify without naming it. Mom. My mom. The bustle of the airport disappeared, the two of us there together in our little pod of reunion.

"I'm sorry," I whispered.

"Me too," she said. "I'm sorry too."

She stepped back a little and gripped my shoulders tightly. She looked hard into my face, and then scanned my body from my toes to the top of my head. I almost expected her to start counting my fingers to make sure they were all there.

"Are you okay, Syd?" she said.

"I'm fine, Mom. I'm totally fine." And she pulled me into another hug.

On the drive to my dad's she told me how things would go in the fall. She said she would let me return to Linden Hill Country Day. "I can't imagine coming this far," she said, "and then switching. I've worked too hard to keep you at that school to let you blow it now." I didn't feel particular relief at the news. It was more like I'd known all along that was how she'd feel in the end.

"Thanks," I said.

She reached across the gearshift and took my hand. "I want you to know," she said, "that I decided about school before you called me from the hospital. I also want you to know that I'm not sure if I ever meant it, about making you change schools. I may have just wanted to scare you."

I felt a little annoyed that she wouldn't just come out and admit this in a definite way. But then I thought, maybe she didn't know herself. Maybe none of us can ever know, for certain, what we're doing, or what we want, at any given moment.

"You know, Syd," she said, still holding my hand. "I never meant to be the kind of mother you couldn't come to. All that time I was mad because I couldn't trust you. But it turns out you couldn't trust me, either."

"I'm sorry," I said.

Her eyes were on the road, but I could see tears spring up, and she squeezed my hand tighter. "Don't you ever be sorry," she said. "I'm the one who's sorry, Sydney. More than I can tell you."

I sat quiet for a minute, trying to remember if I'd ever heard her apologize to me before. I couldn't be sure if this was the first time, or if in the past I just hadn't been listening.

"But you know," I said, "the truth is I did come to you. Maybe not right away, but when it really mattered. And you did exactly what I knew you would do. You came through for me."

She let go of my hand to wipe her eyes with the back of her palm. Then she reached back and pushed a crazy strand of hair behind my ear.

"Thanks for that, kiddo," she said. And we rode together, quiet and smiling a little, all the way to my dad's.

Now my mom calls to check in a few times a week. On Sunday nights I'm allowed to call a friend. The first time I called Brendan. He had just won a role in an independent film and was headed back to Canada—Vancouver this time, the opposite coast. He told me that as soon as he got home he'd Googled all the Pittsburgh papers for a news story about a guy found dead under a tunnel last summer.

"Did you find anything?" I asked.

"No," he said. I think we were both disappointed as much as relieved.

Now it's Sunday again. My body has returned to normal, no more cramps or blood. In a couple of weeks I'll probably get my period. Every morning I eat a huge breakfast and every night I eat a huge dinner. But for lunch I only have some fruit from Campbell's farm, and with all the biking and gardening I haven't gained much weight.

It's weird to think that while I'm here in this other universe, Jane, Silas, and Bucket Head are rowing on Lake Keewaytinook with a new group. I picture them seeing Jane peel off her shirt for the first time, or listening to Silas's guitar, and I have to fight back a stab of jealousy. I'm thinking about asking Dad if I can go back next summer. I'd be glad to do the same cycle: a month on the lake followed by a month on the farm. Maybe the year after that I could even be a counselor. Lifeguarding suddenly seems a pointless bore in comparison.

For dinner tonight Kerry prepares homemade pizza on the grill. I helped her roll out the dough. We cover one with homemade pesto, the other with homemade tomato sauce. Everything is from the garden. Everything is healthy and good. I can't imagine having nightmares here anymore, no matter what scary predictions my dad makes for the future. Right now—in this moment—we're all safe. I'm willing to let that be enough.

Do I ever feel guilty? Do I ever feel sad? Sometimes. Tonight I look around the table. I see my brothers and sister gobbling down their pizza—Rebecca's cut into teeny tiny squares—and I wonder where that missing person might fit, what he or she might have been. But the feeling passes quickly. I understand that I did what I had to do, and if I occasionally feel like I need forgiveness, it's not very hard to grant it myself. In the end it's impossible to regret a future that terrified me so completely. What I mostly feel is gratitude at having my old life back, the way it's supposed to be. It's almost like I had the chance to travel back in time and right something that had gone terribly wrong.

"Sydney," Kerry says after dinner, as Dad collects the dirty plates, "do you want to call one of your friends?"

I think of who I might call. I've got Cody's number upstairs, tumbled into my single drawer in the room I'm sharing with my little brothers. I know he'd be happy to hear from me. And I'd love to hear Natalia's voice. She's been e-mailing Brendan, so I've gotten most of her news from him. She won't be at Country Day in the fall, though she's not going to Switzerland.

"She's going to live with her sister in New York," Brendan told me. "They're sending her to Brearley. It's an all-girls school."

"I know," I said, silently wishing the Miksas luck with this new strategy.

Now Kerry puts her hand on my shoulder, and I realize I haven't answered. "Sydney," she says again. "Want to make a call?"

Outside it's grown dark. Through the screens I can hear all the good summer chirps and buzzes. I've had a long day in the sun. My body is bone tired in the best possible way, and if I closed my eyes for even a second I would feel the first gentle threads of sleep. I know that in a couple of weeks I will be back at my mother's house. I will return to school, and my old life, with a fresh understanding of all that's been rescued. And I will definitely call Natalia, my best friend, to hear all her news. I will certainly call Cody, to discover whatever possibilities lie between us.

But for right now I'm tired. I'm happy to be just one person, with a long day behind her and another one ahead. "I think I'm fine tonight," I tell Kerry and my dad. I love the purity, the honesty, the lack of secrecy in that single sentence. There's nothing in the world I need except a good night's sleep. *I'm fine tonight.*